Kyle swung the

"No kiss this time?" Harmony asked, testing him. Her chin was high.

"That's right." He spoke quietly enough that it didn't carry into the lobby when he said, "You want to know something I'm afraid of?"

"What've you got, superhero?"

"That whatever's happened between us tonight wiped out everything that came before it. Is that what you want?" he asked.

"Are you kidding me?" For the first time, he saw the nerves behind her brave front. Her chin quavered even as she jabbed him with her finger. "Why do you think I didn't say anything before? You think I *want* to lose my best friend?"

He didn't reply.

She lifted her shoulders in a helpless shrug. "But I guess...at the end of the day...I'm not half as noble as you are."

Dear Reader,

A hundred years ago, Lucy Maud Montgomery wrote, "No matter what life might hold for them, it could never alter that. Their happiness was in each other's keeping." *Anne of Green Gables* has clearly stayed with me.

When I set out to write the fifth book in my Fairhope series, I had no plan to draw on books I read as a young girl. I suppose it is no surprise, however, that irrepressible Harmony's flaming red hair and her lifelong affection for noble Kyle drew subconscious parallels to a certain orphan from Avonlea and her dear friend Gilbert Blythe. By the second chapter, Kyle began to refer to his Harmony as "Carrots" and there may or may not be a reference to that infamous slate-breaking incident...

I've always had a soft spot for the friends-to-lovers romance. Harmony and Kyle take it a step further, because when your hero is a tried and true navy SEAL and your aviatrix heroine is an expert in aerobatics, matters like life and death are never far behind.

I have loved every moment of writing this series, mostly because I get to watch characters like Harmony and Kyle dream big, grow up and realize, like Anne, how close to home happiness truly is.

Happy reading!

Amber Leigh

AMBER LEIGH
WILLIAMS

—

Navy SEAL Promise

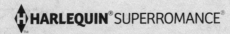
HARLEQUIN® SUPERROMANCE®

Recycling programs
for this product may
not exist in your area.

ISBN-13: 978-0-373-64048-5

Navy SEAL Promise

Copyright © 2017 by Amber Leigh Williams

Printed in U.S.A.

Amber Leigh Williams is a Harlequin romance writer who lives on the United States Gulf Coast. She lives for beach days, the smell of real books and spending time with her husband and their two young children. When she's not keeping up with rambunctious little ones (and two large dogs), she can usually be found reading a good book or indulging her inner foodie. Amber is represented by the D4EO Literary Agency. Learn more at www.amberleighwilliams.com.

Books by Amber Leigh Williams

HARLEQUIN SUPERROMANCE

Wooing the Wedding Planner
His Rebel Heart
Married One Night
A Place with Briar

Other titles by this author available in ebook format.

For my moon child, brighter than the sun.
Read books, cover or no cover.
Gather seashells, whole or broken.
Make ripples on the pond.
Mostly, breathe fire, rebel baby, and
light up the world with who you are.

And for that person, my person—you know
exactly who you are. This SEAL belongs to you.

PROLOGUE

HARMONY SAVITT LOVED nothing more than pulling Gs in her high-performance aircraft. She loved doing all the rash, death-defying maneuvers that made spectators gasp and her parents nauseated.

As a pilot, she was gutsy. A certified barnstormer. She'd graduated at the top of her class from the tip-of-the-sword aerobatics academy she'd moved out west to conquer.

She knew good and well that her parents back home in Alabama would've preferred that she'd never caught the flying bug. If she gave it all up now—maneuvers, air shows, flight in general—and returned to small-town life with her feet planted solidly on the ground, they'd only be too pleased.

However, they'd touted purpose and dreams from the moment they knew she was listening. They'd encouraged her to be who she was, what she was, without compromise. And so she had.

Regardless of all that, it wasn't three minutes into the first show of the season in Oshkosh, Wisconsin, that she felt it—something she rarely felt behind the controls of her Pitts S2S. She pulled rapidly out of formation and radioed the tower that she was coming in hot.

She landed with a skip and a bounce, ripped off her flying helmet. Emergency personnel ran at her with hoses and med bags. "What is it? What happened?" they cried out. She nearly mowed them down as she ran for the first hangar, clawing the air and cursing with every step.

She rounded the structure, grabbed the wall and aimed for the cleanest patch of tarmac she could find.

Sick. Sick, sick, sick.

Where was Mom to hold her hair back now?

The personnel kept a respectful distance. By the time she was done, she'd ejected her entire breakfast. She'd also broken out into a fine cool sweat, and her limbs weren't the least bit sturdy.

Sturdiness was her mien. She was *never* not sturdy. Whether it was pulling those happy Gs or rolling over in a barrel, she prided herself on a cast-iron stomach and rock-steady hands at the controls. Airsickness had never been a problem.

"Hey, winger. You sick?"

This from her mechanic. Harmony fell back into a crouch and leaned against the cool metal building at her back. Planes stormed overhead, tearing, roaring, whistling. In the distance, the sound of cheering echoed off the tarmac in a merry cacophony. And still her knees shook like the ground was quaking.

She lowered her head until her long fire-engine-red rope braid fell heavy against her stomach. "I don't get sick, Danny," she muttered. "Ever."

Her mechanic snorted. "Those cookies you just tossed are bound to disagree with you. If you ain't sick, you're pregnant." And he guffawed because the thought of balls-to-the-wall Harmony Savitt pregnant was…

Impossible.

It took a bit of time, but she got up. Unzipping the neck of her flight suit, she fanned herself and scurried back to her plane. She did a quick check to make sure the bumpy landing hadn't jarred anything loose. The weakness chased her back to the hangar before she could even think about gearing up for the next phase of the show.

She hosed her face off and did her best to cleanse the taste from her mouth by drinking half a bottle of tepid water. When the backs of her eyes went fuzzy and her ears started in with a chorus of white noise, she had to sit down and put her head between her knees.

While she was there, she counted. She counted days. Then weeks.

"Hell in a handbasket," she cursed. The nausea was fading, but the shakes remained. This time they weren't just from weakness.

Something else Harmony Savitt didn't get was scared. But the truth was all but written in front of her. Her long-held tenet of embracing the natural turbulence of life went up against denial—denial of what she'd most likely been carrying around with her in the cockpit of her S2S. Pulling 10 Gs. Slipping. Stalling. Spiraling.

"Shit." She covered her mouth and made a dash for the port-a-john.

She was exhausted, bedraggled—on the verge of a breakdown, the kind *other* people had. Not her.

"Harm?"

Head low, she squinted. The voice was familiar. For a few seconds, she thought she'd conjured it out of some nausea-induced haze. The hand that came down on her shoulder was real, though. Hard and real.

"Carrots. You okay?"

Her heart lurched. Only one person in the world called her Carrots.

"Oh, God." It came out on a wavering prayer. Prayer—another thing she rarely engaged in.

Turning her head, she rested her cheek on the back of Kyle Bracken's hand and thanked the maker for summoning him here to this place so far from home where she had suddenly been feeling so wretchedly alone. Peering up, she felt a weak, relieved smile pull at the corners of her white-pressed lips.

They froze in place along with the rest of her. Sure, it was Kyle. Crystal-clear blue eyes like untouched lakes in Scandinavia. A face like a dream—sharp-cut and hard-boned, it was marked hither and thither by scars, old and new. It was always tan, the freckles peppered across his nose and cheekbones nearly faded by the same sun that had imprinted them there in youth. His cheekbones were high and wide. The only thing soft about him was the slight button nose he'd been graced with by his tiny, fierce mother.

It was a good face. She'd known it all her life, so she was aware, more than most, of the kindness behind it, as well as the inclination toward mischief. There was courage there in boatloads, integrity, too, and the propensity of a warrior living in stunning synchronicity with a heart forged from full-fledged gold.

Some of those new scars…they were reminders of his latest deployment where, less than a year ago, he'd been medevaced from deep conflict after a near-fatal run-in with a frag grenade.

None of it gave her pause. Not anymore. She'd abandoned the end of the flying season last summer when she heard he'd been injured and had sat for weeks at his bedside, trading shifts there with his mother, his father, his sister and his then-fiancée. You couldn't keep a tried-and-true Navy SEAL down. She knew it because her big brother, Gavin, was a SEAL, as well. He and Kyle had survived BUD/S together, fighting through every wall to earn their Trident and their place in the good fight.

And they'd taken someone with them on their way to petty officer status. Someone who'd come to mean as much to Harmony as either of them. Someone she'd come to love, too, over the last few years.

Someone she suspected was jointly responsible for her fears and misplaced cookies.

Kyle offered her a ghost of a grin. When she was a girl, that smile had held the power to bring her to her knees. It wasn't the expression, however, that made her go to them now.

It was the uniform. Full dress blues.

If Harmony knew anything about Kyle Bracken, it was that he didn't flaunt his SEAL status. He rarely donned his uniform stateside unless it was required. T-shirt, jeans, ball cap—those were his go-to threads. Seeing him decked out in white cap and shiny medals struck another chord of fear in her, far worse than the last.

"What're you doing here?" she asked. Though she knew. The sister and the girl of military men *always* knew.

The grip on her shoulder squeezed as the smile on his face tapered off. "Harm. I wish I could tell you I came for the show."

She was holding her breath again. She reached up blindly and gripped his jacket. "Kyle. *What are you doing here?*" The words came through her teeth. They were clenched, near clattering.

Those eyes. They told her before his mouth could bring itself to move. Those Scandinavian lakes were as deep with sorrow as they were wide, and something broke inside her to see it. To know.

"It's Benji," he said. "I'm sorry, baby. He's dead."

CHAPTER ONE

Five Years Later

AN ILL WIND blew Kyle into his Alabama home
port. As he docked his beloved one-man sloop,
the *Hellraiser*, in its rightful slip, he felt change
in the air.

By the pricking of my thumbs—

Looking south, far off south, he saw nothing but cerulean skies skidded with small white
fat-bottomed clouds. It was June, however, and
though temps were climbing fast into the blistering nineties, the breeze was high. Off the
Hellraiser's stern, the Stars and Stripes flapped
raggedly, the line ticking a cadence off the metal
flag pole.

—somethin' wicked this way comes.

The dawn, too, heralded change for the shore of
his coastal home, he remembered as he checked
the bilge pump and turned all power off to the
cabin. This had been his home away from home
for the past week and a half, while he sailed
from Virginia Beach near Naval Amphibious
Base Little Creek, down the Atlantic seaboard,

around Florida's jutting peninsula and its glittering green keys. Watching the day break like a fire-soaked phoenix on his restive swath of the Gulf of Mexico, he recalled the old adage: *Red sky morning—sailor's fair warning.*

Kyle had hoped that that warning was for what lay behind, what had drawn him to the refuge of the sea to decompress from his latest conflict as a Navy SEAL.

At sea, he could breathe. He could disconnect from the chaos and violence of his chosen profession. He could clear his head and reinvigorate his soul.

It had been harsh, the last string of operations. Harsh enough to wake him every night in the bunk of his sloop. But the cradle-like motion of the sea had helped beat back the tightness in his chest. And up on deck, with the salty wind in his hair and his sea-legs beneath him, he had slowly been able to realign the molecules between head and heart.

Out at sea, he wasn't Chief Petty Officer Kyle Bracken. He was just a sailor having his go at the age-old existential clash between man and nature.

He loved his job. He loved his brothers-in-arms. He loved fighting the good fight. But even warriors needed a reprieve. Even the trained elite needed to unplug and get back to self. The little tropical cyclone he'd run into just off Cedar Key had been a welcome reception. A challenge. He'd turned the sloop's bow right up underneath its cloudy, disordered skirt and sailed right through it.

It had been headed northeast, but the wind had now shifted, Kyle noted. He knew before his feet hit the dock of the marina, without switching on the weather radio. He had lived through enough summers on the Gulf to be able to sense the change in barometric pressure. Hell, he could practically taste it.

That damned storm was headed straight this way.

He spotted the man on the deck of the houseboat two slips down and whistled loudly. "'Ey, Nick!"

The white-headed gentleman turned. His face was leathered and bronzed, his beard bushy and white enough to rival Santa's. He was wearing the same Hawaiian-print shirt as always, and the exact style of sunglasses that had died out sometime after the Kennedy assassination. "Hey, boy. Where the hell've you been?"

"Can't say," Kyle claimed, gripping the shiny silver rail on the *Hellraiser*'s port side. Nick had been calling Kyle "boy" since his first visit to the marina alongside his father at the age of seven. Kyle might have changed a good deal since their first meeting, but the salty seaman living on the houseboat had not.

Maybe he *was* Santa Claus.

"Still a person of mystery," Nick grunted.

Kyle lifted a shoulder in answer.

"Saw your old man out and about…oh, Wednesday, I think it was," Nick said, scratching his forehead.

"Yeah?" Kyle asked, lightening at the mention of his father.

"Gearing up for that big show this weekend up at that airfield of his. Reckon you heard about it."

"Huh." Big show. Airfield. Neither his father nor his mother had mentioned either in their weekly emails or the short phone calls they'd managed to grab with him over his last week of deployment. Though words like *big show* and *James Bracken* were no strangers to each other. And James did own an airfield, among a litany of other strange and wonderful things.

"Your folks know you're in town?" Nick asked.

A grin managed to climb over the lower half of Kyle's face. He hadn't known when his vessel would bring him into port. That combined with the stormy run-in had kept him from contacting his parents.

Besides, he liked the element of surprise.

The far-off wail of a weather warning reached Kyle's ears, and he straightened as Nick's head swiveled in the direction of the houseboat's wheelhouse. They both listened for a moment to the radio before Nick glanced back at Kyle, his caterpillar brows vee-ed. "What the sam hell did you bring home with you? Weatherman says that cyclone's spun itself into a ripe-old tropical storm. Headed this way."

The grin washed slowly from Kyle's face as he picked up on the rest of the weather warning. It seemed the calm he'd sought in the waters that straddled Fort Morgan and Dauphin Island, the lull of the Eastern Shore and the bay that, to him, represented the flow and pace of what life should be, was about to be rudely disrupted. What *had* he brought with him?

Nick hocked loudly and spat a stream over the rail before he added, "Go on, boy. Tell your mama you're here." He raised his glasses and peered across the empty slip. "Or I will."

Kyle gave a nod. "Yes, sir." He began to gather his things from the *Hellraiser*'s cabin when Nick called to him again.

"It's good to see you back."

"Were you worried about me, Nick?" Kyle asked, teasing.

Nick's laugh was a rusty tumble. Just the thing for a sailor as old and crusty as he. "Maybe."

It was as heartfelt a sentiment as Kyle had ever heard the man utter. He nodded. "See you out at the airfield later?"

Nick barked. "Your crazy old man might've traded his sea legs for a pair of wings." He stomped one rubber boot onto the deck of the houseboat. Kyle was surprised the ancient decking didn't splinter under the abuse. "My place is right here."

"Uh-huh. You might wanna shower," Kyle suggested. He raised a brow at Nick's questioning frown. "I can smell ya from here."

That rusty laugh climbed into the air and followed Kyle belowdecks.

AFTER LONG ABSENCE, most sons brought their mothers roses.

What Kyle brought his he wrapped doubly in cotton swaths and stuffed carefully into the mid-leg pocket of his cargo pants. His motorcycle was housed under the awning next to his mother's old bay cottage where he'd left it so many months ago, locked and chained and maintained no doubt by his father whose many professions included auto mechanic. He slung the travel bag over his shoulder and fired up the bike before speeding off along the shoreline.

It took minutes to reach the gravel lot just off South Mobile Street, Fairhope's scenic highway. Kyle spotted the familiar sign for Flora. Adrian, his mother, had built her small business from the ground up to support herself and her young son after a disastrous first marriage. Kyle had spent many days after school behind the counter of the flower shop watching her work. If he was restless or naughty, she'd send him off to one of the neighboring small businesses owned by three women who had become aunts to him in everything but blood.

Attached to Flora on the bay side was Tavern of the Graces, owned by Olivia Leighton and her husband, Gerald, a bestselling author. Olivia had taught Kyle how to play pool and darts and how to woo chicks. Later, she'd taught him how to mix drinks and hold his liquor—not that his mother knew any of that. The now third-generation establishment was operated chiefly by Olivia and Gerald's first son, William, these days.

Above Flora was the gleaming display windows of Belle Brides, bridal boutique and operating center of buzzy wedding coordinator and couturier, Roxie Strong. Kyle had tried to avoid Belle Brides as a kid. Most everything was off-limits there. However, Roxie always kept sweets behind the counter, which she used to her advantage whenever she needed stand-ins in lieu of mannequins.

Finally, beyond the shops and Flora's greenhouse, there was the inn. The white antebellum structure was a real gem. Framed by gardens and supported by great columns, Hanna's Inn was lovingly tended by Briar Savitt and her husband, Cole. They'd lived on the third floor for years and had only just expanded into a new wing.

Construction looked to be complete, Kyle noticed as he parked his motorcycle in front of Flora and took off his helmet. Leaning back on the seat, he removed his gloves one finger at a time. He wasn't normally a fan of alteration, but the demand from the inn's guest book had all but screamed expansion as far back as Kyle could remember. And the design was swell. He'd bet Briar was pleased as pie.

He always felt warm when he thought of the innkeeper. She'd often cooked for him, baked for him. Long before she married Cole and gained Gavin as a stepson, she'd let Kyle sleep in the linens she tended as religiously as the landscaping. He'd done homework at her kitchen table. He'd laughed himself silly chasing a giant Irish wolfhound named Rex across the kempt lawn—a lawn he'd regularly mowed as a teen to keep his Jeep full-up on gas.

He'd caught crab for supper from the traps tied off her dock, had learned to fish and swim there, had tied his first skiff there. It was also there he'd kissed a girl for the first time, hunkered down in the butterfly bushes. Amelia Blankenship. They were almost eleven. She wore pomegranate lip balm.

He'd slipped her the tongue, and she'd told his mother. He then spent two weeks sulking without video games as penance. But not two years later Amelia started cornering him behind the lockers at school looking for a French partner, and all was forgotten.

As Kyle shifted from the leather seat of his

hog and planted his hard-soled riding boots in the gravel, he wondered if he'd be able to stick around long enough to catch the sunset from Hanna's. There was nothing like the view from her sunporch at the day's end.

He should know. He'd seen the sun set most everywhere.

The bells chimed over the door to Flora as he entered the shop, the sound as comforting as it was timeless. He stuffed his gloves in the riding helmet and tucked it against his side. The girl—well, woman—behind the checkout counter and the old-fashioned cash register was built like a willow branch. She had short-cropped raven-colored hair in a punk-ish sweep. There was a teensy diamond stud in the crease of her nose and several others creeping up the shell of her ear. She wore black makeup, black clothes. She always dressed in black, even in the thick of summer.

She was a carbon copy of his mother without the red hair neither of them had managed to inherit. Adrian's freckles had faded out long ago, but they remained on Kyle's sister, dark and splattered every which way across pale features. Still, the woman before him was so small even holding her as a child in arms, arms that had felt clumsy and reckless, Kyle had wondered that they could be so closely related.

He was eight when his mother married his biological father, James. And he was just shy of ten when the sibling he'd wished for with every fiber of his being was at last born. Not a brother like he'd wanted. But a sibling just the same.

When the door closed behind him, encasing him in the fresh, sweet-scented showroom, she didn't look around. Her head bent over a large open book, she recited in a bored monotone, "Welcome to Flora, Fairhope's finest florist. How may I assist you?"

"Damn," Kyle muttered, backtracking. "This ain't the cathouse."

Mavis's spine straightened. Her head whipped. Dark eyes pinned him to the spot, the muscles of her face momentarily slack in a rare show of surprise. "Kyle?" It wasn't so much a question as a demand. "You're home," she stated, combing him.

"Just."

"You didn't call," she said, accusing now. A well-worn scowl pulled at her insouciant mouth. "Typical of you to just show up and give everybody the shock of the month." A fist came to rest against her hip. "Jackass."

"Pipsqueak," he threw back.

"Nimrod."

"Tightwad."

"Meathead."

The corners of his lips moved. "Meathead?"

He watched hers waver. "Yeah. That's what I said. *Meathead.*"

He couldn't stop it. He broke into a fond grin. "Get over here."

Mavis had never been one for public displays of affection. Despite that and the tough love she volleyed routinely back at him in spades, she moved toward him. When he wrapped her tight against his chest, she stood only slightly stiff in his embrace.

"Miss me?" he whispered, his cheek against her hair.

"Eh."

A quiet laugh rumbled through him before he let her go.

She gave him another study. "At least you're intact. Wilderness Man."

Kyle skimmed his knuckles over the unruly beard. "Yeah, I could probably do with a shave, huh?"

"You're going to need a bush-hog to rid yourself of that mess." Eyes widening, she asked, aiming to tease, "Didn't lose any more of the family jewels, I take it."

He hissed through his teeth. "Can't afford it. What's left is here, standing right in front of you," he added when she continued to eyeball him, waiting for a solid answer on the health front. She blinked, and the relief was gone, but the glimpse of emotion he gleaned made his stomach tighten just the same. "What about you? How're you doing?"

"No complaints." When his brows hitched and he scrutinized her much as she'd scrutinized him, she repeated, "I said *no* complaints."

"Good," he said after a second's longer study. Mavis had been treated for epilepsy since she was a little kid. "And how's business?"

"Fine," she admitted.

"Mmm-hmm. Any, uh—" he fanned his fingers in the air "—*sightings* lately?"

She smirked, banding her arms over her chest. "You know that's confidential."

Mavis had an unusual job description and loose hours to go with it. When she wasn't tied up doing paranormal investigation, she filled the needs of her parents and their various industries—Flora, Carlton Nurseries, Bracken Mechanics and his father's latest and fondest project, a start-up company called Bracken-Savitt Aerial Application & Training. Or B.S., for short. "You're being careful out there at least," he said. "Right?"

"God, Kyle. It's not like I chase zombies or supervillains or whatever it is *you* do."

"Just ghosts and ghouls," he asserted. He digressed. "Where's Mom?"

"Greenhouse," she told him. "You better have brought her something. Seeing you's bound to knock her over."

He flicked the end of her button nose. She dodged and swiped. Bringing her against his side, he pecked a quick kiss to her temple. "Plans for dinner?" he asked as he backtracked to the entry door.

"Wouldn't you like to know?" She crossed her eyes at him.

He rolled his at her and pushed his way out into the heat. "I'm still waitin' for directions to that cathouse."

"Drive hard due west," she called at his back. "When you hit the bay, hold your breath and keep going!"

He chuckled again when the door closed behind him. He followed the path through the silver sale buckets and past an impressive display of succulents planted between the slats of an Old West wagon wheel. Around the side of the building, a wheelbarrow overflowed with annuals and a pineapple-shaped fountain burbled just before the wide-parted doors of Flora's greenhouse.

He heard the clomp of the stem cutter before he was even part of the way through. Inside, it was sweltering. The hanging plants and tables of vegetation soaked up the humidity. Kyle was already sweating under his cotton T-shirt when he rounded the corner and saw his mother chopping the stems off her latest delivery of fresh roses. The blade swung down, decisive under the guiding stroke of her hand. She worked by rote, quick, efficient in a red apron labeled with the Flora logo and thick work gloves to ward off any ill will from thorns.

He reached into the leg pocket of his cargoes

and pulled out the wrapping with his offering inside. "Howdy."

Adrian's head rotated quickly, and she stopped. It took her a moment. Kyle knew with the beard, and his hair grown out a good ways, that the resemblance between his father and himself was striking. He watched it sink in. Her hands fell away from the cutter, and her mouth parted. With her, the emotions bled through him easily and he let them, smile going soft. "Is this where you keep Dad's testicles?" When she continued to gaze, slack with surprise, he went on. "Mav and I. We've always wondered."

Her lips closed and her throat moved on a swallow. Though her eyes filled, she pulled in a breath and offered him a smile in return. "Why do you think I germinate the best bulbs in five counties?" The mist in her eyes grew until she blinked. She lifted her shoulders, taking him in. "Oh, my God, Kyle."

"Hey," he said, as her hands rose to her face and she lowered it into them. He crossed to her and spanned his arms around her. It was easy to hold her, much as it was once easy for her to hold him. When a silent sob tremored through her, he cradled her closer and rocked, side to side. He gave a small, cajoling laugh. "Mom. Hey, it's okay."

"Did something happen—to send you home early?"

"I'm fine. My rotation just ended."

She pulled back slowly. Raising her hands to his face, she took a good conclusive look at him. Where Mavis had been satisfied with words, Adrian knew better. She looked deep, beyond the eyes, searching. "Something's happened."

He shrugged it off. "It's over. I'm home."

"You are. I'm happy. So happy." Hugging him around the middle, she sighed. "Was your father in on this?"

"No." Kyle chuckled. "No, he's off the hook."

"Have you seen him?"

"Not yet. I saw Nick at the marina. He said something about an air show."

"It's something B.S. put together," Adrian said. "For charity. And, of course, advertising. He's flying a vintage training plane from the '50s. I've spent the better part of the day trying not to think about what happens when that man gets behind the yoke of an outmoded bucket."

"He's a good pilot."

"He's a show-off," she said plainly.

"Can't a guy be both?"

"Harmony's there, too," Adrian added.

"Harm." Kyle warmed at the news. He'd known Harmony from the day she was born. He'd marveled over her—her growth, her can't-touch-this attitude, her remarkable go-hard personality and the unquestioned strength that held those around her together. Being with Harmony was like finding a new penny somewhere unexpected, and not just because of her Zippo Flamethrower hair. "How's she doing?"

Adrian's smile wavered by a hair. Only a hair. "She likes being back in the air, and your father's determined to make sure she stays there this time around."

"Why wouldn't she?" When Adrian's eyes skimmed to his shoulder, he ducked his head to bring her attention back to his face. "B.S. isn't in some kind of trouble already?" Thus far, none of his father's ventures had failed. To hear the man tell it, the agricultural market had been ripe for new sprayers. "It's been barely a year since they cut the ribbon."

Adrian shook her head. "I couldn't tell you everything. I don't think even he's told me all the nitpicky details, but there've been problems. Prospective clients slipping away. Contracts breaking up over mysterious circumstances. And the holes need plugging now to keep the belly of the business off the ground. Until then…" She lifted her brows, eyeing him from underneath them. "This needs to stay quiet. I'm not sure Harmony knows half of what I'm telling you."

"She's fifty percent of the business," Kyle pointed out.

"Yes, but your dad told her from day one that this was a sure thing," Adrian said. "She put her faith in his word, as well as her money, name and reputation. If B.S. goes under, it won't be without a fight on your dad's part. Or mine, for that matter."

Kyle frowned over the wave of information.

Adrian crossed her arms over her chest. Mavis had looked much the same moments ago. "Did you sail home?"

"Always do."

"On the *Hellraiser*."

"What else?"

"Did you stay close to shore?"

"Mostly," he claimed.

One of her brows twitched. "Please tell me you didn't sail like an idiot through that storm."

He hedged. "Huh."

"Kyle Zachariah Bracken."

They both were born Carltons. Adrian had been married to Radley Kennard at the time of Kyle's birth. However, she'd wanted to give Kyle her name in lieu of her first husband's. When James came back into their lives, solidifying the family unit, his mother had asked Kyle's advice over what to do with their name.

He liked the idea of them staying Carltons, sharing what had been theirs together for so long. But he'd also finally gained a real father—one hell of a father—and he'd wanted to take his name. So, to James's amusement and pride, Kyle and Adrian took up the name Bracken to please themselves as well as him. "In my defense," Kyle said slowly, "it wasn't a tropical storm at the time…"

"You sailed through a hurricane and didn't have the decency to call your mother," she surmised, unimpressed by her findings.

"Are you surprised?"

"Not in the least. But I still have that BB gun I took from your possession all those years ago." Her lips pursed. "Don't think I'm not above poppin' you with it."

Kyle finally extended what was in his hand. "Then now's a good a time as any…"

Adrian took the bundle gingerly. "What's this?"

"A surprise. Careful," he added as she unrolled the cotton wrapping. "It's not the cuddly type."

Adrian carefully unveiled the offering. She cupped it in her hands with the cotton bunched between her skin and the thorns packed close along the stem. "Kyle," she breathed, every trace of censure vanishing. "Where did you get this?"

"That's…classified, Mom." When she tutted at him, he said, "I did some research. It's native to Madagascar. They say it migrated to the Middle East in ancient times as well as to small areas of India. They call it the Crown of Thorns."

Adrian gazed at it in wonder. Kyle's mother had seen most every flower under the sun. He loved nothing more than bringing home something exotic, something she hadn't seen before. In his parents' bedroom at The Farm, she kept a shadowbox full of treasures he'd found through his years of service. Bending her head low over the pink blossoms, she sniffed for fragrance. "It's different. I like that. Is it dangerous?"

"Poisonous, from flower to stem. And it'd make a fair pincushion."

It might as well have been a puppy, the way she lifted it to look from another angle. She beamed. "You did *good*. If you're right about the poison, it'll do well to keep your dad in line, too."

Kyle swallowed. "I missed you, Mom."

She gazed at him, the light in her flickering as she focused on what was behind the eyes once more. "Something did happen over there. But I missed you, too. And I'm glad you're home."

CHAPTER TWO

THE WARPLANE HANDLED like it was the 1940s and the war was on again. Harmony strapped into the cockpit of the old bird with the giddiness of a child and took to the sky, climbing high, the nose reaching for the blue, white-peppered expanse.

"No tricks today, ace," the voice of her radio-man advised. "Just do some nice fly-bys and get the people going."

"You're a buzzkill, James," she called back. "I'm just stretching the lady's legs."

What legs! The engine had fire and pizzazz. It was bred for dogfighting and hell-for-leather ma-neuvers. The idea brought gooseflesh to Harmony's skin as she banked, coming around.

The trim airfield spread out below her, a jutting green carpet. Two lines of exhibition planes were queued on either side of the runway. Hundreds of faces from the metal bleachers were turned up to the sky, watching the fighter live again. "Hold on to your hats," Harmony warned, going low.

A curse blew through the headset of her fly-ing helmet as she dipped over the bleachers and climbed again, gaining airspeed. "Well. Hats are in the wind," James observed. "You nearly ripped the blouse off the congressman's wife."

"Then we're certain to make the papers." She banked again. "Relax. Are the good people smiling?"

"They're *verklempt*. Nobody ever said you don't put on a good show."

"Just sit back and enjoy it, why don't you?" she suggested. "Coming in again…"

Even she whooped as she made the next sweep. This was worth all the hassle they'd gone through to get the summer show off the ground. They'd haggled for weeks with FAA regulations. With well-trained pilots, they'd managed to rustle together all the right paperwork and get the all-clear from the powers that be.

God, it felt great to be in the cockpit. No way she would ever give it up again. There wasn't anything she wouldn't give to stay airborne.

Well, there was *one* thing she wouldn't give. Harmony's gaze strayed to the three-by-five photograph she'd taped to the control panel for luck. Her daughter smiled back at her over a ruffle-lined shoulder, curly-headed and coquettish. She was the reason Harmony couldn't try any of her old barnstorming maneuvers, though the temptation sang. She was the reason Harmony heeded James's warning and performed fly-bys instead of loops.

Gracie Bea, who'd lost one parent before she

was born, was the general reason Harmony toed the line. Because no matter how trained she was, no matter how well-maintained the warbird might be, she couldn't take risks. She took enough on a day-to-day basis. Aerial application wasn't low-level aerobatics, but it still held its share of dangers.

Harmony liked being the pilot mama who taught her daughter not to slow down but to run and climb, whoop and holler. Yet she knew her limits, and she heeded them as she'd heeded few other limits in life, even gravity, because no child deserved to grow up an orphan.

It hurt enough that Bea would never know her father, Petty Officer Benjamin Zaccoe—Benji.

"Last pass," Harmony informed James through the radio. "Ready down there?" A frown pulled at her lips when he didn't answer. "James?" She was already going in for a dive. She pulled off the final fly-by and tapped her headset. "Tower, do you read?"

Communications must be down, she mused. Wheels down, she executed a safe, only somewhat flashy landing that brought the bird to a standstill in front of the rows of spectators who clambered to their feet and cheered her as she rose from the cockpit and waved. She'd dressed the part in a vintage flying helmet and sheep-lined leather jacket. As had been her trademark in flying days past, she wore her hair in a thick braid over one shoulder.

The warm reception brought her flight buzz to a satisfying conclusion. She stood on the wing of the fighter, gave a salute, and prepared to hop to the grass before she saw James approaching.

"Nice flying, ace." He nodded, impressed.

She pulled off her helmet. "I lost comms."

He reached out to grasp the wing's edge. James was well over six feet tall and had aged well. Very well. His hair and beard were still thick, with some salt and pepper sprinkled through. His tan face only looked worn around the corners of his eyes where laughter had inscribed itself. "Sorry. It was me," he admitted.

"Why?" she asked. "What happened?"

"I was distracted," James told her. He turned toward the row of B.S. personnel on the ground. "You can blame that one over there."

Harmony squinted. Well-worn T-shirt, cargo pants, battered baseball cap over hair that curled brown under the rim and bordered on unruliness. The beard was full enough to rival James's, and the smile wove a wide path through it. Blue eyes winked at her from under the brim of the hat.

"'Ey, Carrots," he greeted.

She nearly shuddered. "Kyle!" Hopping down to the grass, she got a running leap on him.

"Umphf!" he groaned under the impact, breaking into a low-rumbling laugh as he grabbed her up off the ground in a fierce hug.

Some hugs had the power to heal all manner of woes. Some were as vital as the bodies they brought together. Harmony tightened her hold around Kyle's neck. For a moment—a small moment—she let all her anxiety bleed through to the surface where she never let it stray. Not when he was away. She couldn't think about what he and her brother, Gavin, did. She couldn't think about the risk of losing either of them where she'd already lost too much.

Ducking her head into Kyle's shoulder, she felt her brow creasing and the muscles beneath quake with the effort to hold it back. Beating it under, she breathed deep and smelled sunshine, Zest soap and sea salt—smells that were so very Kyle.

He was back. It was her turn to feel *verklempt.*

"Talk about a hero's reception," he murmured.

Her lips curved. "Mmm-hmm."

"Harm?"

"Hmm?" she mumbled. She felt a bit fuzzy-headed as she pulled back in his embrace. "Oh." Loosening her grip, she let him set her on the grass. "Sorry. I just… I missed the hell out of you."

All the fuzziness faded, and her focus sharpened, everything zeroing in on him. As a girl, she'd felt a magnetic pull toward him. He might've known her since she was a baby, but Harmony was a woman, damn it, and Kyle Bracken was a man, a soldier, that women noticed.

"You look the same," he said.

She swore sometimes Kyle still saw her as his best buddy Gavin's little sister. Did he look at her and see the four-year-old who'd wrecked her bicycle in earth-scorching fashion on the gravel outside his mother's flower shop? Or the eighteen-year-old he'd tossed into a mud puddle in front of his navy friends? "Is that good?" she asked.

He reached up, touched her hair. Just a brush above the temple where some flyaway strays had pulled free of her braid. "Couldn't be better."

She ignored the missed breath and balled her hand into a fist. Throwing it into the rock slab of his shoulder, she knocked him back half a step and startled a short laugh out of him. "You don't call. You don't write. You just show up out of the blue to let us know you're—" She stopped herself just short of saying *alive*. She licked her lips and shook her head. "You're nearly as bad as my brother."

"Ouch," he said, his good humor fading by a fraction. He touched his shoulder. "You've been working on that jab."

"I'm a mama now, K.Z.B.," she reminded him. "Somebody's got to step up their game. Since Benji can't be here, and with you and Gavin gone more than half the time, I'm the only one left to teach Bea how to breathe fire."

His face went solemn at the reminder of Benji,

of Kyle's own continual absence. She saw a spark of guilt there. Harmony hadn't meant to hit him in the tenders. It was easy to forget he even had tender spots. He was built exactly as what he was—an elite fighter. He didn't exactly wear his emotions on his sleeve. He wasn't trained that way.

He just got back, she reminded herself. She knew better than most how long it took a soldier to settle after returning home—physically, emotionally, psychologically. And Kyle's heart reached as wide as the warm Gulf waters. Switching gears quickly, she said, "Bea will be thrilled to bits when she sees you."

"Not as much as me."

"Are you staying at The Farm?" she asked, referring to the farmhouse and acres of horse pasture, fields and woods that belonged to Adrian and James. "You could come by. Though you probably want to settle in first."

"I'll stay at The Farm for a little while," he acknowledged. "I'm not sure Mom would have it any other way. It's not much of a walk from their place to yours."

That was true. She lived on Bracken land in the mother-in-law suite. When Kyle's grandfather, Van Carlton, passed away, he and James had built the cozy little house for his grandmother, Edith, while the Brackens moved their family of four into the farmhouse she had no longer wanted to keep up. The arrangement had lasted little more than three years before his grandmother moved to a retirement village in Florida.

When Harmony returned home after Benji's death, she'd accepted the Brackens' invitation to live in the empty suite. The arrangement worked for all parties. She couldn't have very well brought a squalling newborn to the inn like her parents had wanted. They might like the idea of having their grandchild so close, but they also had an established business to run.

And Harmony liked the Bracken lands. She'd enjoyed raising Bea there with not much but honeybees and squirrels for company. The Farm was a rich place to raise a child. Bea had learned to ride in the last year. Adrian and James had even bought her her own pony. The Brackens themselves were generous landlords, understanding and unobtrusive. And it helped that Harmony's business partner was only a hop, skip and a jump away. B.S. butted up against The Farm and Carlton Nurseries, meaning the commute to work wasn't half bad either.

"Come by," Harmony invited. "See Bea. I'll make macaroni."

Kyle hissed, reaching for his waistline. "You know my weakness for your macaroni. Just as you know a soldier's got to watch his form."

"A spoon or two won't kill you," she said, slugging him again in the stomach. Her knuckles did little more than ricochet off the abs underneath his T-shirt. The man was a machine. There were strong men. Ripped men. Then there were men like Kyle who were made of stronger stuff—concrete and rebar. "I'll make it for Bea. You can gank a few bites off her plate if it makes you feel better. I'll even throw in a free trim." She motioned to his neckline. "You're getting long in the back." Overseas, he often let it grow out, but hair as thick as his didn't last long at home without a trim, particularly in the summer.

He scrubbed those peeking brown curls. "It didn't bother me 'til the humidity hit. Mavis could do it, but it's a foolish man who asks her to take scissors to his head."

"You're afraid of Mavis," Harmony noted. She shook her head. "I thought you big SEAL types were fearless."

"Not entirely."

"What else are you afraid of?" she asked experimentally.

He turned thoughtful. Again, his smile slipped. She wondered at the hitch before it vanished, and he responded. "Sharks."

"It's a good thing you're home then," she pointed out. She touched him, to assure herself again that he was really here. "You won't find many of those inland."

"I guess." He looked over her head, saw the

people watching and waiting. "I shouldn't keep you. Your fans'll want a piece of you, too."

"Work, work," she said, grinning.

He bent down, placing his lips against her cheek. "Amazing flying out there," he told her, lingering. "I'm proud of ya."

"The biplane's next," she told him, ignoring the little stir in her blood. It *was* little, after all. "You could tag along."

He barked a laugh as he backed off, knowing her penchant for flat-hatting. "I live dangerously enough on your mac-and-cheese."

"Ah, come on!" she chided.

"Not on your life, Carrots!" he shouted back. Lifting his chin to her, he disappeared into the throngs of spectators to join James, leaving her as spooled up as she had been in the cockpit of the old warplane.

DUSK FALLING ON The Farm was the essence of tranquility. As night approached, there was both a hush and a crescendo. Everything stilled. Even with the sun gone from the sky, the heat didn't dwindle, but it banked, the air breathable once more. As the light faded, the sound of night bugs—crickets and cicadas—escalated. Amphibians struck up the tune, adding throaty backup vocals to the noise of the backcountry twang. Their combined pitch heightened to that of a diesel engine. After his time away, it was like a homecoming symphony from Mother Nature's Philharmonic.

The mosquitos were out, but the farmhouse's back porch screened them from feasting on flesh. Through the open window, Adrian and Mavis could be heard arguing lightly over the dish washing.

On the porch, James puffed a cigar. In his youth, he'd been a man of many vices. He was no longer controlled by substances. His weekend after-dinner Montecristos were his only remaining weakness. He tipped his head back, blowing rings into the air, looking every bit the striking, aging pirate. At fifty-four, he still cut an impressive figure, especially in the flickering light of Adrian's tiki torches.

Kyle soaked it all in. The sweet scent of his father's stogie. The familiar tumble of the land, rising and falling under wild grasses to the stable and pastures. A horse nickered in the distance. The animals' slow-grazing silhouettes were fading against the inky backdrop of trees.

Some pockets of the world remained untouched. That certainty was what Kyle escaped to when the fighting was over. Change was inevitable. Cities moved forward. Small towns turned to progress. Backcountry places like this developed. People changed. Grandparents passed. Engagements broke. Teammates burned out or chose to leave the service to save their families. Some of them never saw the beauty of their final homecoming.

The Farm was rare. The way of life went on unceasing, the pace unbroken. It persisted and endured. Yet that shift in barometric pressure could be sensed here, too. The storm was gaining speed in the Gulf and hadn't altered course. It would make a wet landing somewhere between Perdido and Pensacola. Home and business owners were already battening down in preparation for the first seasonal run-in with the tropics. Soon Kyle would help James and Adrian stable the horses, round up the litter of puppies spring had given them and board the windows.

The storm was small enough not to worry too much. The Farm would most likely remain unscathed. For now, Kyle drank an icy glass of tea and let his father smoke. "How bad is it?" he asked out of curiosity.

"What's that?" James asked, turning his head from the view.

"The aviation industry," Kyle indicated.

James took a final puff from his cigar, eyeing Kyle over the brown stump. Releasing a ragged stream of smoke, he leaned forward in his patio chair and stabbed it out in the tray at the center of the table. He'd take the tray out in the yard and dump it before going back inside, so the ashes didn't get caught up in the breeze and dirty Adrian's furnishings. Such courtesies between Kyle's parents were simple and commonplace, performed with unspoken poignancy that was touching in the extreme. "It should be booming."

"But it's not," Kyle surmised, daring his father to challenge the assumption.

James did a few more quick stabs with the Cuban before depositing it in the tray. Dragging a hand through his mop of hair, he settled back with a creak from the chair. "There've been some ruts in the road."

"And?" Kyle posed the question again. "How bad is it?"

James folded his hands over his middle. "I've been a businessman for thirty years. I haven't lost one entrepreneurship yet, and I'm not going to now."

"No matter the cost?"

James hesitated. He glanced toward the window where Adrian and Mavis were talking. When he spoke again, his voice lowered to a murmur. "Those two are the chief reasons B.S. has to survive."

Kyle frowned. "There'll be collateral damage if it doesn't," he realized, trying to read James. It wasn't easy. The man could bluff like a maverick and not just at the poker tables. "What did you mortgage? The cottage on the bay isn't big enough. Was it the auto shop? Please tell me it wasn't Flora or the nursery."

"It wasn't any of those," James mused, no longer meeting his son's eye. "It was a sure thing. Byron Strong went over the business plan. The best advisers on the coast took a look at the specs. The application market was ripe for new pilots. The only issue was lack of local training opportunities, but we fixed that with the teaching base of B.S."

"So what's the issue?"

"I don't know, exactly. We've had two big contracts fall through based on minute technicalities. We've had farmers shy away after weeks of negotiation. Even advertising has had its windfalls." James released an unsteady breath. "It was The Farm. I mortgaged The Farm to get B.S. off the ground."

James might as well have pulled a WWE and hit Kyle over the head with his chair. For slow-winding seconds, he felt as if he were being choked out by one of his SEAL teammates.

Dragging oxygen into his lungs, he worked to clear the bright pinpoints in his head that told him blackout was imminent. Gripping the arms of his chair, Kyle stared at his father in something close to horror. "You…gambled The Farm?"

"Like I've been trying to explain to you, it wasn't a gamble."

Kyle pushed up from the seat. He braced his hands on his hips and walked to the far side of the porch. There were potted plants in most every variety hanging from chains, stacked on shelves and pedestals…and he couldn't breathe. "Son of a bitch," he hissed.

"Kyle," James said, climbing to his feet, too. "It'll be all right. We won't lose. *I* don't lose. The Farm is your birthright. Nothing's going to change that."

"Mom let you do this?" Dark gathered on the porch with only the torches to make up the distance between him and his father. "She knew what you were doing?"

"Of course she knew," James said, insulted by the insinuation that she might not. "I'm always up-front with your mother. You know this."

"Did you sell her the same old line of bull— that it was a sure thing? That we'd all come out smelling like roses?"

In a weary motion, James dipped his hands into his pockets. "Son. You're angry. I get that. But there are no lies between your mom and me. There's no subterfuge. We couldn't be what we are if there was. It's the same with you. Haven't I always given you the truth, straight up?"

"Yeah, but it wasn't like that in the beginning, was it?" Kyle asked. He was on the verge of furor and he went there. "All those years ago. You didn't exactly tell her why you missed the first part of my life. Why you left her when she was seventeen, pregnant. She had to find out for herself what kind of man you were before us."

James stared, stricken. They'd rarely spoken

in heated terms. They'd never hurt one another.
It had been their silent understanding from the
moment James had come back into Kyle's and
Adrian's lives, a way of making up for all those
lost years.

But The Farm.

Some things were sacred.

Hurt worked in the creases of James's face,
looking for purchase. Yet he spoke levelly. "Have I
ever done anything to make you question my loy-
alty or motives? You're my life, Kyle. You, your
mother, Mavis… You're my whole life."

"Then why didn't Mav and I have a say in
this?" Kyle asked. "You didn't do this for us. You
did this to satisfy your own need for thrills on a
day-to-day basis, Howard Hughes."

"I did this," James said, placing each word with
care, "for our home. Family-owned agriculture is
dying. Farms like ours are breaking up and being
put to auction. I needed to do something."

"You did it for yourself," Kyle maintained. Another thought struck him, and it brought on great
big flame balls of ire. "And what about Harmony?
How much does she have riding on this? She lives
here, too, Dad—her and Bea. This is their home.
She's staked money, probably most of what she
has to her name. Her name itself is stamped on
the business. You lose B.S., what does that mean
for her? You won't be able to pay back all she bet."

"No one's going to take a loss," James said, the

first signs of frustration bleeding through. "No one."

"How much have you told her? She's your partner. Her training is your big ticket item. What does she know?"

A pronounced frown took hold of James's tight features. "I don't want her to worry."

"But there's no reason to worry, right?" Kyle said, tossing the assertion back at him. He shook his head. "You're a piece of work."

"Kyle," James said as Kyle shoved through the screen door.

"I need a minute," he said as he descended to the grass and kept walking. He had to walk. The fighter in him was taking shots, and it needed to stop before he could face either of his parents again. He felt betrayed by the one person in the world who shouldn't have betrayed him. His father had thrown his so-called birthright against the wall like spaghetti.

If Kyle stayed, he'd say something he'd regret. *Do* something he'd regret.

He'd walk until the sting of his father's actions numbed. Even if it meant walking all night. The Farm went on for miles.

CHAPTER THREE

SOMETIMES A GIRL needed to see the moon. Especially if that moon was a strawberry moon.

"Mama," Bea moaned as she gazed at the rising moonscape through the paper tube of her makeshift glitter-dotted telescope. "It's not *right*."

"Not right?" Harmony said. She was on her knees in capri pants in the middle of the dusty path that led from the gate of the Brackens' farmland to the mother-in-law suite. She peered at the horizon. Rising over the trees was a wondrous, dusky red full moon. "That's it. Right there."

"But it's not a strawberry," her four-year-old insisted, disappointment laden in her voice.

Harmony felt the urge to laugh. Bea's seriousness kept the brevity from breaking the surface. Clearing her throat, she said in the practical tones her intuitive preschooler would appreciate most, "It's only called a strawberry moon."

"Why?" Bea asked, features squelched as she gazed, skeptical, at the impressive nightly specter.

Harmony pursed her lips. "Well, it's red. Like a strawberry."

"Tomatoes are red."

"True." Harmony nodded.

"And Mammy's tulips. And puppy noses."

"All valid points." And Harmony did smile, because the thought of a Puppy-Nosed Moon was too amusing to resist. She loved Bea's mind. She loved its precociousness and the great kaleidoscope of imagination that kept it from maturing too quickly. "But I think it's called a *strawberry moon* because... You remember talking in day school about the first people who lived on this land, the Native Americans?"

"Uh-huh?"

"Well, those same Native Americans needed to know when their strawberries were ready for picking. So the moon would paint itself up like a strawberry to tell them."

"Oooh." Bea tilted her head, as if viewing the moon through a new lens. "It looks like blackberry juice."

"It does, doesn't it?" A heady breeze stirred the trees into a whispering frenzy. It brought the smell of salt far inland, an early herald of the storm. Shifting from one knee to another, Harmony drew the folds of her sweater close. Planes would be grounded for the next few days until the damn thing spun itself north to the Plains and petered there.

June brought pop-up thunderstorms. It was a fact of life in the low south, but that didn't stop her from feeling restless. She'd been grounded too long before James came to her with the proposal for Bracken-Savitt Aerial Application & Training. Summer was prime running time for crop dusters with fields ripening toward harvest, and yet the seasonal weather was a nuisance and a half.

Bea shifted from one leg to another then back. Harmony picked up on the telltale impatience, identical to her own. "Have you seen enough of the moon tonight?"

"Can I have a bath?" Bea asked, swiping her small round palm over her brow. Blond curls clung, damp, to her temple. "I wanna bath."

It took some effort not to roll her eyes and remind her daughter that she'd firmly refused bath time not two hours ago. Settling for a sigh, Harmony stood up and helped bring Bea to her feet. "Bath time sounds good."

"With Mr. Bubble?" Bea asked, hopeful.

"With Mr. Bubble," Harmony confirmed. Dusting the frilly skirt of Bea's fairy outfit and the petticoat layers underneath, she took the lead to the house.

Bea's head turned sharply at the sound of rustling in the high-climbing vegetation. "What's that?"

"Probably an animal," Harmony said, tugging Bea along and eyeing the bushes warily. A *big* animal. Creature sightings were everyday happenings on The Farm. Aside from the horses and dogs the Brackens raised, there were squirrels, raccoons, reptiles and insects in abundance.

The crashing in the undergrowth grew louder. Bea's mouth dropped. "Mama," she whispered. *"What is that?"*

"I don't know." She stepped halfway in front of Bea to protect her.

Bobcat?

No. *Bigger*.

Deer?

"It's a bear," Bea said, eyes as round as the moon.

"It's not a bear," Harmony said doubtfully. Then she frowned. *Is it?* All of a sudden, she found herself wishing for the hot-pink high-powered stun gun her father, a former police detective, had given her for her sixteenth birthday. In case of a break-in, she kept it in her top dresser drawer under the naughty lingerie she never wore.

Bea's hand tightened on hers as branches snapped and tossed. Harmony licked her lips and tensed. Whatever it was would have to go through her…

A swath of moonlight fell on the T-shirt-clad figure, and she breathed again. *Just a SEAL*.

He turned to go up the path, then stopped when he saw them, frozen and watchful.

A very surly SEAL, Harmony observed.

"Hi," he greeted shortly.

"Hi," she returned. She nudged Bea. "See? Not a bear."

Kyle tilted his head to the side to get a look at the girl hiding behind Harmony's leg. "Hey there, little wing."

Energy zipped from the bottom of Bea's frame to the top. She gave a short squeal, tearing off from her hiding place. She launched herself at Kyle as he went into a crouch, arms spread wide.

"'You'll fly like a bee!'" he shouted. Then he tossed her, giggling and kicking, into the air. "'Up to the honey tree, see?'"

"I see!" she shrieked. "Again! Higher!"

Kyle grunted, tossing her up toward the stars.

After the third toss, again Bea cried, "Again, again!" and Kyle eyed Harmony.

She shrugged. "You brought this on yourself," she told him.

"Yeah, but you made it," he countered. He threw Bea up one last time.

As she came back down, Bea latched on to him around the neck, much as Harmony had earlier in the day, and didn't let go. Nuzzling her cheek against his, the smile in her voice was clear. "I missed you!"

Any trace of the sullenness Harmony had glimpsed when Kyle had trudged out of the thicket vanished quickly. He folded his arms over Bea's back, letting one hand stray into her vivid curls.

"Missed you, too, Gracie Bea." Turning his lips into her cheek, he closed his eyes and rocked her from side to side.

Harmony tried not to melt too much over the pair. She failed. Bea's pink high-top sneakers dangled free, four feet from the ground. Kyle's hard muscly arms tightened around her, his hands splayed over her slender back, soothing. Those hands were made for fighting, for pumping rounds through an M-60 machine gun. They were calloused and rough. They could put a man down in seconds. Yet they cradled the child of his buddy and his best friend's sister, and his expression was putty. Soft, soft putty.

What chance did a mama have?

Harmony sighed a little, sliding one hand slowly into the back pockets of her capris. She gave the pair another moment, two, before stepping forward. "Bea." Touching her other hand to her daughter's back, she let out a laugh. "Bea. Let him breathe, baby."

"She's fine," Kyle assured Harmony, meeting her gaze through a tuft of downy hair that had blown across his face.

"She's choking you."

"Not since I joined the navy have I been so happy to be choked out," he admitted.

Harmony patted the ringlets just beneath the

hand Kyle used to crib Bea's head to his shoulder. "What are you doing out here?"

He shuttered, giving a slight shake of his head. "Walking."

"Walking?" She eyed the tree line he'd been blazing a trail through. *Give the man a machete and he could pave the way to town.* "You were fighting kudzu. We thought you were a predator."

"Oh, yeah? And what are the two of you doing out?"

Bea's head lifted finally. "Me and Mama found the strawberry."

"Strawberry?"

"Strawberry moon," Harmony said, gesturing toward the sky. "It's tonight."

"It is, huh?" Kyle asked, hitching Bea on to his hip. She pointed and he nodded sagely. "How about that, little wing? They hung a strawberry in the sky just for you."

"I can't eat it," she said, crestfallen. "I love strawberries."

"Don't we know it?" Kyle set Bea on her feet. He crouched to her level. "When you lay your head on your pillow and dream, I bet you'll be able to reach out and grab it."

"How will I get all the way up there?" she asked, her dark wondrous stare seizing on his.

Harmony rubbed her lips together as Kyle eyed her briefly over Bea's head. "You could climb up on my shoulders," he offered.

"You'll be there?"

"If you want me to be." He dug his fingertips into her ribs. She shrieked. "Do you? Huh?"

Bea wriggled. "Yes, yes!" She snorted and squealed as he kept tickling. When he subsided, she settled down with a smile, rubbed the hair plastered to her brow again, and asked, "Will you come home with us?"

"It's late," Harmony pointed out. "Kyle probably wants to go back to the farmhouse and rest. He's been gone a long time."

"A *long* time," Bea echoed.

"What's a few months to buddies like us?" Kyle suggested.

Bea placed her hands on his cheeks. Rubbing her palms over the soft texture of his beard, she said, "We could watch Stuffins."

"Stuffins," Kyle repeated, clueless.

"Doc McStuffins," Harmony elaborated. "Disney. She's allowed to watch one episode before bed. I'm sure Kyle would rather finish his walk and go home."

"Actually," he said, "Stuffins sounds perfect."

"Really?" Harmony asked as Bea cheered his decision-making skills.

"Really. If you don't mind." He smirked. "Mama."

Harmony rolled her eyes as Bea sounded off with a chorus of *pleases*. "I don't have mac-and-cheese. Tonight's leftovers."

"Chitlins and dumplin's," Bea informed him very matter-of-factly.

"*Chicken* and dumplings, baby," Harmony said when Kyle's brow peaked. To him she added, "I don't feed her pig intestines. I swear."

"They're not so bad." When Harmony and Bea's noses wrinkled in sync, Kyle grinned in a wicked sort of way that resonated from the past. "Come on. You'd try them once."

"Only if you wolf that big strawberry down first," Harmony suggested.

Kyle frowned at the moon. They both knew he was allergic to the fruit. It'd always puzzled Harmony—someone as strong as him, felled by a berry. "Did, ah, these leftovers come from your mom, by chance?"

Harmony ran her tongue over her teeth. *He* was allergic to strawberries. But unlike her mother—the culinary goddess of the south—*she* was allergic to cooking. "Yes. But I mashed the taters."

"With the raw bits left in?"

"How else would they stick to your ribs?"

Bea tugged on his hand, and Kyle followed her, rising to his feet and swinging their linked fingers as he fell into step with Harmony. "Now, that sounds like a treat."

"You didn't eat with your family?" Harmony asked as they began to walk down the lane to the suite.

"I did," he admitted. "Mom made her glazed

Andouille-stuffed pork because she knows that's all I think about when I'm away. But when I'm really tired of MREs, I've been known to think about Briar's chicken and dumplings."

"Anything else?"

"Your freaking macaroni and cheese," he noted. "Though it is bound to kill me eventually."

She smoothed her lips together, pleased to make the cut.

"And if your mother's thinking about making a blackberry pie or her coq au vin anytime soon…"

"I'll be sure to bring leftovers home for you." Harmony picked up the hint.

He sent her a sly sideways smile. "Thanks."

Bea skipped ahead, buzzing with excitement. The wind swept up her hair as it tossed through the alley of trees arcing like an awning over the narrow pathway. Honeysuckle blossoms tumbled down, a soft white rain. The sweet fragrance teased up memories of summers long ago. Summers when life was still simple, rich and undefined. "I envy her," Harmony mused as she watched her daughter caper toward the lights of the white-framed house. Kyle turned to question her. She explained, "She gets to grow up at The Farm. Could childhood be any better?"

A frown toggled Kyle's mouth, and he looked at the ground as they kicked honeysuckle blossoms up under their feet. "No."

"I was so jealous of Gavin when we were kids,"

she pointed out. "All those weekends he got to come here and run wild with you."

"You came with him," he remembered.

"Not as much as I wanted to." They walked on, quiet together. Almost at the point of lollygagging. The night was one of those lulling complacent ones, tepid and inky, luring people outdoors like a crooking finger. "And, anyway, you boys reveled in leaving me behind."

"Not true." When she arched a brow, he digressed. "Not *entirely* true. Not on my part."

She smiled at bit over the admission. "Have you seen him? Gavin? He hasn't called in a while. I know he's all right. Dad tells me. He gets emails. I know y'all are on separate teams and you take turns on the hopper, but I was hoping, in the crossover, you might've seen one another."

"I haven't seen him," Kyle said shortly, that frown pulling at his mouth again.

Harmony licked her lips. "I know the new job in DC has kept him tied up when he's stateside. Still, it'd be nice to have him visit."

A line burrowed between Kyle's brows. "Job?"

"He didn't tell you?" Harmony crossed her arms, oddly chilled. She knew things hadn't been the same between Kyle and Gavin since Benji's death. Their business was their own, and, when it came to the details of service, they kept it that way. Harmony understood even as she bristled at the not knowing what had gone amiss between her brother and the friend he'd once claimed was like a brother to him.

"No, he didn't," Kyle stated. The frown deepened. "Harm, when was the last time you talked to him?"

"A while."

"What's a while?"

She thought about it. "Must be six months now. Maybe seven."

"Seven…" He trailed off, perturbed. "Did he visit then?"

"No. He rarely does." At Kyle's curse, she added quickly, "There's been the job. And I know he has a life. From the sound of it, there might have been a girl at one point…" When Kyle only shook his head, she trailed off.

"So you spoke on the phone," he surmised. "What about?"

She crawled back into her memory. The conversation had been brief, stilted. Yawning absences did that to the tightest of siblings. "He talked about work. He asked after Bea, made sure Dad was telling him the truth and all's well with him and Mom and the inn…"

"Nothing else?" Kyle asked.

What was he waiting for her to say? She took herself back over the conversation with Gavin but couldn't think of anything more. "Don't think so. Why?" she asked. Though nothing changed on the surface, she could all but hear the hum of Kyle's indignation building. "Do you know something I don't?"

He seemed to hesitate. His outer shell was as good as a bullet casing. He kept tight to that casing. "He should be here."

"If you're here," she calculated, "then isn't his team rotating to active?"

"The team is," he said and nothing more.

Harmony was growing irritated, too. "He's my brother. If you know something, tell me."

"It's not my place," he said shortly. "He should be the one talking to you about this. When was the last he came home?"

Harmony sighed. "I don't know. Last summer sometime."

"For how long?"

"He stayed overnight at the inn and left the next evening. Mom and Dad both wanted him to stay longer. We all did."

"Why didn't he?"

"He said he had training."

"You believe that?"

She rolled her eyes heavenward, tired of the third degree. "I don't know."

"He visits once a year and is hardly around for twenty-four hours when he does. That's bullshit, Harmony. I know it. You know it. *Everybody* knows it."

"Maybe it's hard for him to be here," Harmony suggested. "You ever think of that?"

"Why should it be?" Kyle asked, finally turning his face to hers. There was anger there, and he opened up just enough for her to see the genuine mystification behind it.

"Because it's a reminder," Harmony replied. "The town, the inn, The Farm… They're all reminders of Benji. Because Bea… She's all that's left of her father. She looks like him. She acts like him. God, Kyle, look at her. She even walks like him. Sometimes it's difficult to process. Even for me."

Kyle shrugged. "I'm here. Right?"

She measured the breadth of his stance, the realness of him.

"Why shouldn't Gavin be?" he challenged. When she kept walking, his voice gentled. "Bea's his niece. Flesh and blood. That's no simple matter."

Harmony licked her lips. "No. It's not. But since Benji died, Gavin's driven straight back into that big tough lone wolf mentality. He always had it, deep down. But then Benji…" She shrugged. "You know he was there, don't you? The night Benji was killed? When Benji was shot. He was there when he—" she licked her lips again and made herself say it "—when he bled out. He carried him out on his back."

Kyle nodded, eyes forward.

"It's hard to say," Harmony noted, "still. It's hard to think about. It never won't be. But to have been there…" She let out a shaky breath. "I don't know how he carries that around with him. And part of me doesn't blame him for being the lone wolf. I don't even blame him for not being here. Because maybe that's his way of coping."

Kyle fell into thoughtful silence. The surly bent of his mouth was back.

Harmony had the absurd notion to feather her fingertips across it to soften it once more. She rolled her eyes, moving her shoulders back to loosen them. "We do appreciate it." When he turned to her, she added, "*You* being here. You always show up, hard times or no. That's big. Don't think I don't notice."

He searched, eyes roving from one of hers to the next. His mouth curved at the end. Acknowledgment. Gratitude.

On the wind, a honeysuckle blossom skittered across her face. It danced into her hair and tangled. She reached up to pry it loose.

Kyle beat her to it, tugging it free.

"Thanks," she said, tossing her hair back.

Methodical, he used ginger fingers to extract the long green stem where the nectar lived. He pinched off the petals, discarded them. "You know what honeysuckle makes me think of?"

"No," she admitted, watching how he handled the fragile parts of the minuscule flower with infinite care.

"Springtime at Hanna's. I knew it was spring

when the honeysuckle vines burst on the trellises. You could smell them a block away."

"I used to hide there," she said. "Whenever I did something I shouldn't have."

"A frequent occurrence," he remembered, smiling at her sideways.

"Yes," she said with a nod. "Poor Mom. I gave her more hell than she deserved."

"Growing up'll do that to you." Holding the stem up, he offered her the small bead of nectar dripping from the end in a motion that was as natural as the wordless shift from spring to summertime.

Harmony tipped her head back without thinking, accepting. It felt natural, sure. But she was very aware of his eyes on her face and the momentary brush with his laser focus. And she felt hot.

She frowned. She could blame it on June or the tropics. But she'd had these brushes with him since she was a girl. A girl with a crush so boundless and hopeless, it had nearly cracked her in two.

Before Benji, before womanhood, there had been only Kyle. Her daughter wasn't the only young'un who'd ever been enamored with K.Z.B.

Turning her eyes to his, she closed her mouth around the drop. It was barely enough to taste. When his gaze held hers, she swallowed because her pulse began to work in double time. His beard drew her attention. "You need a shave."

As she walked on, she breathed carefully. She

was burning hot beneath the skin. It'd stopped being a problem for so long, she'd forgotten how difficult it was to cool. *Go big or go home* had always been her go-to phrase. It was typically her body's response to everything, as well.

Sometimes that was nothing short of hell.

Kyle was still off-limits. Military. She could not under any circumstances love another military man like she'd loved Benjamin Zaccoe. And, frankly, she'd thought she was done with this hot mess she'd developed for Kyle. Before she'd moved out West and thrown herself into school and piloting.

It had helped that Benji had been stationed at Coronado by that point and had visited often. It helped seeing him fresh out of BUD/S. A new Benji. Hard-bodied, disciplined, with that cheeky grin peeking through, a hint of the troublemaker she'd known back home where he'd cracked jokes about her gangly build and ginger mane.

It had helped that, without Gavin around to police things between them, Benji saw her in a new light, too. No longer the petulant tagalong but an adult. *You're a frigging force of nature*, he'd sized her up after watching her train without an instructor for the first time. *You know that?*

The only thing that had threatened to slow down the snowball of their relationship was Gavin and Kyle's opinion on the subject. Benji had come away from a few days with them on the Gulf with bruises and five stitches in his forehead. He'd come away smiling, nonetheless, with cautious blessings from his bosom buddies.

It had helped that Kyle had been involved in a serious relationship as well, one that had gone as far as the potential of marriage. Laurel Frye had been the bane of Harmony's existence from the moment she started tagging along behind Kyle, too. The whole fairy-tale romance had started in early high school. Kyle had been smitten with Laurel, which had made the whole affair worse for Harmony.

High school sweethearts were rarely lasting. It had seemed that Kyle and Laurel would be one of those rare exceptions…until his first tour and the frag grenade that had torn through his left leg. Laurel wasn't the only one who'd wanted him to quit the teams after. Harmony had gone so far as to reason with him not to re-up. But Laurel's voice had been louder. And when he did go back close to a year later, her voice was the one that had grown embittered.

Kyle and Laurel's relationship hit the skids shortly after. By that point, Benji was dead, and it was clear that Harmony was going to have to raise a baby alone.

Not alone, Kyle had assured her. By phone. By email. He was right. A single parent she might be, but she hadn't been alone like she thought she'd be. Not even in the delivery room. Kyle had returned just in time for the early labor. He'd driven her to the hospital, sat with her in the delivery room until her mother was there to relieve him. And he hadn't just checked in through the years as Gavin had. There had been FaceTime between him and Bea. For the little girl, he'd been an example of what a man should be. Not a father. He couldn't replace Benji and had no intention to. He'd been, as always, a friend. Harmony hoped she and Bea had returned the gesture in kind.

Because that's what they were. Friends. That was what they would remain, she was sure as she mounted the small steps to the little screened porch and held the door open for him. He entered the house that smelled like dumplings and Briar Savitt's peach pie, Bea slung comfortably over his shoulder. As he brushed past Harmony, he even turned his head and winked.

Steady, she told her insides when they started to quake. *Steady as she goes, girl.*

We are not *wrecking through this flight path again.*

CHAPTER FOUR

"SHE'S ASLEEP," KYLE ANNOUNCED, hushed, as he returned to Harmony's kitchen where she was doing the dishes. He reached back for his neck and tilted his head to work out a crick.

"How many stories did she ask for?" she smirked, knowing.

"A dozen," he said. "She still likes *Where the Wild Things Are*. That was—"

"My favorite," Harmony said, nodding. She turned to him, drying her hands. "You remember that?"

"Reading to you was always the better part of my day," he told her.

Her lips seamed and pressed inward. She scanned his face before her attention seized on the hand massaging his neck. "You didn't lie down with her, did you?"

"She asked me to."

"Kyle. She sleeps in a daybed."

"So?"

"So," she said, "you're *six-four*. I know SEALs are trained to sleep anywhere, but how did you even—"

"I was half off," he admitted. "It's all right. She was asleep in five minutes flat."

"You're a bona fide teddy bear."

"I can accept that." He nodded. "As long as I still get to shoot bad guys."

She laughed. "Isn't that what teddy bears do when children fall asleep? Defend them against the monsters in the closet?" Laying her hands on the back of one of the chairs surrounding the small round table between them, she asked, "Ready?"

"For?" he asked, blank.

"That trim," she said.

"It's late. You still wanna?"

She pulled out the chair. "Have a seat. I'll get the shears."

To Kyle, the ritual was more sentimental than anything. After the frag had torn through his lower body, he'd been in and out for weeks thanks to the powerful pain meds. His first lucid memory was waking up in a military hospital, disoriented. Then... Harmony. Harmony leaning close. Fingers skimming through his hair. It took him a moment or two to realize that she was giving him a trim and that she'd shaved his beard down to the fine black stubble he preferred off-duty.

When she saw his eyes open, she'd stopped. Said his name. Fighting against the sensation of cotton-mouth and the anxiety of not knowing where he was, he replied with, "Carrots."

She'd gone misty-eyed. It occurred to him then

that he hadn't seen Harmony cry since she was in diapers. There was a wavering fear that she would break down and that seeing her do so might break him down, too.

She held it together, like a boss. "It's good to have you back, K.Z.B." And, after offering him a sip of water, she went back to trimming his hair, smiling.

She'd gone a long way toward holding him together over the agonizing months he spent recouping.

As she combed his hair now, he felt all the tension in his body slide toward extinction. As she raked wet fingers through to dampen his hair, her small nails teased his scalp. His eyes closed. Comb in one hand, shears in the other, she silently, meticulously went about the task of snipping the thick curls growing toward the nape of his neck.

He'd spent a week on the *Hellraiser* trying to lose himself amid wind and tide. He'd come home, a task that usually brought him necessary reprieve. But it wasn't until now, he realized, that he'd felt truly relaxed since departing Little Creek.

Her hand rested on his head. "You're not sleeping, are you?" she asked in a low voice that trickled down the back of his neck.

Kyle blinked. Had he been? "Why?"

"Your head started to bob."

"Sorry." He cleared his throat. He sounded groggy. "Long day, I guess."

"We've kept you up." She snipped strays one by one. He heard the drone of the buzzer. Using the hand on his head, she pushed his chin to his collarbone. "Let me get your neckline."

She buzzed him down to his shirt collar, then walked around to his front. Bending to his level, she squinted at her progress.

Kyle studied her. Hers was a chameleon face. From one angle, it had the potential to be soft and feminine. From the other, it could be sharp, inflexible, even cold. All her life, she'd had a notorious mercurial habit of flying from one mood to the next. Her features reflected that well.

Unlike him, she'd never favored one parent or another. Aside from the warm honeycomb irises that had been imprinted by Briar, Harmony's eyes were narrow and feline. By turn, they could make her look catty or uncompromising. Her red hair in particular proved her to be the perfect Savitt-Browning hybrid—a genetic toss-up between Cole's dark brown and Briar's ash-blond. She was athletically built. Tall and leggy. In fact, she'd out-inched her old man by the time she was legal. She'd never been curvy. She was more angular, and each one of those intriguing angles came with its own road hazard. *Caution. Speed Bump. Sharp Turn Ahead.*

Erring, his study fell upon her lips.

Slow Down. No Crossing. Dead End.

She wet them. The lazy river of his blood began

to eddy and flow. As she reached out to test the evenness of his ends, her outer thighs nudged against the inner seam of his, and she caught her lower lip between her teeth.

He felt taut again, but in a way which spoke of his six-month deployment and the lack of anything besides male companionship over that time. His thigh muscles flexed as something unfurled there, around his gut and the base of his spine.

Her teeth were slowly releasing her lip, letting it round gradually, red and wet. A strawberry ripe for the plucking.

No Thru Traffic. Wrong Way, Moron!

Kyle snatched himself out of the off-color reverie. *Blink.* It was Harmony's face in front of his. *Carrots.* He'd read her to sleep with Little Golden Book stories as a kid. He'd watched her learn to walk.

He'd taught her to ride her bike, damn it. To swim. Soon the Little Golden Book readings had warped into E. B. White, Beverly Cleary, Roald Dahl, Laura Ingalls Wilder. He'd even spent one sulky summer speed-reading through a tattered copy of *Anne of Green Gables* for her. And ever since, he'd called her "Carrots" in consequence.

He'd watched her grow into a skinny-legged teen, then a self-possessed adult. He'd watched her and Zaccoe collide headlong. When something unexpected and timeless had grown out of that collision, he'd watched their destinies entwine. He'd been happy for them.

He'd been the one to tell her Benji was KIA. He'd stood next to her on the tarmac as his brothers-in-arms carried the flag-draped casket off the angel flight.

He'd been the first person to learn she was pregnant while she bent over Benji's face one last time in the visitation room at the funeral home. She had wept then, tears dripping off the end of her nose combined with long piercing cries that belonged in the wild to some poor felled animal with no chance of mercy.

He'd cradled her baby in the crook of his arm and wondered not for the last time why fate had left him alive and taken Benji.

A space of a lifetime passed between blinks. Kyle tried to reassert himself in that space, but all he got was disorientation akin to what he'd felt in the hospital upon waking after being blown up by that mother-humping frag…

"Kyle?" Harmony's gaze had zeroed in on his. She stilled.

All trace of relaxation was lost. So taut was he from head to toe, he felt like a live, loose electric line, crackling and precarious.

Yellow lights were flashing behind his eyes. *Danger Ahead*, the signs read, one after the other. He tried to get the message across to his body. Half of it was log-jammed by panic. The other was need-bound and gluttonously wondering still what that strawberry would taste like if he leaned forward…and nibbled…

You sick bastard.

The words were in *his* head, but they sounded doubly like Gavin.

Unlocking the breath trapped in his lungs, he exhaled tumultuously. Her honey-crisp eyes were out of focus, but they were there, framed by thick black fringe he'd never noticed before. There was a tiny beauty mark trapped like a tear beneath her right eye. How had he missed that?

Invoke ninja smoke. "Thanks, I gotta go." One sentence rear-ended the other as he stood, removing the towel she'd draped over his shoulders before the trim.

Harmony rose, too, and touched the collar of his shirt. "I didn't nick you, did I?"

"No. You're fine. *I'm* fine." He nearly ran into the jamb of the doorway that led from her kitchen to her living room.

One forbidden mouth. Years of training, instinct and self-awareness in the toilet.

"You forgot your hat," she pointed out, chasing him with it.

"Thanks." He squashed it down over his new do. *Don't follow me, woman. If you know what's good for you, you will not follow me.*

"You'll come back, right?" she asked from the door as he found the screen door of her porch.

Doubling back, he asked, "Come back?"

"For mac-and-cheese," she reminded him. "Bea'll be devastated if you don't."

"Ah, yeah. Rain check on that." Because she waited, he realized how rude he was being. It wasn't her fault he hadn't been with a woman in so long his testosterone had gone loafing after her. Holding the screen wide, he leaned against the rising wind that wanted to rap it shut and trap him in her comely circle. "I owe you."

"You're back," she said in answer. "A haircut and macaroni are small change compared to Bea's Kyle home from battle."

It snagged him, the thought of Bea dreaming her dreams and climbing up on his shoulders to touch the moon. "Tell her I'll see her. Tomorrow night. You'll need to get your shutters up."

"You let me worry about the shutters," she told him, "and get your butt over here for dinner. Deal?"

Kyle nodded. "You all right, Carrots? Out here alone?"

The slant of her eyes narrowed further. "Locked and loaded." And with a salute, she added, "Petty Officer, sir."

"That's Chief Petty Officer to you, ma'am." Kyle touched the brim of his hat and backed down the steps when a laugh answered. It was a laugh timbered in brass like the tubes of the wind chimes she'd hung from the eaves of the porch tossing against the rising wind. It was a "crazy person" laugh. A "don't give a damn" laugh. It was his favorite laugh in the world.

It was one of the myriad items he could add to the list of the sexy things he'd never noticed were sexy about Harmony. And that was *bad*. Real, real bad.

BRACKEN MECHANICS DIDN'T look like much, but the family business had been Kyle's home away from home for most of his existence. In case the building itself didn't draw enough attention, the vintage lineup of cars outside did. Shiny, waxed—they were just a few of his father's many toys. But the garage itself was modest, a block structure made of rust-colored brick crowned only by the Bracken logo.

Kyle had learned everything there was to know about car engines, domestic and foreign, under its unpretentious roof. Long before training courses at Coronado, he'd learned how to maneuver in a stick shift versus an automatic, how to draw as much horsepower out of a car's engine without overworking it and how to fix most motorized problems known to man.

When restless nights following deployment stalked him on land, there was one last vestige of peace to strike at. That was suiting up in a pair of coveralls and getting greasy beneath the hood of whatever the motley crew his father had long-employed was working on at the garage.

"Manifold's cracked," Murph "Hickory" Scott said, the words muffled somewhat by a wad of Copenhagen. He snorted, giving Kyle an earful of nasal congestion. He was Marines, retired, hard as hickory—true to his moniker—and still carried Vietnam with him behind the patch over his left eye. The shrapnel bugged him at the onset of rain, so today he was more ornery than usual. "Distributor cap, too."

"Made in America." Kyle leaned against the open hood, elbows down. "Parts'll be easy to come by. It's just cleaning her up. That'll be the trick."

Wayne "Pappy" Frye beamed at the thought. "Yes, sir. Needs everything down to seat cushions." He didn't look it, but Pappy was approaching eighty, a hobby-man who had taken the job alongside Hick in Bracken Mechanics's early years, not because he needed revenue but because he *worshipped* cars. Like all Bracken employees, Pappy was as good as family. But as Kyle's ex-fiancée's grandfather, Pappy and Kyle had nearly been family by law.

Pappy kicked the treads of the old Trans Am. "Good tires." He caught Kyle's eye. "Have you heard about her mystery origins?"

"A lady of intrigue?" When Hick grunted and chewed, Kyle pushed up from his elbows to the heels of his hands in interest. "Don't keep it to yourselves."

Pappy and Hick exchanged glances. When the latter raised his brows, Pappy took it upon himself to illuminate Kyle on the subject. "Two days ago, Mavis came in early for some filing business and found this beaut waiting patiently outside. A Trans Am wasn't on the roster, so she called your dad up to ask if he knew anything about it."

"Did he?" Kyle asked.

"She said he was as surprised as she was," Pappy elaborated, "but asked no further questions, insisting on seeing it for himself. Later that morning, we found him standing much as you are now having a look under the lady's bonnet. I asked him if he knew whose car it was. He would only say it belonged to an old friend."

"He's got a good many of those," Kyle speculated. His father had once worked the underbelly of the GTA circuit. Then after getting cleaned up, he'd worked for NASCAR, among other things, before returning home to Fairhope and building a respectful name for himself through small business.

"Yes, but this one seemed…sentimental," Pappy continued. "We're guessing this old friend isn't an old rival at the poker tables." He exchanged another look with Hick. "We were hoping you might settle the mystery. If he's bound to tell anyone other than your mother, it's you."

Kyle pulled the brim of his hat down over his eyes as he stood back from the car. He crossed his arms, feet spread. James wasn't in the shop today; he was out at the airfield. Kyle might've liked to have been there if last night's conversation hadn't lingered. The walk after hadn't quite done what it was supposed to, and, despite the brief clutch of tranquility he'd felt at Harmony and Bea's, the odd turn of events there had made him doubly agitated.

He was barely fresh off a homecoming, but he needed to get his head right before he returned to The Farm or his family. Maybe most especially to Harmony and her strawberry-shaped mouth.

Goddamn. He shifted slightly when the image hit and made him taut in the loins again. Pivoting his thoughts in the opposite direction, he plugged back into the Trans Am. "What's he planning to do with it?"

Hick sniffed. "He's been coming in every night, asking me to meet him."

"After hours? What for?" Kyle asked. His father rarely worked overtime at either the airfield or the garage. He liked going home to his wife, who, for him, reaffirmed the grind of life on the straight and narrow.

"Don't know exactly," Hick opined. He snorted unceremoniously. "At first I thought he'd want to start breaking down the engine. Mostly he just looks at it like some complex algebra problem he can't solve."

"Strange," Pappy said.

Kyle agreed. James Bracken, a man never unsure of himself. "Why the hesitation?"

"We were hoping you'd know," Pappy admitted.

Kyle walked around the car, studying its unpolished lines. Dents. Scratches. A paint job was the least of her worries. But she could ride again.

The license plate on the back bumper snagged Kyle's attention. "MERCY," he read out loud.

"Maybe it's a gift from the gods," Hick proposed. As both Kyle and Pappy frowned at him in turn, he gesticulated in a brusque motion toward the car, "As benediction for past crimes. Christ. He's been on his best behavior for now on thirty years."

Kyle fought a grin. "Are you waxing poetic on us, Hick?"

Hick scowled, uncomfortable. "Ah, to hell with ya'."

Kyle chuckled. He'd grown to like Hick as much as Pappy. The man had battled PTSD for well on a decade after his time in the service, a fact which Kyle hadn't known until after his recovery and several time-consuming talks working overtime in the garage alone with the man. Through the long hours, he and Hick had developed a quiet understanding of one another.

"Say you're right, Hick..." Pappy shook his

head at the unlikelihood of the scenario, but a smile worked at the creases of his mouth. With two fingers, he smoothed his Roosevelt 'stache. "…why a broken-down Trans Am? Why not a Cobra? Or a Ferrari?"

"Do I look like I commune with the righteous?" Hick muttered.

"So how 'bout asking him for us?" Pappy nudged Kyle. "I think I speak for every man here—and Mavis—when I say that we'd love to know who she came from and what Jim Boy plans to do with her when he's done figuring her out."

Kyle spared a glance for the sky through the open doors. A stiff breeze blew in steady drafts. It kicked up sand from ditches and spread it across the lot. The vintage cars would have to be moved inside within the next hour. "I'm sure he'd tell either of you if you ponied up and asked."

The quick cacophony of knocking broke through the chatter. Kyle glanced back at the half-walled office. Mavis peered through one of its three-sixty windows and offered him a brisk come-hither motion. "'Scuse me," he said to the men. Ducking his head through the door, he asked, "What's up?"

Mavis cradled the phone between her shoulder and ear. Pulling her mouth away from the receiver, she covered it. "Customer complaint. Wants to talk to my superior." She tuned in to the caller and uncovered the mouthpiece as her spine straightened. "Yes, he's a man. What's that got to do with anything?" Her mouth fell open. "Now listen. Just because *I am a woman* does not mean I can't tell you that the service you received last week was quality and you wouldn't find better anywhere south of Demopolis. This is your fourth service and your third complaint in two years, Mr. Lowman. That's right; I remember. If you don't like our work, then why haven't you taken your Chevy to one of those dime-a-dozen, select-service auto chains they stick on every corner? And *another thing*—"

Kyle eased back against the door, smiling as his little sister chewed the chauvinist on the line down to size. He knew his father would've moved heaven and earth for her to give up her spooky line of work and take up the banner of executive assistant at Bracken Mechanics. She could be a bit of a rough diamond, but among her various talents she could boast an eidetic memory, a talent for negotiation and bargaining, and an excellent knack for reading people. She also knew as much about cars as Kyle. She'd refused their father's many offers, however, and had stuck to part-time bookkeeping and payroll.

As Pappy approached the office door, Kyle nodded for him to join him. They split a stick of gum. Pappy took the only available seat in the office, kicking back with his heels on the desk.

Before Mavis finished talking Lowman down,

Pappy's head bobbed, and he snorted, startling himself out of a snatched nap. When he peered at Kyle and saw the raised brow, he reluctantly lowered his feet from the desk.

"Not getting any sleep at home?" Kyle wondered.

Pappy yawned until his jaw popped. "Ah, it's the great-grands. They've been staying with us for a few weeks. You forget how noisy the parent life is." Shifting on the chair, he opened a newspaper on the desktop, wetting his fingertips to flick through the pages to the auto section. "Laurel's getting a divorce, you know."

Caught off guard, Kyle frowned at the man. "No. Really?"

"Yep," Pappy said with a grim nod. "Stress got to her. Joey's hours. He kept taking extra shifts, especially when the last couple of babies came along. Twins."

"Twins," Kyle said, trying to digest it. "Holy shit."

"Laurel quit her job at the school to take care of the brood. She loves those babies, but she never could get a break. In the end, she and Joey realized they couldn't get back to one another. Pressure broke them."

"She okay?" Kyle asked, shifting against the jamb. It was odd, talking about his ex in this manner.

"Ah, she'll be all right," Pappy wagered. "She's

working again, teaching summer school. It's been good for Alva, having all that time alone with the children. And Laurel's starting to stand up straight again now that some of the burden has been lifted."

"I reckon so," Kyle muttered. "Especially with... How many kids did you say?"

"Four."

Kyle might've choked. *"Four?"*

Pappy chuckled at his reaction. "Yes, sir. Her and Joey managed to turn out four in four years."

It *sounded* like a lot. Still, Kyle didn't know quite how to take the news of the divorce. It wasn't long after their long-term relationship had gone belly-up that Laurel had taken up with Joe Louth, a local firefighter. It hadn't been long after that that the two announced plans to marry. Laurel had always been vocal about her desire for traditional family life, down to the kids—a whole baseball team's worth. Before Joe, before BUD/S, she and Kyle had talked about making that a reality.

The damn frag changed a lot of things.

It wasn't a surprise to him that Laurel had moved on to make her dream of marriage and kids a reality. Nor was it a surprise that she'd grown weary of Joey's firefighting hours. She'd barely lasted through Kyle's first deployment.

Mavis finally hung up the phone. Pappy chuckled at her smug expression. "Ah, honey, ain't no mistake. Hearing you take J. T. Lowman down a few pegs cheers me up somethin' fierce."

"It wasn't the worst part of my day," she admitted, shredding the complaint report methodically down the middle. "Sorry, bro. Guess I didn't need you after all."

Kyle held up a hand. "You lullabied Pappy into an afternoon siesta and saved me a hassle. Good work." He pushed off the jamb and walked back into the garage.

It was beginning to feel crowded with Hick and a few of the other boys rounding up the show cars and parking them bumper to bumper in the empty service stations. Kyle smiled when one of them tested the motor of his father's old Mustang, revving it so the deep-throated growl of high-performance ponies galloped up the walls in a chill-inducing charge. A few of the boys leaned out of the cars to whistle appreciatively. Kyle applauded. He'd fallen in love with the noise early, much as he'd fallen in love with the laugh of a strident redheaded girl.

The last had always been platonic. *Decidedly* platonic. He'd never wanted to kiss Harmony. Never thought about kissing her. Never thought overtly about any particular part of her body. Especially not her mouth in all the colorful imaginative ways he had over the last sixteen hours…

He didn't want this. Any of it. It threatened to take one of the most important relationships in his life and rend it in half. What had seemed ironclad yesterday was now on the verge of being crushed beneath the heel of his boot—like some intricate origami bird. Sure, it looked sturdy, but how well would it hold up under the flat side of his shit-kickers?

Kyle had to lock it down. If it meant retreating to all the training techniques he'd learned through the years, so be it. The white-winged crane that was him and Harmony and, partially, Bea's connection was crucial to each of them. And, damn it, no bad mission, questionable homecoming or lack of female companionship was going to undermine it.

He found himself facing the Trans Am again, this time from the back. The word MERCY caught his eye once more.

Something crawled down the back of his neck. A feeling he didn't like. It was usually his chief indicator that something was about to go terribly wrong on a mission. The Spidey sense had saved his life more than a time or two overseas as well as the lives of his teammates.

As much as he'd like to give the engine another look, he sidestepped the car, giving it a wide berth. No, he didn't know where or who it had come from. At this point, he wasn't sure he wanted to know.

It smelled like trouble in Goodyear tires and a double coat of dust.

CHAPTER FIVE

"THIS IS JUST EMBARRASSING," Mavis mumbled, slouching farther into the white rocker on the front porch of Hanna's Inn.

"How long have they been at this?" Harmony asked from the next chair, scarfing a triangular-shaped sandwich. She hadn't eaten since breakfast. Storm prep at B.S. had kept her and the other airfield employees hopping throughout the day. She still had to go home and put up her own storm shutters, but her parents lived on the bay. They didn't just have to contend with the possibility of wind. There was the very real threat of flooding. So she'd come to make sure they were okay first.

While her father and several other strong-armed fellas connected to Flora, Belle Brides and the tavern were still tying down and boarding up, the women had taken a well-deserved break with tall glasses of lemon ice water and cucumber sandwiches.

Mavis frowned sideways at the others. "What's wrong with them? They're supposed to be the grown-ups."

Harmony gobbled another sandwich. "Mmm. Let them have their fun."

"Ooh, ooh," Adrian Bracken said, straightening against the high back of her rocker. "He's coming."

"Yes," Olivia Leighton hissed as she leaned forward to get a better look down the street. "'Bout time. I've earned this today."

Harmony watched, amused, as her mother, Briar, ran her fingers through her medium-length hair and smirked when she caught Mavis inching up a bit in her chair. "Oh, good God."

"What?" Mavis asked, trying to look as surly as Kyle had the night before.

"Look at you, trying to get a peek." Harmony slapped her knee as she sat back and laughed. "You're just like them."

"Am not," Mavis said, offended.

"Are, too," Harmony returned.

"Am not!"

"Are, too!"

"Sh, sh! Girls!" Olivia said, waving a blind hand at them as the object of their fascination finally jogged into view on the sidewalk lining the scenic highway beyond the gravel lot.

He wore red running shorts, low-cut socks, running shoes and nothing else except a black band around his bicep that held a portable speaker. Music followed him, the crash of heavy metal angry enough for Mavis to appreciate. He'd been bronzed by the sun and was fit to please.

A fine male specimen indeed. Harmony slowly licked a dab of dill cream cheese from the corner of her mouth and reached for the cool glass on the small table next to her chair. The temperature was rising.

A shrill whistle cut across the porch, followed by the impressive strain of a rebel yell. When the man's head swiveled, Olivia called out, "Get you some, hot stuff!"

The runner grinned back and jerked his chin in their direction. "Right back at ya, ma'am!"

Mavis groaned and turned fifty shades of red, failing epically to blend in with the yellow seat cushions.

Harmony guffawed. "Do y'all do this every day?"

"We have a standing appointment with Running Man every other weekday," Briar admitted, having the decency to look somewhat embarrassed by the display.

"Rain or shine." Adrian sighed. "He never disappoints."

"Does Dad know about this?" Mavis drawled.

"He knows it's harmless," Adrian replied.

Harmony tilted her head to see her mother better. "Is Bea with the guys? I couldn't find her downstairs."

"In the breakfast room of the new wing," Briar

told her. "A visitor stopped by to help us prep, but she snagged him first."

Kyle. Harmony caught Mavis's knowing look and brushed the crumbs from her blouse. The one person who knew about her long-ago feelings for Kyle was Mavis. They were close in age and had grown chummy through the years. Chummy enough for secrets. They never spoke of it, mostly because Mavis found the idea mortifying. No one was more relieved nothing had come of Harmony's crush on Kyle than his baby sister.

Someone clattered up the porch steps and Harmony turned her attention to Roxie Strong. She wore high-arched heels and an immaculate day dress. Nobody ever found a wrinkle on Roxie. She had aged superbly. Though lately she looked tired. Despite her busy hours as a wedding coordinator, seamstress and the taxing business of being a mother of three, she'd hidden the wear that came with her combined workload with admirable ease.

"Harmony," Roxie greeted, embracing her warmly. "I saw Bea earlier. I gave her sweets. I hope that's okay."

"Did she give you the lip?" Harmony asked.

"The pouty one, yes." Roxie nodded. "It's impossible to resist. How do you say no to her?"

"I'm the local bad witch around these parts," Harmony admitted. She narrowed her eyes on her mother. "Especially with the Good Witch on the loose."

Briar blinked innocently. "What? I'm the Mammy. I'm allowed to indulge her."

"Hmm," was Harmony's response. "I'm going inside. Hopefully, I won't find her on the downhill slope of a sugar high."

Harmony left the women to their devices, retreating into the hushed cool lobby. The building encapsulated the essence of her mother's soul. No wonder her father, Cole, had found refuge here. It wasn't easy, the life of innkeepers. But his past penchant for wandering had washed ashore here at Hanna's, and, under its roof, in Briar's embrace, it had quickly checked out.

Growing up the innkeepers' daughter had had the opposite effect. Like Gavin, Harmony was more of a wild thing. Living in the third floor with guest suites below, there had been no running or stomping. She'd learned how to maintain a proper "inside voice" early on. Meeting new people every day and hearing their stories had always been a source of enjoyment. But was it any wonder she'd craved days at The Farm and its wide open spaces?

There was something about coming home, however. As she followed the long, curving hall with its ornate line of floor-to-ceiling windows into the new wing, Harmony trailed her fingertips along the edge of an antique breakfront. The paintings lining the new hallway were local artistry, their subject dedicated solely to bay life.

Today the view was obstructed by wood panels that would protect against surge should the storm bring it.

The new suites were built into the far end of the wing, allowing more privacy. They were larger with modern touches that the old rooms, regardless of charm, weren't able to accommodate. The bed-and-breakfast now boasted ten suites in all—four in the original floor plan, six more in the new. It would open with a spectacular showing in a few short weeks, courtesy of Roxie, whose party planning vision knew no rival. Harmony looked forward to watching the inn come alive in its newfound evolution. Her parents were already training new help to take on a percentage of the expanding workload.

About time, she thought. Briar had held the same staunch notion for decades—since her mother, Hanna, had run the inn from top to bottom until her death, and so could she. Until recently, she'd ignored entreaties to hire a small staff.

It wasn't just the new rooms that had worn Briar down, Harmony knew. The pain in her hands, a gift from arthritis, had gone steeply uphill over the last two years. Instead of admitting it out loud, she'd hired an assistant gardener on the sly. Others had followed—an office boy to answer phones, a maid, another maid… Loosening her hold on the reins was difficult for Briar, Harmony could see, but she was glad her mother was no longer carrying the full load of responsibilities.

The breakfast room would greet guests with coffee and vittles in the coming weeks. For now, it was roped off until furnishings were set and décor had been given the final nod.

The ropes hadn't stopped Bea from sneaking in. Neither Briar nor Cole would've stopped her anyway. Her companion hadn't thought twice about skirting the red velvet cordon or its Please Keep Out sign, either.

The pair had set up a tea service on the black lacquered coffee table in the center of the room. Bea sat on one of the pristine new sofa cushions. She wore a plastic tiara. She held her teacup in one hand, pinkie out for good measure, and a magic wand in the other. As Harmony watched from the doorway, her daughter slurped the remains of her imaginary tea and set it down. "Bibbity bobbity boo!" she chirped, tapping the wand on the end of the cup. As she picked it up again, she addressed her companion. "Would you care for more tea, dear prince?"

"Sure thing, princess." Kyle held out his teacup. In his hands, it looked like something Alice might drink from at the bottom of the rabbit hole. Through his two-fingered hold, there was a teensy, visible fault line along its rounded edge, likely from his handling.

Bea repeated the incantation, flicking her wand

over the rim. "Here are your magic sprinkles," she chimed, picking up a glitter-filled salt shaker her Mammy had loaned her. She tipped it over Kyle's cup.

"Thank you, Your Majesty," Kyle said. He tapped his cup lightly against hers and the two drank, Bea slurping again. "Ah," Kyle said with a nod. "That's the stuff."

"Unicorn biscuit?" she asked, offering him a pink plastic crumpet on a plate. "I had Gar-song make them special."

Harmony hid a snort of laughter behind her hand. Under the shaded brim of his battered cap, Kyle's gaze lifted over Bea's waxen hair and zeroed in on Harmony's hiding place. The amusement that had woven warm filaments around his eyes and mouth staggered. His smile tapered slightly. The glitch bothered her, but the frisson of worry it brought was singed away by the zing of intensity he threw at her.

"My compliments to the chef," he said instead of giving her away. "It's been a while since I had a decent unicorn biscuit."

"Unicorns don't like when Gar-song gives their biscuits to strangers," Bea expounded, nibbling a purple crumpet.

"I imagine not."

"They poke him," Bea divulged. She emitted a conspiratorial giggle. "Right in the—"

The words ended on a shriek as Harmony's

arms wrapped around Bea's middle and she turned the point of her nose into the sensitive place beneath her daughter's jaw. The shriek merged into laughter, sweet clangors of it. "Right in the *what*?" Harmony asked.

"Nothing!" Bea claimed.

"Ah, now I'll never know," Kyle groaned, setting his teacup down with a clack.

Harmony hugged Bea, tugging her on to her lap. She noticed the lace-trimmed handkerchief with the Hanna's Inn crest Kyle had unfolded over one muscled thigh in lieu of a napkin. He was sitting cross-legged with knees raised several inches, thanks to the confines of the sofa at his back. As a result, his jeans, worn soft but still a good shade of blue like his eyes, stretched taut underneath the hem of his gray T-shirt. Harmony cleared her throat, making some effort not to stare at his inseam. She lowered her head to Bea's again. "Did you tell Prince Charming about your new pet unicorn?"

"Mmm-hmm," Bea said with a pert nod. "We're going riding together when the storm's gone."

"Oh," Harmony said. "Playdate for two."

"He said you could come, too," Bea added almost as an afterthought after slurping from her teacup once more.

Harmony darted a glance over the table. Kyle's bronze arms, the pronounced black-inked SEAL trident tattooed on his bicep peeking out from underneath his left sleeve, rested on his knees. His hands were linked. Watching. Demurring again from his laser focus, she still couldn't miss the introspection that muffled the relaxed affection she was so used to seeing. He hadn't moved but an inch or two since he saw her standing at the door. Yet she sensed that nothing about him was relaxed anymore. Even with the ottoman between them, she could feel the strains of tension. The type a watchful panther might coil inside itself while waiting for its prey.

She didn't feel like the hunted. Her heart palpitated, out of sync. The frown. The wariness. It was almost as if he saw the hunter in her. She was the threat.

She didn't like that one bit.

"Ooo, I forgot," Bea chirped. She reached into the picnic basket, rooting around. "The rainbow cake!"

It was a loaf of apple bread wrapped in cellophane. Several slices were gone from it so the pattern on the inside could be seen: rainbow swirls. It was Briar's work, today's special treat for the granddaughter she so loved to indulge. Before Bea could even think about cutting it, Harmony took the plastic knife from her hand. She unwrapped the cellophane on the tray so no crumbs would scatter on the coffee table.

"Kyle first," Bea demanded.

"Yes, Your Grace," Harmony drawled and

rolled her eyes as she carefully placed the first slice on Kyle's plate.

The corner of his mouth lifted in response. He waited until she had cut a slice for Bea and herself before digging in. A line of ardor appeared between his brows as he closed his eyes and groaned. "Mmm. Gar-song's outdone himself."

"Herself," Harmony amended. "And for somebody so worried about carbs yesterday..."

He lifted a noncommittal shoulder. "Between you and your mother, I'm screwed."

"What are carbs?" Bea wanted to know.

"Little bites of heaven," Kyle answered readily. He scarfed several more bites. "They'll get you closer to the pearly gates if you're not careful."

"My daddy's there," Bea said, eyes round as she seized on the word "heaven."

Again, Kyle stilled and the humor drained. "Oh, yeah?"

Bea nodded, wiping crumbs from her lip. "Uh-huh. Mama says he watches over me. If anything tries to hurt me, he sends helpers." She beamed at Kyle. "Like you."

Kyle's intent stare rose again over the top of her head to rest on Harmony's face. Harmony didn't know quite what to say to him. It was the story she'd told Bea when nightmares plagued her. Knowing Benji and Kyle and Uncle Gavin were all fighting on her side helped lull her back to sleep. And Harmony would be lying if she didn't say the idea soothed her, too, during her own rest-less nights when life or single parenthood became overwhelming.

Driving up to The Farm as a kid, she'd always been mesmerized by the two stone lions lazing on concrete pillars at the entrance. Because she'd been as fanciful as Bea once, Harmony began to think of them as Kyle and Gavin, her eternal watchdogs. Like Kyle's teacup, they were cracked now. Weatherworn. A bit mottled here and there. But they never moved. A symbol for her and, now, a comfort to Bea.

Thank God she hadn't lost either of them. Los-ing Benji had kicked the legs out from under her. It had taken a while to get back up. Gavin's absence had grown to ache almost as much as Benji's. Yet she had to keep telling herself he and Kyle were both hers. She had to know they were whole. If either of them fell off those pillars...

Kyle's tension, the arm's length he was hold-ing between them—she'd known it right off be-cause they had an understanding, silent as it may be. He would never not be there for her. He would never not be a friend. In return, she was there for him and was his friend without compromise. And that was that.

She sighed a little, her cheek pressed to Bea's curls. They felt like Benji's whenever he'd let his grow. No, there would be no falling in love again. With anyone. Because the only other man she could give herself to was the one she knew good and well she could never have.

Kyle moved finally, unfurling from his stiff pose. He leaned over the table and chucked Bea beneath the chin. She tucked it in, grinning, because she thought he would go for the tickle zone underneath. He merely wiped missed crumbs. Only Harmony noticed how the touch lingered, tender, and how his expression softened to the consistency of butter. "That's right, little wing." He lowered his chin and made sure she was listening. "Don't think just because you can't see him that he hasn't got people fighting for you. Hear me?"

Her head bobbed in a nod. Bea was rarely reticent. Harmony knew she was taking in Kyle's words, owl-eyed and enthralled.

She wasn't alone.

Warmth seeped over Harmony's lap. It wasn't until the wet soaked through her shorts that realization sank in and she closed her eyes. "Oh, Gracie Bea."

"I'm sorry, Mama," came the meager response.

Harmony could feel Bea shrinking in on herself from embarrassment and tucked away the urge to scold. "It's all right. I don't think it got on Mammy's cushion. Just…me. Come on. Up."

Soggy, they struggled to their feet. "I got her," Kyle said, leaning over the ottoman to pick Bea up by the waist. "You taking her upstairs?"

"Yes. She's got clothes there, and Mom probably has something I can change into." Harmony walked behind them as they backtracked through the window-lined hall into the original wing. Three floors up, Harmony took Bea into the bathroom, rinsed her and found a change of clothes.

By the time Bea was dressed again, they found Cole Savitt standing in the kitchenette with Kyle and a glass of lemonade. Bea bounced into the room, episode forgotten. Her grandfather placed a hand on the back of her head and hugged her to his leg. "There's my garden bee." He patted her on the shoulder as his gaze veered beyond her. He eyed Harmony and her wet pants. Some effort went into quelling the smirk she saw flirting with the muscles of his mouth. "Did you have an accident?"

"Funny." Closer, he looked grungy from prep. Harmony approached him nonetheless, placing her hands on his upper arms, thick with muscle even in his sixties. His hairline was gone. His dark eyes exuded quiet strength. Both her parents were eternally steadfast, the picture of calm. Once she'd held a firm notion that she was secretly adopted.

Pressing her cheek to his, she didn't mind the slickness of perspiration. It didn't matter if he were dirty or clean. She'd never had a lovie or a security blanket. Just her parents and their individual warmth and bouquets. "I'm sneaking into your room. I need something to wear home."

"Go ahead," he said and spared her a peck on the ear. She retreated to the door of the master bedroom, and he asked, "Did you get your shutters up?"

"Tonight," she called back.

"First rain bands will be setting in around six," he warned. "It's five o'clock."

"Stop fussin'. I'll get them up."

"'Stop fussin','" she heard him mutter to Kyle as she disappeared. "Sometimes I wonder who the parent is."

She opened the first drawer of her mother's bureau. A wave of lavender billowed forth. *Speaking of security blankets.* This one was feather-light and fresh. Every item in the drawer was folded into a precise square. "Geez," she murmured as she pulled out an over-long button-up.

She realized she hadn't showered since the day before yesterday. Even with the thought of storm shutters, she soaked for a few minutes in the claw-foot tub, propping her too-long legs on the edge and lying back until her shoulders submerged. It wasn't easy to scrape together enough minutes out of the waking hours for things as basic as everyday grooming. Indulgence felt like a distant comrade.

After drying, she stuffed her shorts and delicates into a laundry bag. Unable to resist, she spread a small bit of her mother's fragrant moisturizer over her hands and smoothed a light layer over the bare surface of her legs.

Damn it, it was summertime. Leg-baring weather. Remembering to shave every other day was a must. She was going every three days as it was, and that was as embarrassing as having urine-soaked pants. Especially in front of—

"Harm? You still back there?"

"Yeah," she answered Kyle's far-off voice. "Just a sec." She threw on the button-up and used the belt she had been wearing to try to bring the ensemble together. It was long, thigh-length, but she had thighs only a giraffe could take pride in, bringing the hem up farther than she preferred. She frowned at her reflection, reaching up to tuck away flyaway strands at her brow. One of these days she would grow used to looking like an awkward Dr. Seuss character.

"'Red. Red. They call me Red,'" she chanted as she left the bedroom suite.

Kyle was waiting at the door to the living room. She opened it and he straightened against the jamb. "Bea says she's lost—" He stopped, eyes taking a steep dive. His brow hitched a good inch.

She closed the door at her back with a rap and pursed her lips, keeping her legs together. For once, a decent thigh gap wasn't on her list of things to achieve in life. Crossing one Sperry-clad ankle over the other, she warned, "Don't laugh. I couldn't wiggle into Mom's jeans if I tried."

His jaw went from slack to firm. Very, very firm. His eyes lifted slowly from the hem of her makeshift shirtdress before landing pointedly on her face where they passed over her mouth in a considering blast, brief but evident.

Harmony went motionless. Dear God. He was looking at her. *Really* looking at her. Her heart revved, pumping her adrenal glands into action. Mouth wet. Tongue tingling. Blood whistling. Her body had been ready for this. She thought it'd forgotten how to operate on this level. But apparently it'd only been lying in wait, for him.

Her brain, however, wasn't so prepared. It saw Kyle looking at her—healthy male to desirable female—and her thoughts flopped off the track like a faulty projection strip. Her damp hands spread on the shallow skirt, and she fumbled with a testy *"What?"*

His study snatched from her mouth. His eyes went wide with disbelief. Horror? He took a step back. A lengthy step. His expression spelled full-on *Retreat!* Shaking his head, he jerked a shrug. "Nothing. It's nothing."

She licked her lips. Her mouth was wet, but her lips were dry. How was that remotely possible? Now she was sweating through the shirt. Folding her hands under her arms, she tried to soften the defensive tone. "Didn't look like nothing," she murmured. Intimacy echoed through the phrase and she chided herself again. *Typical Carrots. From one extreme to the next.*

For a split second, he looked helpless. Battle-tested Chief Petty Officer K.Z.B, helpless.

The weakness vanished. He reeled it in. Even his eyes, those gorgeous Scandinavian lakes, flattened. "I guess Zaccoe was right."

She blinked, struck by Benji's name. "About?"

He hesitated, then smoothed over the glitch. "He used to call you Legs. Remember?"

The memory wafted from far afield. The nickname had come before things had happened between them. It was only after Benji started calling Harmony by her given name that she knew they'd taken the steep dive into love and commitment.

She'd forgotten. What the hell kind of woman forgets?

She closed her mouth to keep the ready exhale from escaping. It would have sounded plaintive and weak. She hated both. Her gaze lowered to Kyle's shoulder. She scrambled to rise from the unexpected plunge. She'd gotten so good at floating. "Right."

"Damn it. I'm sorry." He said it quickly.

It was her turn to lift a shoulder. She grabbed on to the shirt hem when it rose with her movement. "No big deal."

"It was a dumbass thing to say," he argued, self-inflicted anger heating the lakes.

The warmth was a welcome reprieve even if

it was tetchy. She released the exhale, letting it wind slowly out from her nose, making room for cool thoughts. *When in doubt, breathe.* Wasn't that what the grief counselor her parents had arranged for her to see after Benji died told her to do? "What did Bea lose?"

"Miss Puppybubbles?"

She nodded, some senses restored. "Poppinbubbles. Her unicorn doll. The Leightons gave it to her last Christmas. I'll go look for it. Dad's right. I need to get out of here if I'm going to get my shutters up."

"You let me worry about that."

She frowned. "You aren't going back to the farmhouse to ride out the storm?"

Again, anger forked across his facade. "No."

"Oh," she said, wondering what was behind that.

"Besides," he added, "you said something about mac-and-cheese, and since the rainbow cake already broke this week's carb limit..."

She felt a smile creeping over her mouth. "Go big or go home?"

"The slogan's worked well for me so far." His smile answered hers, and, at last, the tension seemed to break between them.

She snatched the comfort of normality and drank from it to relieve the pressure inside her. "All right. Dinner," she agreed. "You hammer. I'll cook. Bea'll sabotage us both with her charms.

Sounds like a date... *Plan*," she remedied. "I meant plan."

"Maybe by then we'll both have removed the foot from our mouths," he mused.

She crossed her fingers and held them behind her back. *Here's hoping.*

CHAPTER SIX

DINNER AT HARMONY'S was a risk. Kyle had considered going to the tavern instead and letting Olivia fix him a few promised welcome-home tonics. He might meet a woman there. An *available* woman.

But due to the storm, the tavern would be closing, too. He couldn't sleep on the *Hellraiser* for similar reasons. So his options were to return home to his folks or dinner at Harmony's. The idea of going home held less merit.

He'd also given his word to Cole that he would make sure Harmony and Bea were tucked up safely before the storm came ashore. So it was that he found himself nailing shutters on the sides of the mother-in-law suite while mentally nailing his restraint over all the damning things he shouldn't be feeling for the woman who lived there. Before the first rains descended on The Farm, he'd secured the house, taken down wind chimes that were already tossing haphazardly against the wind and helped Bea hunt down Lucy, her wandering bobcat mix.

Once during dinner he caught himself going

back to that questionable moment at the inn where he'd imagined sliding his palm decisively up the back of Harmony's visible thigh—farther, underneath the hem of her shirt, skirt…whatever she'd intended it to be.

Bea helped him put a lid on that pot by placing a dry macaroni necklace around his neck and making him join her in an off-key mash-up of *Frozen* songs.

As rain and wind worsened, they camped out as a trio on the small couch in front of the television. It wasn't long into a presentation of *The Black Stallion* that Bea leaned into his shoulder and zonked.

"Storm's not bothering this one," he murmured, amused.

No reply came. He glanced the other way to see Harmony's head back on the cushion and her eyes closed. Her lips were parted, and the line of her breasts rose and fell in slow procession. Upon returning home, she'd tucked the shirt into a pair of jeans. Thank Jesus. Asleep, though, her thigh edged against his in a comfortable slouch, and he knew exactly how it looked—toned, the hue of toasted almonds and smooth enough to glide his lips along.

Stop beatin' 'round the bush and take yourself to church.

Kyle frowned. The disapproving mutter in his head no longer matched Gavin's. It was his grandmother, Edith, now. The interior of the mother-in-law suite that had once been hers no longer gave off strong Edith vibes with toys scattered haphazardly and Harmony's eye-catching color scheme, but sure enough, those were her less than dulcet tones…

Even you need Jesus, Kyle Bracken.

If he squinted off into the corner, he could see Edith sitting in her favorite rocker, foot tapping restlessly to keep the thing in motion, her unchallenged gaze pinning him to the wall like the dry ugly husks of insects her husband had preserved, much to her vexation.

He needed a drink, Kyle decided. But he couldn't move from the couch without waking one or both of the girls. To avoid imagining Edith in the corner again, he took what resort he could find by laying his head back, too, and letting the sweeping soundtrack of the vintage film and the persistent toll of rain sheer on the eaves of the old house lure him to sleep.

Thwack… Thwack… Thwack…

Helicopter rotors swept in an endless circle… A teammate leaned out the open Blackhawk, motioning him forward… His mouth moved brusquely, his voice drowned by the listless rotors, yet the message was clear: haul ass or get hosed.

They were deep in the shit. Kyle was bleeding from the shoulder. The sleeve of his digi-camo was damp.

*This time, he was going to make it out on his
own feet. Despite the dozen or so unfriendlies
coming hard behind him and his teammates.*

"On the ground!"

*Kyle heard the telltale whistle and threw him-
self on to a rocky patch of earth. The sound of
the helo was drowned out by the resulting con-
cussion. The RPG hit close enough to rock him
sideways. He stopped himself from skidding into
a boulder. His ears rang. However, he was able
to see the two bodies lying on the ground before
he heard the sound of another teammate shouting the words he dreaded most.*

"Man down!"

*The guys from the helo laid down cover fire,
enough for Kyle to scramble across the uneven
terrain to the nearest prone squad member. He
cursed as he rolled him over...*

Gavin.

*The world stopped turning on its rotors for half
a second. Kyle's stomach dropped when he saw
his friend's dirt-and-blood-smudged face. Then
training took over, got him moving. Ignoring the
protest from his injured shoulder, Kyle grabbed
Gavin by the front of his vest and hauled him up.
Gavin was no slouch when it came to weight lifting. Kyle grunted as he hauled his solid form over
his non-injured shoulder and took the first limp-
ing steps to the Blackhawk...*

Bullets sank into the ground behind him. They

*pinged off rock, making him move double-time.
"Son of a bitch," he groaned as he battled his
way uphill. "You better be all right, you son of a
bitch." Each word came to a point.*

*He wasn't going home again without Gavin. He
wasn't showing up at Harmony's hangar again
to tell her that someone else she loved was dead.*

*Thwack. Thwack. Thwack. The helo blades
sped up, ready to lift off. Another team guy
jumped down from inside and ran toward them.
"Come on!"*

*Neither the helo nor the fellow SEAL seemed
to be getting any closer. Another blast drove Kyle
on to his knees. Gavin's body slumped limp off his
back, out of his grasp.*

*Maybe neither of them were making it home
this time....*

*The thought pissed him off, amped him up. Kyle
once more grabbed Gavin and jerked him into a
sitting position. "Wake up!" he shouted. "I know
you can hear me!"*

Gavin's eyelids flickered. He made a noise.

*Kyle shook him. "Goddamn it. Open your eyes,
Gav! Helo's waitin'!"*

*"Yeah?" Gavin mumbled, eyes struggling to
focus. A wave of pain made his features go tight.
"Ah... Christ!"*

*"Get up!" Kyle said. "I'm not leavin' you in
this hellhole!"*

"I can't see..." Gavin shook his head. He reached for his face. "I can't fucking see."

"Then listen!" Kyle raised his voice over machine gun fire and the fragments of hysteria he heard in Gavin's voice. "I'm going home and you're coming with me."

Clarity struck Gavin's face. Something in his expression shifted. "Home?"

"That's right." Kyle nodded. "We're going home now. Now get the hell up!"

Thwack. Thwack. Thwack.

Kyle blinked himself awake...and sat staring at the ceiling fan rotating above his head. His shoulder wailed, phantom pain slowly tapering off as the blessed relief of consciousness filtered back into play. No Blackhawk. No mountaintop. No enemy fighters crawling up his ass.

No Gavin.

Kyle lifted his head. The muscles in his neck were rigid. He rolled his shoulder forward, sliding both of his arms off the back of the sofa. Bea snoozed, her head on his leg. She'd slumped down to rest in his lap. He stilled, trying not to jostle her.

His legs were tangled with someone else's. His right foot between two socked feet. One socked foot between both of his. It was nice. Cozy. Warm. It took a few seconds for reality to sink in. He might've delayed it. The warmth, the niceness pushed the details of the hot extract farther into momentary obscurity.

Harmony. They were her feet. Those were definitely her legs.

He raised his gaze over her lap, up her torso to her sleeping face.

Ah, Carrots. Look at you.

The softness took hold when she was in repose. That at least hadn't changed since she was a child. Only, back then her mouth hadn't drawn so much of his focus. Red as a knockout rose. Lush enough to draw into his mouth—and bite.

Back then—way back when—the wash of her breath across his skin hadn't made goose bumps trickle down his sensitive neck. Then he hadn't looked at her near long enough to trail his gaze down the long graceful column of her throat, just above the open collar of her shirt where he could see her pulse stirring. Her collarbone nestled the sweet defenseless spot. There life capered, unbroken.

Sure enough, she was a woman. Real and vibrant. Smart, sexy, feminine, vital.

A flash of heat took hold of him. It gripped, digging in with surprising purchase. With claws.

His first instinct was to fight his way free. He made every muscle in his body lock. He cursed inwardly when he realized he had to shift his body into Harmony to slide Bea's head from his leg. When did she start smelling this good?

He cradled the back of Bea's head, positioning a throw pillow under it. Tugging the blanket off the back of the couch, he let it fall over her, covering her from neck to toe since she was still wearing her short-legged overalls.

To slide off the couch, he had to reposition himself farther against Harmony. His ribs rubbed right up against all those angles. There was softness there, too, he discovered. It was inviting. So was the sleepy sound she made as he dragged himself up to standing.

His brain was spiraling down, down. Where it would stop was a mystery.

Was it going to stop? Kyle turned off the television which had flipped to blue screen. Letting his feet lead him, he found himself circling the kitchen. The rain was still drilling against the boards.

"Are you okay?"

He turned away from the dark window in front of him and faced her across the small dark room. She just stood there; her arms locked across her chest. Somehow, she looked small, framed by the light from the living room. The house was silent. It was a strange juxtaposition with the storm wailing away outside.

It might've just been the two of them alone in the little house in the woods.

Not alone, he told himself sharply. "I'm sorry," he murmured. "I didn't mean to wake you."

She studied him. Her arms dropped to her sides. She skimmed her hand along the curved rail of a dining chair. "I know something's wrong." She took a step, treading slowly. "And maybe I should keep quiet. But you've seemed...on edge."

If she got too close, if he felt his restraint slip any further...he could always beat his way through the wall. What match were a few plies of Sheetrock and an inch of siding to a desperate two-hundred-pound asshole?

"You know you can talk to me," she asserted. Then she stopped, rolled her eyes. "Unless, of course, it's classified or whatever."

"I'm fine," he said, the delivery blunt.

She seemed to hesitate. "Benji used to talk to me. At first he tried not to. Then one night...one *bad* night, it all just spilled out. From then on, there wasn't much he held back in terms of detail. If you want to talk, only you're afraid I can't handle it—"

"No," he said, putting a definitive end to the conversation. "Yes, my mind's stuck in a boggy place right now, but I'll work it out. It's what I do."

She licked her lips. "Must be nice. Not needing anybody."

He scanned her features. Each and every one. The corner of his mouth twitched with a ghost of a smile. "You can't rankle me into spilling my guts. I know your tactics."

Shifting back on to one heel, she added, "I just hope you're not withholding because you're trying to protect me in some way."

That was exactly what he was doing. He couldn't lie, either, and tell her he wasn't.

She nodded. *Hard to read*, Laurel had accused him of being time and time again, particularly after his training began. His mother or Harmony entered the picture, and it all went to hell. "I can take a lot," she reminded him.

"I know you can," he said, kindly. He traced her features again, lingering this time on each. "I know."

"But you still won't tell me." She sighed. "Bea's right. You are a prince."

"I'm not," he warned, voice dropping in low warning. "I'm not a prince. All right?"

Confusion webbed across her brow. It fell away at the strange noise from outside.

Thwack. Thwack. Thwack.

"What the hell is that?" Harmony asked.

He crossed the gap between them, unthinking. His fingertips lifted to her lips, not quite touching. They listened as one.

Over rain, over wind… *Thwack. Thwack. Thwack.* Then… *Pop. Crackle. Pop.*

He cursed, loud. Then he grabbed her by the waist and pushed her to the floor, bracing his body over hers as the roof of the kitchen collapsed.

"THERE'S A TREE in your kitchen. There's no way you're going in to work."

Harmony scowled. There was indeed a tree in

her kitchen. Or...what was left of one after James and Kyle got ahold of the chain saws. Pine needles littered the floor along with a good bit of moisture. She could see the sky through the trusses. The storm had broken sometime in the early morning, well after she and Kyle had swept Bea off to the farmhouse after the near-miss with the forty-foot pine.

Adrian was keeping Bea distracted there by getting her to help unstable the horses and feed the Brackens' menagerie of animals. Harmony had followed the men back to the mother-in-law suite to assess the damage, and Mavis had hitched a ride. The roof would be patched before the end of the day, the men had told her in no uncertain terms. Thank goodness for the storm shutters, otherwise she'd have three broken windows on her hands, too. Her dining room table and chairs were still intact. Small mercies. The only damage, aside from plywood and shingles, was a few dishes—nothing irreplaceable.

Harmony thanked God Bea had been snoozing safely in the living room when it happened. And that Kyle was so quick on his feet. Otherwise one or both of them would be sporting an impressive goose egg, or worse.

Mavis was right, however. Harmony wouldn't be flying today. The phone at the farmhouse had been ringing off the hook from the early winking hours with requests for flyovers and damage assessment. But she had a mess to clean up here.

Something tapped against her foot. She spotted the frog making itself at home amid the branches and needles and gave him a good scoot toward the open door with the end of her broom. "Ack. They're getting bigger. Do you think if I fire up the FryDaddy they'll scatter?"

Mavis, a part-time vegan, nudged the frog in the right direction with the toe of her combat boot to aid its escape. "Could be worse. I think there's a gator living in the river under my dock. And don't forget we have some species of snake the size of—"

"If I find a snake in this house, I'm lighting a match," Harmony warned. She could tolerate most wildlife. Snakes were not among them. She stooped to see out the open kitchen window. Over a line of round pine logs, she spotted James and Kyle. "I stopped hearing the chain saws half an hour ago. What're they doing out there?"

"Standing around jawing, from the looks of it," Mavis observed. She switched to James's deep Southern drawl. "Well, son, that there's a tree." Digging into Kyle's slightly deeper intonations, she added, "Nah, Daddy. What we're lookin' at here's a *Pinus palustrius* or, in layman's terms the 'piney longleaf.' What d'ya say we load up the shotguns and use it for target practice?"

There was half an inch of standing water in her

kitchen, yet Harmony felt a sure smile coming on. Reason number 999 why she and Mavis had remained close friends well into their twenties— she could always put her in a good mood. "You realize those cavemen are your tribe."

"Ugh." Mavis took the broom. "I'll finish sweeping. If they're going to patch the roof, you're clearly going to have to light a fire under their asses."

Harmony took glasses of sweet tea outdoors for incentive purposes. The air was thick and stagnant. The ground sloshed under her big rubber Wellingtons. Tree frogs ran at her approach. If the idea of frog-gigging didn't make her squeamish, there were several baskets worth of appetizers hopping around. It would at least cut down on the racket she knew they'd be putting up tonight while she was trying to put Bea to sleep. Such was life in the country, the life they'd chosen.

She advanced on the menfolk who were having what sounded like a hushed argument. "You boys thirsty?" she asked and watched them conspicuously falter. She took in their matching surly expressions. It was ridiculous the way their hair fell the exact same way over their foreheads, how their brows stooped over their eyes in a show of argumentation. Fighting the urge to tiptoe into the clearing, she cleared her throat. "Oh, don't stop all this brooding on my account."

She bent at the waist and set the glasses neatly

on top of the tree stump. Straightening, she placed her hands on her hips and looked from one man to the other. James's eyes wouldn't quite meet hers, which was odd. Odder still that Kyle wouldn't look at her at all, turning half away with his ax dangling at his side.

She frowned at the both of them. "If you two are experiencing your first father-son disparity, I'll confiscate the ax and give you some room. But if whatever's happening here has something to do with me, I'll ask you to clue me in." When the two of them only exchanged wary glances, she tilted her head. "Like right now, please."

Kyle slowly dropped the ax blade to the ground. Leaning against the handle, he jerked his chin toward the crude tabletop. "Notice anything weird?"

"Should I?" she asked, facing the stump again. She stared at its level surface, rough but almost perfectly planed.

Her eyes narrowed. She felt her mouth open. The question behind it fell away as her mind drew a simultaneous blank. "It's…it's *cut*," she managed finally.

Kyle nodded, grim and silent.

"Did either of you do this?" she asked.

"No, darlin'." James's grip closed on her elbow, as if he were afraid she might sink into the mushy ground. "It's unlikely the wind did it either, especially this low to the ground. It would've splintered."

Harmony held up a hand. "Someone *deliber-*

ately cut down this tree. Who would do that? *Why* would they…" And then she saw it. The beeline the falling tree had made for her kitchen wall.

Not only was it a clean cut. The angle was perfectly in line with her house.

It was Kyle who stepped up to her now. He said nothing, but she could feel the anger juddering off him. He might as well have been jackhammering with it.

It took her a moment to come to her senses. Her fist clenched around a handful of his damp shirt. James's hold was hard now, as if he sensed the jelly in her knees.

Thwack. Thwack. Thwack.

She sucked in a breath. She'd heard it. She'd heard *him*.

A noise escaped her. She didn't recognize it as her own.

"Carrots."

She shook her head. "I—" Something was rising inside her. The urge to toss the nice breakfast frittata Adrian had made before they struck out that morning. The fleeting urge to deny everything. *What the hell kind of a person would…?*

The feelings behind the denial threatened to burn her from tip to tail, but she grabbed on to them because they were solid, not futile like the others. She let the ire spread until she was immersed in it, until it threatened to singe through the skin of her face. Fisting the cotton of Kyle's shirt, she ground her teeth, bringing him closer. His front buffed against her side, and her lips peeled from her teeth. "Who was this jackwipe? I wanna know who he is."

She felt more than saw James and Kyle exchange glances again over her head. James cleared his throat. "It was raining. Any tracks he left are as good as gone."

"He's done this before," she said, again examining the evenness of the stump, the definite angle at which the pine had fallen. "He's a regular frickin' lumberjack."

"Close to it," James confirmed.

"Harm…"

"Bea," she said. She turned her face up to Kyle's and confronted him. "Bea was there. She was sleeping."

"Yeah," he growled. Wrath boiled off of him, steaming through his mask of composure. She saw it firing beneath the surface of cool blue lakes.

She muttered a curse as foul as she'd ever uttered. She bristled when an arm rose between her and the stump. Kyle's. It wasn't near comfort or restraint enough to stop the fire tornado in her blood.

CHAPTER SEVEN

"YOU CAN'T SLEEP THERE."

Disbelief colored Harmony's face as she pinned Kyle to the wall with an incredulous stare. "What are you talking about? That is my home. People typically *sleep* in their homes."

"Somebody tried to hurt you last night," Kyle said. He stood on one side of his parents' kitchen. She stood on the other. His mother and Mavis sat astride bar stools on the far side of the breakfast counter. His father leaned against the refrigerator. Cole stood next to Harmony in the wide doorway leading to the den. Briar was there, too, somewhere in the house distracting Bea so Kyle didn't have to mince words. "If they weren't trying to do you a big harm, then they were sending a message."

"A barbaric message," Mavis muttered. "Why didn't they just smear chicken blood on the door? It's just as crude, less work."

"The point is," Kyle interjected "neither you nor Bea need to go back to the mother-in-law suite. Not until we know more."

"You can both stay at the inn for the time being," Cole agreed.

"Bea can go to the inn," Harmony granted. "I'm not leaving."

"I'd prefer you stayed away, too," James weighed in, earning himself an injurious look. "Let us search the woods around the house. We might find a lead. Then—"

"Fine. Search the woods." Harmony's eyes swung, hot, to Kyle. "Set up a security feed around the house. I don't care. But I am not leaving."

"Harmony…" Adrian said, joining the conversation with care. "This might not have been the act of a single man. We don't know who or why or where he may be now. If whoever's behind this is brazen enough to trespass this far on to our land and cut down a tree in the worst of last night's weather—" her gaze collided with Kyle's "—God only knows what they're capable of."

Kyle nodded. "Exactly." *Thank you, Mom.* There was worry there. There was worry all around the room. He couldn't say he wasn't brewing the worst of it.

Releasing some of the untapped pressure, he pushed off the sink's edge and crossed the room to Harmony. Dipping his head, he said, "I'm sorry."

"It's our home," she said. "It's the place we go to be. We can't…" She ended on a shrug that was at once brusque and helpless.

"Oh, hell," Mavis spoke up. "I'll stay with you."

Kyle whirled on her. "What? No. Stay out of this, Mavis."

"No," she said. "All we're doing is going around in circles."

"What're you going to do to chase off an intruder?" he asked. "I don't think voodoo will get you very far."

"I don't know," Mavis said in a faux saccharine voice. Her dark eyes were a shade beyond glacial. "Why don't I use you for practice?"

"She'd be better off with a witch doctor."

"I know a good witch doctor," Mavis offered. "I'll give her his number."

Harmony rolled her eyes. "I don't need voodoo, the local witch doctor or anything else! I need my house to be mine and Bea's again. Now, if you'll excuse me, I've got to go Shop-Vac my kitchen and stack a mountain of firewood. Sorry for the chaos, Adrian."

Adrian smoothed her hand down Harmony's arm in consolation as the latter bypassed her for the door. When Kyle moved to follow, Adrian did the same. She clung to him, bringing him up short of following Harmony. "She's angry. She's in shock. The safety and security of her home and child have been disrupted. Just let her walk it off."

"She'll come around to it on her own, Chief," James said.

Kyle shifted back to his father. Beyond him,

Kyle spotted the doubt on Cole's face. "Yeah, because Harmony's always been a pushover. Am I right?" He sought Mavis for an answer. She pursed her lips, declining to riposte. Letting his mother's grasp slide away, Kyle slapped the door open and exited onto the porch. Through the screen, he saw Harmony go around the barn. He pushed through the screen door. "Wait up, Carrots!"

Harmony tossed a glance over her shoulder. She sped up.

He sprinted after her, catching her beyond the horse pasture where a small footpath converged in the woods. "Your stems might be impressive, but they're gonna have to move faster than that."

"If you think you're going to change my mind," she said instead of slowing, "you can turn around and go back to Mama."

With her quick gait and lengthy strides, she wasn't just eating the ground up. She was gobbling it. "Slow down."

"Is that an order, Chief Petty Officer, sir?"

"Harmony!"

The command behind her name brought her up short. She braced her hands on her hips, and her shoulders lifted over several near-panting breaths. Kyle circled her. When Harmony was on edge, she was best left alone like his parents had warned. But he couldn't let her go back to the suite alone. He planted himself in her path, waiting for her to catch her breath.

"I have a taser," she informed him.

"The creep has an *ax*. Beyond that, he's whacked out of his mind. What the hell's a taser got against a psychopath?"

"Oh, God," she scoffed. "You don't do melodrama, Kyle. Don't disappoint me and start now."

"Don't disappoint me!" he rebutted. He jerked a finger in her house's direction. "Don't be foolish enough to go back there. Not until the police investigate."

"What're they going to find that you can't? Are *they* going to tell me to stay out?"

"They'll likely tell you to stay with somebody, like we tried to. And, for the record, *not* with a voodoo witch doctor."

"I won't leave The Farm. My life's here. My work's here. *Everything* is right here!"

The fire burning through her was high and bright. *Jesus, what a woman.* He took a deep breath, released it. "Fine."

She frowned. "Fine?"

He nodded. "Stay at The Farm, but you're sleeping in my bed."

For the second time that day he saw her falter, speechless. He realized a second too late what the words implied and backtracked. "Not with me. I don't want you in my bed. No, that's not right. Ah, hell…" *I'm a moron. I'm a dirty rotten moron.* He bit off the rest through gnashed teeth.

"You can stay in my room at the farmhouse for the time being. I'll find somewhere else to crash."

"You just spent two weeks at sea," she pointed out. "Six months before that outside the country."

"So?"

"So you're finally home and you're going to give up your room for me?"

"It's better than lurking outside the mother-in-law suite all night hoping you don't mistake me for the lowlife and zap fifty-thousand volts of electricity into my pelvis."

She pressed her lips together. "If I'm at the farmhouse, you won't be up all night anyway pacing in front of the windows?"

"No, I will be," he said honestly. "But at least this way you'll have me and Dad. And Mom sleeps light. There's one more bonus, too."

"What's that?" she asked.

"If you really don't want Bea to leave, the bed's big enough for two."

"She'd rather sleep with you," she suggested.

What about you? It took a moment to wipe the suggestion. No decent alternative filled the void, so he stood and waited for her to make a decision.

The challenging light in her flickered. Her chin finally lowered. "How in God's name am I supposed to stand my ground when you keep looking at me like that?"

Like I would rather sleep with you? Again, he sealed his mouth shut. *For Christ's sake.*

"Like it's not which house I'm choosing," she continued. "It's as if I'm choosing whether to trust myself or you."

He hesitated. Then he risked losing the sheer glass containment he'd built around himself and stepped toward her. "You're strong. I get that. You can take care of yourself. You're even armed. Not just with a stun gun—I'm willing to bet those stems can give a legit roundhouse kick. But Harm..." He laid a hand on her shoulder, edging in closer. He opened himself up and let her see something he never showed anyone. He let himself be naked for her. "They call men like me when they need someone to do the jobs nobody else can. But I don't go into that fight without my team. Guys I trust to have my back more than anybody else in this world."

Her eyes seized on his, and he saw the grace of understanding beginning to seep through.

Grazing his thumb across the neckline of her cotton tee, he touched the skin of her throat, close to that life point he'd practically wallowed over last night. "You and me and Bea..." His brow creased. "We're a team. Aren't we?"

She licked her lips, silent as she shifted from one foot to the other.

"Team members look after one another." He closed the gap, winding his arm around the back of her shoulders. He gathered her to his chest. "I've got your back, Carrots. Just give me the high ground to fight it out if necessary."

Her arms lifted loosely around his waist. Her brow rested against his sternum. Again, her fists bunched around hanks of his shirt, as if she were tethering herself against him. As if he was the only anchor line she had left and she'd forgotten.

He heard her lungs working in deep resonating drafts. Her hands stopped clutching. Spanning wide over the line of his back, they progressed up to his shoulders where she hooked them. Lifting her face, she sought him.

When her head came to rest against his collar, he was forced to take a couple plunging draughts of his own. He packed the cleansing air into his lungs until he was filled with the smell of pines and her.

"I don't want you to have to fight anymore." She spoke in a quiet voice so unlike Harmony. The grip of her arms tightened. "Not for me. Not for anybody."

The line of his throat and jaw were nestled against the side of her head. He didn't trouble either of them to remedy the situation. Not when he was beginning to understand that he needed this as much as she did. His voice was rough. "It's what I do, sweetheart."

"You've done more than anybody should have to."

"Ask me if it means as much over there as it does here."

"Damn it, K.Z.B." A sigh trembled out of her. It caught him off guard—it seemed too vulnerable a sound to come from the Harmony he knew. In all the dimensions of her he'd seen, was there one he hadn't been exposed to—a softer version? "Is it any wonder we love you?" she finished on a whisper.

The breath he emitted was half laugh, half shock because the phrase *love you* hit him on target, and he couldn't shake the sense that he was standing exposed in the crosshairs without his trusty body armor. More, that somehow he was opening himself up to take the slug in the center of the chest. *Kill shot.*

"Did you ever think of asking whether or not I want you to fight for us?" she asked, pulling back.

He frowned at her. "No."

Her brows arced at his instantaneous and uncompromising response. Her surprise melted away, split apart by mirth. Her features went soft again, eyes drinking in his. "Wow. It's been a while since I've wanted to laugh at anyone and hit them at the same time." Then she lifted up on her toes. He saw her intent before she angled her head sideways. Her eyes lowered briefly to his mouth.

The split second stretched, slowly grinding the Earth's axis to a halt. All the years they'd known one another hung in between. The hungry motor of his heart dragged that split second out, pistons firing loud into the morning lull of the forest.

She licked her lips again, then touched her strawberry mouth to the edge of his jaw. He fought an agreeing noise rising from the depths of his throat as she lingered another second. Then another before lowering herself back to her normal height, pressing those lips together again. She smiled at him, reaching up to his hairline. "I missed a little, here."

He was going to grab her. He was going to grab her and kiss her. *Please don't be packin' that taser now, Carrots.*

His mother's voice came swinging through the errant thoughts like a wrecking ball. "Kyle." When both he and Harmony turned as one to see Adrian standing on the path, she said, "Sorry. I'd like a word."

Kyle scarcely nodded as Harmony moved away. She glanced at him before choosing the direction they'd come. Back to his parents' house.

He'd thought he would be able to breathe easier knowing that she was where he would be. But nothing was easy now.

When Adrian tilted her head and studied him, he kept his arms at his sides, trying to fit that mental body armor back into place. It wasn't the summer heat making his palms sweat. The women in his life were to blame.

Adrian reached up to the point on his brow Harmony had caressed just moments earlier. "She did miss."

He swallowed. Okay, he could stop feeling naked anytime. "Mom, she's—"

Adrian shook her head. "I'm not here about Harmony. I didn't think I would be interrupting."

"You didn't," he said quickly. He tried to sound indifferent. He failed.

As he found his feet and walked a little ways down the path and back to his mom, Adrian shrugged and uttered, "All right." Locking her arms over her chest, she strengthened her tone. "I came looking for you because I want to know what is going on between you and your father." Before he could dismiss her, she made a discouraging noise. "He hasn't slept since you got back. He's been working himself blind for the past two days. And you treating him the way you have…" She blew out a disbelieving breath. "Kyle, it's not just baffling to me. It's downright hurtful."

"Mom—"

"Now if this is about B.S. and the mortgage, I can understand your frustration. But don't you think it would be better to try and help the situation?"

"What can I do?" Kyle asked. "He's literally given away the farm."

"We're still here, aren't we?" Adrian indicated. "He hasn't given it away. On the contrary. He's doing everything he can to save it, and he could use support from everyone."

"Everyone, Mom? Last I checked, Harmony was still in the dark about this."

"She'll be informed if your father's preventative measures fail."

"You realize you've involved me now in this?" Kyle asked. "He's got me lying for him now. *To her!*"

"She has enough on her plate without worrying about B.S.'s fate, especially in light of what happened last night!" Adrian's eyes went to slits as she scrutinized his set features. "And whatever it is you're hiding about her brother…"

Kyle's spine straightened. "I'm not hiding anything."

"Oh, please, Kyle," Adrian admonished. "Your eyes aren't for lying, however much the rest of you might be trained to do so. Harmony knows you're keeping something from her. That's what Mavis says, anyway."

"Jesus. Will Mavis ever stay out of the middle?"

"It's not in Mavis's nature to back down from those she loves," Adrian reminded him. "Nor is it yours. Which is why I'm so surprised at you, behaving as you have these last few days."

"I'm angry," Kyle admitted. "And both of you oughtta let me stay that way."

"It's punitive."

"He deserves it."

"This isn't about anger," she ventured, searching him with uncanny motherly intuition. "This is about fear."

"Fear," he echoed, punching the word back at her. It was riddled with derision.

"This is about change and your fear of it," Adrian said. "Which is why you're running after this thing threatening The Farm and Harmony, guns a'blazing. Because the things you love most and thought were unchangeable are suddenly at risk. Why else would you be acting so defensively toward your father, toward me—toward everybody? Even Harmony. Excluding what I saw just moments ago—which I'll refrain from telling my good friends Cole and Briar about, by the way. We've got enough divide on our hands without involving them, as well."

He started to deny it, then stopped. "I don't know what's going on here," he added, voice dropping away completely because he was at a loss as far as Harmony was concerned.

"Yes, I can see that," she observed. "Yet another reason you're so scared."

"I'm not scared," he bit off, unable to admit it even to himself. He was a SEAL, damn it. If he felt fear, he didn't show it. He channeled it, utilized it. What place did fear have in a situation like this? What action was there to be had when he'd just finished charging Harmony with waiting until police arrived?

"No?" she challenged. "Not one bit?"

Again, he found another fledgling response slipping away.

"Underneath that tough Bracken skin and SEAL bravado, you're shaking like a newborn foal," Adrian assessed, "and you're just as frustrated with yourself over it as you are with everything else. You won't come to terms with anything that's going on until you accept that. Change is inevitable. So get rid of your anger before you're the one who does damage no one can undo." She blinked several times as her voice thickened. "You're the heart of this family."

"Shit," he said when the emotions and the words struck him. "Mom."

"Did you know that?" Her small chin began to wobble. "You are the heart and soul of all of us. Be careful. Be *very* careful, Kyle." When he nodded obediently, she turned quickly before she broke down in front of him any further.

Kyle saw her hand lift to her mouth as she followed the path home.

Why didn't she just reach down his throat and finish the job? On second thought, taking that straight shot to the chest might be easier if the open onslaught of the last few days was to continue over the next few weeks.

CHAPTER EIGHT

"You've got to be joking."

The break in the Piper Pawnee Brave 300's engine's timing made Harmony glower. She finished her third sweep low over the feathered green heads of corn, pulling up with less than her usual thrust. Circling wide, she played the caution card, listening again for the split-second off-timing in the pistons.

It might've flown over the head of a less experienced pilot. But to her, the hitch in the Piper's giddyup was no less subtle than the swift, hind kick of a mule. She checked and rechecked her gauges.

Ducking the crowns of silos, she trimmed her speed and went in for another pass, tuning her ear to the drone of the engine and the vibrations along the one-seater's fuselage. She knew them well. She knew them like the terrain of Baldwin County. She knew what belonged. She knew instantly what did not.

"Piper. Piper. Do you read?"

She ignored the summons from her headset, releasing the spray over the next row of stalks.

Near the end of the field, she muttered, "Come on, Brave. Talk to Mama."

After requisitioning the Piper for Harmony's use, James had painted the sprayer red, like her. She had added her own touch to the cockpit door beneath the B.S. logo—a black decal in the form of her air sign, the Water-Bearer.

"Mother ship, calling the Enterprise. Report your position. Over."

Harmony gritted her teeth as she circled back around for another pass, ignoring the tower boss once more. A few more sprays and she would be done. Then she'd return to the hangar for diagnostics.

Damn it, she'd just calibrated this puppy.

"Piper, Piper! Do you read?"

"Arg!" Harmony snapped the mic stick from the visor of her flying helmet, positioning it over her mouth. "Piper to Tower. Completing my final run at Solange. Over."

"What's with the radio silence, ace?"

She dumped her load, then circled back around for another go. She enjoyed the work but preferred to keep the chatter to a minimum. "Trying to do my job." She chose not to mention the hitch. Not yet.

If word got back to James, he'd tell her to scrub, immediately. Harmony didn't like the idea of abandoning the field. They'd already had to fight for weather windows over the past week. Not to mention that the contract with Solange Agg called for work a bit wider afield, which had been a triumph of only the last three months. It was too soon for any hint of incapacity or unprofessionalism to enter into it.

Solange proprietors, the brothers Farrow, had toiled these lands with their own hands for so long under the Alabama sky, they had leather backs and sun-pocked faces to prove it. While they might have taken somebody like James Bracken on reputation alone, they'd looked askance in Harmony's direction, measuring and somewhat skeptical.

Harmony put a little more distance between herself and the silos, making wind adjustments. It was starting to blow at a northwesterly slant. She noted the blue dots of clear sky peeking through the white furls rolling in from the south like waves off the Gulf. "No rain chances today. Gotta take advantage."

The slight bump in the seat made her curse through her teeth, shallow enough to avoid radio transmission. The second hitch was more minor than the first. So minor, she might not have caught on to it if she hadn't been trawling for deficiencies. The photo of Bea taped to the console drew her eye briefly. "I'll finish and head back."

"Someone's been hanging around for you. Wants to see you pretty badly, from the sounds of it."

"Huh." There were no meetings on today's itinerary. "Put them in my office and ask them to wait another forty-five minutes if they can. And ask Seb to meet me at the airfield."

"Sure thing. Over."

"Piper out."

She should've been enjoying this. The vast panorama spreading above and beneath her. The drone of the Piper met only by silence. The proximity to the top of Earth's dome. She loved manipulating the empty matter of the sky. She loved fighting the forces humankind should've been bound by—wrangling the invisible dynamics and particles of wind and matter.

There was no room in the small cockpit of the Piper or any other aircraft for uncertainty. As she set a course for home, she felt unease creeping along her spine. Between her and James and their master mechanic, Seb, the Piper and all other aircraft at B.S. were meticulously tuned. Efficiency and safety went hand in hand in their business model, along with accuracy afield. These principles were the bedrock on which both the application and training parts of B.S. had been founded. The planes themselves were top-of-the-line, as tried and tested as those piloting them—herself chief among them.

She batted back the first clutch of apprehension building at the base of her skull. Charting the flight she already knew by heart, she mentally took herself through the landing pattern. *Get her home*, she mapped. *Get her to Seb. See what's up.*

The Piper touched down without any further glitches. Seb, gruff and short-legged, met her on the tarmac. As she detailed the flight, the flaws sounded slighter than her apprehension. Seb agreed to give the plane a look-over, but as Harmony walked to the tower offices, she couldn't displace her frown.

Was this paranoia?

"I blame this on you, Kyle," she muttered to nobody but herself. She'd watched for two days as he patrolled the woods and grounds around the mother-in-law suite, kicking up leaves. He'd shown her mussed cobwebs in the corner of one of the windowsills on the outside of the house. *Definitely tampered with*, he'd told her.

You're losing your mind, she'd told him.

Though Harmony and Bea were both still installed in Kyle's room at the farmhouse, the police had turned over no leads, just as she'd known they wouldn't. She maintained for Bea's sake that the delay was due to roof repairs—and not because Kyle, James, Adrian, Cole and every other adult in their lives seemed united in keeping them from their home until more was known about the mysterious whereabouts and malfeasance of the perpetrator.

Whether or not the weirdo was found, Harmony didn't plan on telling Bea anything more about it. If her daughter was going to have nightmares, they would be about bears and clowns. Not faceless lunatics who were as real as the ax they evidently had to grind.

Harmony pushed through the door into the air-cooled building where B.S. came together in all its endeavors. Her office was sparsely furnished. On the walls were various awards and citations. On the desk were a few framed photographs of Bea and Harmony's parents. She eyed the water cooler through the glass door. Her mouth was dry as dust. When she swung the door open, though, she saw the person sitting in the leather-bound guest chair.

The woman got to her feet. She was small. She wore short shorts and a tank top to combat the heat. She shifted the baby in her arms to her hip. "Harmony! I was beginning the think you weren't coming."

Recognition evaded Harmony for a moment. Then she saw the red birthmark cupping the point of the woman's chin and the past brought it back to her. "Torrance," she replied. "Wow. It's been…"

"Five years, at least. I know." Torrance offered her a smile. Harmony noticed it was stilted at the edges. She also caught the glint of sympathy behind the eyes.

The last time she had seen Torrance Letter was around the time of Benji's funeral. Torrance was a SEAL wife. She and her husband, Mike, lived across the Florida line in the suburbs of Pensa-cola. Mike and Benji had bonded at BUD/S when they both nearly washed out during Hell Week.

Whether the teams were overseas or back home, the community of SEAL wives and families was a close one. They banded together particularly in the event of a SEAL's death or injury, offering familial support or presence at a bedside. Harmony had actually met Torrance while Mike and Benji had been working up to their first deployment. They'd shared their concerns over pizza and beer. It had been refreshing, knowing the unique experience of being a Navy SEAL's girl wasn't a lone one.

There had been outpourings from the other wives, of course, in the wake of Benji's death, and it had continued after the funeral. There had been phone calls, emails and the occasional visits to check that she and Bea were doing okay, if they needed anything. As a whole, the gestures had been heartfelt, some timely, especially during her pregnancy. However, over time Harmony had realized that they were hurting more than helping in the moving-on process. Hearing those outpourings, seeing those faces had made her ache for the days when she'd been on the other side, waiting for her solider to come home.

It was a world she'd never be part of again.

Harmony eyed the baby. He had a sweet face and big blue eyes to match. His fingers were in his mouth as he threw the look right back at her. She felt her jaw go soft. "Who's this little guy?"

"Oh," Torrance said, bouncing him a bit. She tugged his hand down and wiped his fingers with the ready cloth on her shoulder. "This is Liam. Sorry for the drool. He's starting to teethe."

Harmony lifted a shoulder. "Comes with the territory. I hadn't heard you and Mike had a baby."

"Yes," Torrance said with a bob of her head. She beamed. "Finally, right? Liam just turned six months. We had a party and everything. Ridiculous, I know, but Mike was home on the day, so we said, 'What the hey?' and went all out."

"He's a cutie," Harmony said, tugging on a miniaturized tennis shoe.

"How's Bea?"

"Raising Cain and proud of it," Harmony remarked. After a split second's hesitation, she picked a frame up off the desk and passed it to Torrance. "Growing so fast, I'm afraid to blink sometimes."

"Aw. Look. Just like Benji," Torrance observed.

"Yeah." Harmony cleared her throat. Annoyed by the perspiration she felt on her brow and under her black polo shirt, she sidestepped the desk for the water cooler. "What are you doing here?" she asked as she filled a paper cup. She gulped it then tossed it into the corner trashcan.

"Oh, you know…" Torrance forced an easygoing gesture after carefully setting the frame back in its place. "I was kinda in the neighborhood. We hadn't talked in so long. I figured I'd take a chance you were around."

If Torrance had dropped in only to say a simple hello, Harmony doubted she'd have waited over two hours to do so, especially if she and Liam had a long drive back to Pensacola. Coming to stand behind her desk, Harmony planted her hands on her hips and waited.

Liam whined and Torrance turned her head to his. When he reached for her ponytail, she indulged him by letting him take a fistful of hair. Cupping the back of his head, she brought it gingerly down to her shoulder where he closed his eyes. She readjusted, cradling him with both arms against her chest. Lowering her voice she said, "I was wondering… Have you heard from your brother lately?"

"Gavin?" Harmony shook her head. "Not really. Why?"

Torrance seemed to stop herself. She reached into the pocket of her shorts and pulled out a pacifier. Offering it to Liam, she settled him again and licked her lips in a nervous motion. "I overheard Mike talking. We met some friends down in Panama City for Memorial Day. Some other team guys, their wives and kids. Anyway…your brother's name came up."

When again Torrance paused, Harmony dipped her head. "Yeah?"

Torrance blew out a breath. "Well, Mike said something about him refusing help from anyone. That his family didn't even know. It bothered me, so much so that I let him and the guys have it. I said that if Gavin didn't notify his folks, then one of them should've, screw bro code."

Harmony held up a hand. "I'm sorry. Notify us of what?"

Torrance's face fell. "Oh, God," she breathed. "You really don't know."

Harmony's stomach turned. "Know *what*? What's wrong with my brother?"

Again, Torrance shook her head, this time faintly. "I'm not sure, exactly. It's not good, from what I have heard. I tried to get it out of Mike, but you know how the guys are. As soon as I made noise about coming to see you, he started battening down. Wouldn't open up. I'm sorry to bring this up to you like this. But I figured you should know that Gavin's been injured at least."

"Yes," Harmony agreed. Her voice sounded flat. "Thank you."

Torrance eyed her uncertainly. "Are you okay?"

"Fine," Harmony said. She brought her hand to her brow. "I just… I need to talk to my parents. I need to talk to…" *Kyle*.

The name came to her instantly. And with it, clarity. He'd known. He'd known something was up with Gavin, but, like Mike and the other SEALs, he'd battened down. Bro code. Soldier code. Whatever it was, it was tight. So tight even Harmony's understanding with him couldn't break it.

That didn't sit well. That didn't sit well at all.

Feeling flushed and heated, Harmony gestured toward the door. "I'll walk you and Liam out."

"Harmony," Torrance said when Harmony came around the desk, latching on to her arm. "We've missed you. Me and the other girls. If you'd ever like to have lunch or something…"

Harmony nodded away the rest of the invitation. "Thanks, Torrance. I'll call you. But now I've got to…"

"Right," Torrance said, backing off. "I hope everything turns out okay."

Harmony ducked her head and nodded. *Oh, was one soldier ever in for it.*

THE MAN FROM Philly had tourist written all over him. His floppy fisherman's hat might as well have had the price tag dangling from it still. It did little to hide the bright pink coating of sunburn on his face. The burn clashed horribly with his electric-green Hawaiian-print shirt. His legs emerged from his Eddie Bauer shorts and above his Crocs in the same hue as Elmer's glue.

He checked his Rolex compulsively and shifted from one leg to the other as he waited for Kyle to finish changing the back right tire on his eco-friendly Odyssey. Kyle made sure the lug nuts were firmly in place as he said, "It'll just be a moment, Mr. Palmer."

"Appreciate it," the man said. "It's a long drive."

"Headed out of town?" Kyle asked, trying to ease Palmer's impatience.

"Yes. My wife has family in Charleston."

"That is a long drive," Kyle agreed. "I'll just check your tire pressure before you get underway."

"Jeffrey!" The wife approached. Now here was somebody who knew how to accessorize a sunburn, Kyle noted. She wore a hot-pink hat that any fine-bred lady on race day at Churchill Downs would've envied. With a matching blazer to boot. She used the hat to swat flies. "Jeffrey! I swear there're more of them today than there were yesterday. It's like the locusts of plague!"

Amused, Kyle watched her frantically swish a lovebug off her husband's arm. Her eyes were wide with fright. "Should we be concerned? It's clearly a *swarm* of some kind."

"Ah, it's nothing to worry yourself over, Mrs. Palmer," Kyle assured her. "This here is the phenomenon known commonly to locals as lovebug or March fly season. And unless you're attached to the paint on your front bumper, it's harmless."

"I've never seen a fly with two heads instead of one," Jeffrey muttered, flicking one offender off his wife's hat.

"It's actually two flies." At the blank answering stares from each, Kyle expounded. "It's mating season."

"Oh," Mrs. Palmer said. Her mouth rounded, and she looked taken aback. "Well, that's... interesting."

"Mmm. Multitaskers." Kyle stood up with the tire gauge, job complete. He took the shop rag out of his back pocket and wiped his hands. "Gives new meaning to the mile-high club."

"Heh," Jeffrey uttered by way of a chuckle. "Lovebugs, you say?"

"There're plenty of names for them. Lovebugs. Kissing bugs. Honeymoon flies."

"It's sweet. I suppose."

Kyle had a feeling Mrs. Palmer thought the lovebugs more perverse than anything. "They're a nuisance, but scientists say they're beneficial to plant life. Larvae feed off decayed vegetation. Swarms take place twice a year, in spring and late summer. They can last for weeks."

Hick slammed the hood down on the Odyssey, done with the oil check. "I saw 'em once in December."

Kyle hooked the rag back in the pocket of his coveralls. "Yep. You're full of baloney, Hick."

Hick stepped back from the van. Turning his head, he spat a stream of Copenhagen on the pavement. Mrs. Palmer drew back from the dark splat, clutching her husband's sleeve. "Swear to the Almighty," Hick claimed. "It was Christmas of '88. They looked like snow, driftin' real slow-like. Rising instead of falling. Black as night. Like the devil's blizzard."

Kyle grunted. The swarm did look like snow now that he thought about it. He frowned. They were going to be scrubbing the bastards off every bumper that came through the garage for the next month. He addressed Hick again. "Give the head-lights and bumper a wash. We'll wipe the wind-shield down, replenish the wiper fluid." To Mr. Palmer, he added, "That should get you through our neighbor Tennesseans' hospitality. Beyond that, you'll have to give your bumper another wip-ing. Don't let the bugs sit on your grille any lon-ger than that. They'll eat right through the finish."

"Thank you," Palmer said, surprised once more. He held out a hand to Kyle. "You've been more than helpful, Mr…"

"Bracken," Kyle answered, pumping the man's fist.

Palmer's gaze strayed to the tattoo peeking under Kyle's sleeve and the navy T-shirt visible underneath the opening of his coveralls. "You're military."

It wasn't a question. Kyle paused briefly as the man's eyes rested on the trident. "Yes, sir. Just returned home, actually."

"From deployment?" Palmer asked.

"Yes, sir."

"It's peacetime, isn't it?"

"Peacetime," Hick grumbled as he buffed love-bugs off the bumper.

Kyle stifled a frown. If Hick scrubbed any harder, he'd be the one eating paint off the Odyssey. "There're jobs needing to be done whether war's on or not."

Palmer measured him for a few seconds more, letting go of his hand. "Well, if we pass through again, I guess we know where to come for repairs."

"We look forward to it, Mr. Palmer. Ma'am." Kyle touched the bill of his cap as the missus followed the man to the van. "Have a safe trip."

As the Odyssey disappeared around the corner, Hick took out his tobacco tin and made another wad. "Man looked at you like you're the new harbinger of plague."

"Mmm," Kyle said noncommittally. He watched Hick tuck the wad into his cheek. "I'm glad your aim's off. I'd hate to replace the lady's shoes. They were Italian leather."

"Who says I was aimin' for her?"

Kyle gave a half laugh, pushing the brim of his hat up and tucking it back down over his brow.

"Hey, sailor."

The tone was much sweeter than Hick's. Kyle's head swiveled in the direction of the lot to find a curvy female in long gray slacks and a white eyelet blouse. Her smile was soft and feminine, just like the rest of her. Intimate, too, a reminder of bygone days. She took off her sunglasses in a slow motion, as if to get a better look at him.

Laurel. He loosened an exhale from his chest. "Hey, gorgeous."

Her eyes, as gray as her slacks, circled his features once, then again before Hick made a noise in the back of his nose and throat, making her blink. "Hick," she said, beaming like the uninviting veteran was a sight for sore eyes. "I didn't see you there."

"You got eyes, girl," Hick grunted as he veered around Kyle, headed back into the garage. "Two of 'em."

"And they're both happy to see you," she trilled after him, grin broadening when he answered with, "Yeah, yeah, yeah." She giggled, her shoulders quaking with the movement. "Charming as always," she acknowledged. Her eyes stilled on Kyle again, and the LED smile warmed by a fraction. "Pappy said you were back."

"Yeah." He wanted to flex his hands. Or something other than stand there facing her like a statue. Just like that, he was wiped back to the adolescent days when he'd first met her and felt just as clumsy and awkward. "You here to see him?"

"I brought him a late lunch," she said, lifting the carryout bag under one arm. "When I got off work, Nana said he hadn't come home during his break, then sent me back out the door with cash and instructions." When he only looked at her, the smile dimmed. "It's okay that I'm here. Right?"

His brow knotted. "Why wouldn't it be?"

"I don't know," she said, tucking a strand of her strawberry-blond hair behind one ear. She shifted her feet. "You don't seem exactly sure about it."

"I'm glad you're here," he asserted. "It's good to see you."

Laurel searched him. When she saw that he meant it, it brought the smile back. "It's good to see you, too. You look…bigger."

Kyle placed his hand over his stomach. "Mom's cooking."

She giggled again. Her nose wrinkled when she laughed. She touched a knuckle to it. "No. I meant…" She flexed her bicep. "This kind of bigger." Lifting a shoulder, she arched a brow. "It's ridiculous. In a good way."

"You look good, too," he returned. And because he felt ridiculous for circling the conversational wagons, he elaborated. "Like Christmas at Bellingrath."

"Aren't you sweet?" Her top lip drew back to reveal white-bright teeth and a clean gum line. "You've always been sweet. You never change, Kyle."

He gave a short sigh. "I was sorry to hear about you and Joey."

The smile fell away slowly. Her eyes strayed to the ground. "Oh. Yes."

Kyle wondered how much he should say. "Pappy says you're doing okay besides. Are you—doing okay?"

"I think so," she said, readjusting the large purse hanging from her shoulder. "It's the kids more than anything. I almost couldn't go through with it, for their sakes. But they pick up on more than we grant them. I think Little Joey... He's the eldest. I think he knew when the energy changed. He and Mikayla—our second—understood that there was discord, even before Joey or I admitted as much. However much you try to shield them, little bits trickle through nonetheless."

"They're okay, too?" Kyle asked. "Now?"

"It's still an adjustment," Laurel admitted. "They're troupers, though. And Joey's been great. Sometimes things just...don't work out. Even the things you thought you needed most."

Kyle gave a short nod, choosing to remain mute on that score.

Laurel tilted her head. "So tell me, do you still hate me?"

He shook his head. "No."

"However much you might have tried?" she asked, testing the waters.

"Maybe," he said quietly. He shrugged. "It's in the past. You did what was right by you. So did I."

"Yes." She rolled her eyes. "Oh, God. I'm such a dimwit. I didn't even think to ask how you are. Your family. Everything."

"I'm fine," he said. It was a lie he'd told so many times, it'd become routine. Standard operating procedure. "Mom and Dad are the same."

"Still into each other?" she guessed.

"And keeping me on my toes," he finished. "So's Mavis."

"I wouldn't expect any less from our Mavey," Laurel said. She'd once been Mavis's babysitter.

Kyle crossed his arms and braced his legs apart. "Other than that, there's not much to tell."

She raised a brow. "Nothing?" When he shook his head, she grinned. "I find it hard to believe there's nobody significant in your life. I mean, look at you."

He thought of Harmony in the woods. Asleep on her couch. Trimming his hair. Before he could deny anything, Laurel leaped on his hesitation, her smile etched and sly. "Is it a secret?"

"Secret," he repeated. He heard the *zip-zip* of an automated drill from inside the garage and cleared his throat. "Well…it's a little embarrassing. I mean, it's Hick."

Laurel busted up laughing. The wrinkle in her nose materialized again as she pressed her hand over her mouth.

"What can I say?" Kyle asked, diverting the truth further. "He's kind of cute in a…starving polar bear kind of way. And don't let the granular temperament fool you. He's a real cuddle monster once you get him alone."

"Stop!" Laurel said, holding her stomach and doubling over. "You have to stop!"

"But we work together," Kyle continued, grinning wide now, too, as he shrugged. "So things are a bit awkward. Plus, I'm not sure what my folks would have to say about the arrangement." He gave into the urge to laugh alongside her when, wheezing, she grabbed him by his forearm. He held her beneath the shoulder to keep her upright.

"Kyle Zachariah Bracken!"

He glanced up at the livid delivery of his name. The laughter dried in his throat at Harmony's approach. She was still dressed in her B.S. uniform and mad as a hornet from the looks of her sharp-angled face. He abruptly let go of Laurel. "What?" he asked.

Harmony shoved the heels of her hands against his chest and pushed him back a step. "I'm going to throttle you!"

"Hey." He stepped in front of Laurel. Harmony was nearly riled enough to maul. "Calm down. You're overreacting."

"Overreacting?" Harmony blew out a humorless laugh. "You lie to my face and I'm overreacting?"

Terror struck Kyle. It spread quickly, ice cold. He might as well have been lying in the freezing surf again on the beach at Coronado.

Someone had told her about B.S.'s misfortunes

and his part in the cover-up and now she was here to crucify him for lying to her.

"I'm going to ask you one more time," Harmony said. "And, I swear to God, if you lie to me, I'm going to feed your ears to Bea's bobcat, one lobe at a time."

He fought the urge to wince and solidified his stance. "Ask your question."

"What's going on with my brother?" she asked, eyeing him beadily. When he blinked and his lips parted, she scoffed. "You know what? To hell with you, K.Z.B."

"Wait a minute," he said, quickly grabbing her by the elbow before she could stalk back to her SUV. He spun her back around in a jerky motion. "All this? This is about Gavin?"

"You're damn straight it's about Gavin," she replied. "Have you been lying to me about anything else?"

"No," he said, grabbing the opportunity by the horns. "No. Of course not."

"Okay," she granted. "So have you? Been lying? Because Torrance Letter was a hell of a lot more forthcoming in the ten minutes she spent in my office this afternoon than you've been for the last week."

Kyle flirted with the idea of studying her shoes instead of looking her in the eye, but he couldn't turn away from those hissing feline slits any more than he could stop feeling guilty. "I might've withheld information."

Her jaw went hard. "Why?" she asked, hurling the question at him. There was fear wavering behind the seething interrogation. When he paused, she shoved her hands into his chest again. *"Why?"*

"Because…" Silently, he cursed himself. He cursed Gavin. The whole situation, he cursed. "Because he asked me to."

"What's wrong with him? If you don't tell me, I'll find out where he is, Kyle, and you won't be the only one who's sorry!"

She'd do that either way. Still, he held up a hand. "Look, a few days ago, I told you how it should be. It should be him standing here spilling the truth. I did my best to get him to come home."

"So he's…" Something flickered over her, showing how deeply her fear had entrenched itself. How far the scenario had gone in her mind. "He's able to come home, if he wants to."

Kyle scowled, again wrestling over what to say and what not to. "There's nothing wrong with his legs," he settled with. She waited, expectant, and he reached up with both hands to tug at the bill of his ball cap. "Goddamn it, Harm. He's blind."

She looked as if someone had struck her. The skin of her throat and shoulders drew taut against her collarbone as her breath seized.

When she continued to stare at him, blank, he released a tumultuous sigh. "I can't do it anymore. I can't wait around for him to just show up. There's a part of me that knows, just as you do, that's probably never going to happen."

All the muscles of her face were bearing down on whatever was rising on the inside. Still, she waited, her command unflagging.

Kyle glanced around the parking lot. He did a double take when he realized Laurel was no longer with them.

"Looks like I scared off your girlfriend," Harmony muttered helpfully.

He rolled his eyes at her and didn't bother telling her Laurel wasn't his girlfriend anymore. He grabbed her by the arm, then held up his hands again, resigned, when she shrugged out of his grasp. "Come on. Let me buy you a drink. Then we'll go see your folks and lay it all on the table."

She went up on her toes. "*You* can lay it all on the table. Then you can apologize to all of us."

As she walked away, he rolled his shoulders back and turned his head to the side, feeling the tension. It was everywhere. He followed her, keeping his gaze on the back of her head, not the movement of her hips as she walked her swinging, pissed-off walk several paces out in front.

CHAPTER NINE

"WE WERE ON a task force. It was the only reason we were paired together. Neither of us said anything to the head shed when we realized we were both chosen. I guess we figured it'd been long enough since things got off-foot between us that it wouldn't interfere with the assignment."

Harmony sat silent on the high-rise chair in the dim corner of Tavern of the Graces, nursing a beer. Since it was a weeknight, most of the tables around them were empty. From the bar, William Leighton had taken one look at them when they walked through the doors and known they needed space. Harmony ignored the hype from the well-played jukebox, which was cranking through a slow Pearl Jam ballad she'd always loved, and focused on Kyle.

He'd taken barely a sip from his own drink. He gripped it on the table, gaze trained on the label. Like her, he leaned against the back of his chair. He might've looked comfortable if not for the muscle spasming along his jawline. "Everything went according to strategy. The enemy didn't catch on to us until extraction. Then things got hot. They came in numbers and nearly had us pinned down. We were almost to the helo when they started launching RPGs. Nobody's sure what happened exactly, but Gavin and another guy from his team, Pettelier—Big Pete—they went down not ten yards to my right."

There was a funny taste in her mouth. Thick, acidic. She'd tasted it before.

Kyle explained further, "We got to the helo. Pettelier was in bad shape, and Gavin…he kept mumbling that he couldn't see. There was shit all over his face."

"Blood," she ventured, sensing him holding back.

Kyle nodded. He lifted the beer to his mouth. "They were medevaced off the carrier. Pettelier's right leg had to be taken at the knee. And Gavin… He'd lost most vision in his left eye and close to half in his right."

Harmony felt the breath leave her again. Gavin. Blind. "Why weren't we informed? The doctors… Isn't it routine for them to inform next of kin?"

"He interfered," Kyle said. "There were at least two team guys with him at all times. He said that that was family enough until he could contact you personally."

"You knew better," Harmony said. "You must've known that was never his plan."

"I knew." Kyle nodded, grim. "I tried to ram it into his head that you, your parents…had a right

to know. He wouldn't hear a word about him needing you. Not because he's a thick-headed asshole.
Which he is, don't get me wrong. But he didn't
want you to see him down. Not until he made it
out of the hospital, into rehab. Until he was stronger." Kyle's expression darkened, and he leaned
his elbows on the table, flattening his palms as
he rubbed one against the other. "I really thought
he'd come home this time. But as soon as he realized his sight wasn't returning—"

"How long ago was this?"

Harmony knew by Kyle's hesitation that it was
longer than it should have been.

"Five months."

"You've been covering for him all that time?"
she asked, incredulous.

"He made me swear on your life that I would
let him do the telling at the right time. I didn't
realize 'til I got back he never came home, never
even bothered to call."

"So…there was never a job in DC," Harmony
realized.

"No."

"And there was never a girl."

"He's still got a mouth. I think as long as he
does, there'll be women. But as a far as I know,
he hasn't seen anyone since it happened."

"When was the last time you saw him?" Harmony wanted to know.

"He was in the hospital for several weeks. I

traded shifts with friends at his bedside. After we finally got the verdict from the doctors about his eyes, I started telling him, 'It's time now. Let's do it.' It would've been easy to get him transferred south, closer to you and Briar and Cole. Over the next week, I rode him hard about it. I said everything I knew to say to get him in gear. Eventually, he told me he didn't need me anymore—or any of the other team guys for that matter."

"Stupid lone wolf." The heel of her hand supported her chin. She let it rest there. The sheer force of all the emotions she'd endured in wave after wave since Torrance's visit was starting to wear. The beer did little to cool the worst of it. But as usual, it brought the heat to her skin. Alcohol and anger always made for a nice Molotov cocktail to cap off any good upsurge in furor. The weight of it all was building alongside the fatigue. It reduced the urge to harangue Kyle further, however much she might think he deserved it. Through the shock and ire, she was beginning to feel the onset of sadness.

She grimaced. Sadness never helped matters. All it did was bring her down. While pregnant and grieving, she'd learned that once the seeds of sadness drilled a home inside her, there wasn't much she could do to prevent them from putting down roots. Colonizing. There they'd stay until they were good and ready to be harvested.

It made her restless, which wasn't great, considering her way to cope with restlessness was by jumping into the nearest flying bucket and letting adrenaline do its work. And until her Piper had been seen to by Seb, she wasn't going back into the skies.

Harmony folded her arms over the tabletop and pressed her brow into the bony part of her wrist. "Where is he now?"

"Hopefully, he's still working through rehabilitation," Kyle explained. "When my team got back to Little Creek, I ran into one of his guys and asked the same. He was real vague on details—acting on Gavin's behalf, I'm sure. He said at least he was getting the help he needed. I assumed that meant he'd come home. Because, yes, he does need rehab. He probably needs a good deal of therapy. But the thing he needs most is the people who love him. He's just too much of a frigging martyr to abandon himself to that fact."

Harmony raised her head. Looking across the bar, she caught Olivia's eye. Her cousin shared a consoling sort of smile before raising the neck of a rum bottle. Harmony shook her head at the offer. The smile faded. Olivia nodded, set the bottle down and made her way to the phone at the end of the bar. Harmony had little doubt who she was dialing.

She pushed against the edge of the table, straightening her arms. "Okay," she acquiesced, "here's what's about to happen. Either Dad or

Mom, or both, are about to walk through those doors." She nodded to the entry, which was propped open to let the breeze carry through. "Ready to come clean?"

"I was ready to do this five months ago," Kyle said, sounding as weary as she felt.

"It'll hurt worse now." There was accusation behind the warning, and she ramped up on it because she *was* still angry at him. "I'm pretty sure this is going to kill Dad."

"I'm prepared to apologize."

Harmony took another bracing gulp from the beer that was going tepid beneath her hand. "I wouldn't be opposed to the idea of you groveling a little bit."

Kyle looked conflicted. It was hard to look at him. Her pillar. Her big stone lion with uncomfortable guilt written all over him. No doubt, he was a man of honor. He was a man of his word. He'd kept it to Gavin. He still valued his relationship with her brother enough that he hadn't broken it, even when that friendship had suffered. Even when, she saw now, it had tortured him to do so.

She didn't want to forgive him. She didn't want to look at him and see all the shiny wonderful things that were Kyle.

Spinning her beer on the table, she tipped it so she was staring down the barrel. Things started to blur as the silence between them lengthened. Unable to stand it, she said, "I almost wish I could hate you." She bit the inside of her cheek and jerked a shoulder. "But it seems I can't. At least not completely."

"Carrots…"

She closed her eyes. "I am mad as hell at you, so I'd refrain from calling me Carrots."

"You're always Carrots. Especially when you're mad as hell."

She blew out a breath because the temptation to laugh and break through the sadness and returning grief knocked loudly. "Shame I don't have a slate to break over your head."

"Do you see me pulling your pigtails?"

When she looked up, there was a smile in his eyes—quiet and reaching. Her lungs stopped working. He was still shiny. He was still wonderful. He was still hers. Her very own frigging Gilbert Blythe.

The light in him faded, and his mouth formed a grim line. "Ask Dad what's going on with B.S."

"B.S.?"

"Yeah," he answered simply, pulling his beer into his middle and crossing his ankle over his knee. "Ask him."

"Have you been lying for him, too?" Harmony asked, feeling the "carrots" rising up her neck again.

Kyle sniffed and chose to pick lint off the knee of his coveralls. "It was Mom. She asked me not to say anything."

She ground her teeth, containing the urge to jump on him and his honor and put a wallop on both. "Anything else you're covering up?"

He looked at her again. She gleaned awareness, kin to what she felt for him whenever he was near. She saw another veil of guilt, which he shed quickly—safely behind that big gleaming suit of armor. He looked away and said under his breath, "Nothing a good sermon wouldn't cure, I'm told." The wariness crept back over his countenance. He straightened. "Here they come."

Harmony glanced around and watched her parents enter the tavern arm in arm. She grabbed her beer and his.

"Where're you going?" Kyle asked as she stood.

"To tell William and Liv to bring us all another round," she informed him. "At least give the good folks something to fortify themselves before you deliver the biggest blow of their lives."

Kyle deliberated. Then he shifted his weight to the left. Reaching into his right back pocket, he pulled out his billfold and took out two folded bills. He passed them to her by the tips of two fingers. "Tell your cousin to bring the top shelf. Straight, hard, with no delay and to keep it coming."

By the time Kyle left Tavern of the Graces, it was late enough that the sky had gone dark. Not a tinge of color abstracted the horizon. He wandered down close to the water, doing his best to embrace the lukewarm zephyr along the shore. Heat lightning fizzed across a distant cloud face and ghost lights flashed and died along the surface of the rich estuary. He smelled the sea and heard the languid stir of water.

The lure was there not to return to The Farm. He craved this. The call from the *Hellraiser* was strong in his blood. He was feeling too raw, and he missed the Gulf.

Harmony had left the table before he'd finished speaking to Briar and Cole. He thought she'd gone back to the inn to relieve one of the maids from babysitting duty. When he saw the figure standing near the dock, he realized different. He took a cleansing breath before crossing the lawn to her silhouette.

She stood up to her ankles in water. Her shoes were littered with her socks on the sand. Standing very still, letting her toes sink into the silty clam-strewn bottom, she stared off into the distant storm. Her shoulders were high, her chin level. There was a challenge, a dare, written all over her. Just as he'd sailed into a cyclone to get here, she silently beckoned the rolling thunderhead closer.

Not everyone looked into a storm and said, "Bring it," especially when their world was already tattered at the seams. Where Kyle had seen the storm on the Gulf as a distraction from the conflict that always came with duty, he knew Harmony was something of a different beast. She needed the storm to reassert her strength, to prove again to herself and others that she was a survivor. That no matter life's trials, she would get through.

Her fighting spirit was the chief thing he'd always admired about her. In light of all the ill-advised feelings that were stirring inside him whenever she was near, that spirit was another unquenchable reason he had for beginning to need her.

He gave her another moment, two, before he said her name. Her head rotated slowly. He was right. There was challenge there. The impact came with a one-two punch when he saw her eyes damp. No tears beneath, yet they were red and bright and came swinging at him with surprising force. She turned away quickly and, with a frustrated swipe of her sleeve, made sure there was nothing to clean up before facing him again.

"All right?" he asked quietly.

"Fine." Her answer was dim but unwavering. Again, her dogged strength rode at the forefront and blazed an approving trail inside him.

The conversation with her parents hadn't been any easier than expected. When Harmony excused herself and Briar escaped to the ladies' room, Kyle had given Cole a few of the grittier details he'd held back from them. Details from the op, Gavin's surgeries and the gray mood he'd sunk into after.

If Harmony had known he'd held back, she'd

have come swinging at him with more than her eyes. He'd been right to hold back, though, he observed. At least for now. "You sure you're fine?" he asked.

She gave a quick sniff and looked off toward the Fairhope Pier in the distance. "I shouldn't drink," she said, admonishing her weakness. "It makes everything soft."

Her, soft. Color bloomed from the column of her throat and had mushroomed over her cheekbones. But she was steady on her feet, and her speech didn't run together as he knew it did when she'd gone overboard with the Patron. Her lids were long, heavy, almost at half-mast. The malice had lifted at last. A relief. "Yeah," he said, "but sometimes it lets things leak through. Things you've kept on ice too long."

Her gaze crawled back to his. With her head turned sideways, she eyed him in the low golden wash from the dock light. It kissed the water around her, painting light over the ripples. For a moment, he could imagine her as a vibrant, forbidding variety of sea goddess. One of Triton's own.

After a while, she shook her head. "Whatever it is, I can't go to Bea." She lifted a hand to the inn sleeping on the grassy gardened slope beyond. "Not until I get a handle on it. She knows me too well, and it's not a short drive back to The Farm."

"So don't," he suggested.

"Don't what?"

"Don't go back tonight. Sleep at the inn with your parents instead."

Her drawl deepened mockingly. "This is about that dern bandit."

"He's more than that."

She only scowled. "You don't want to go home tonight any more than I do. Well, you don't have to," she added quickly when he chose not to respond. "Nothing's turned up over the last few days."

"Yeah, but you'll go back to the mother-in-law suite." He knew. "You'll leave Bea here with your parents, just in case, and go back while my back's turned."

"I need to go home," she insisted. "Just like you need the *Hellraiser*."

"Why go?"

"It's *home*. What's the first thing you need when you get off the boat?"

"Don't confuse want with need, Harm. It's dangerous."

"Maybe in your case," she retorted.

"What's that supposed to mean?"

She gave him a swift once-over, width to width. Then another, slower, up and down. Those half-mast eyes blinked, languorous. Behind them, something stirred like the water around her. She rubbed her lips together, drawing his attention to them.

What was she doing looking at him like that? Like ripe winter peaches. What *the hell* was she doing?

He bent to pick up her shoes.

"Where are you going?" she demanded when he began walking up the slope.

"To walk you home. Where else?"

She groaned at his recalcitrance. He heard her splashing her way to shore. "You're as pigheaded as Gavin."

"Thanks," he said, refusing to slow. When she caught up a bit, he asked, "Will they be okay? Your parents."

"Dad won't sleep 'til we get Gavin back. Everything will be better once he's here. They don't say it, but all he and Mom have wanted these last few years is for Gavin to come home and stay."

It was as hard to quit the SEAL teams as it was to stay in. To quit your team, your boys, to live knowing you'd hung up your gun while they kept putting themselves in the fight... All that combined with Gavin's lone wolf issues... It wasn't any wonder his buddy had stayed away from home.

Things were different now. Gavin's service was effectively ended. SEALs needed 20/20. Gavin was skilled in the art of the fight, but visually impaired didn't clear basic navy med checks, Jedi or no Jedi. "It's not going to be easy—convincing him to come back."

"Who says we're giving him an option?"

His brows steepled. "So, you're gonna hog-tie him and toss him into the trunk of your getaway car?"

"I'm hoping he'll see reason once we talk face-to-face," she mused. "But if he's more obstinate than normal, yes. Into the trunk he goes."

"I'd like to see that," he decided. He sped up as they passed through the garden. It was darker there, more fragrant, suggestive.

"Slow down," she ordered him.

"No," he returned, flat.

She sped up, level with him now. "I need to say something to you."

"There you go with that need thing again," he said. "Go on ahead to the porch, Carrots."

She put on another burst of speed, flipping around and planting herself in front of him on the path.

Kyle came to an abrupt halt to keep from plowing into her. He took a breath. There was urgency building inside him, bringing the pressure up to whistling. He could tell her what she needed and that was to get the hell out of here. He closed his eyes and told himself to level off before planting his hands on his hips. "Don't push me." He strung each word out low in his throat so they were clear.

True to form, she ignored the hint, tilting her chin up like she had in the face of the thunderhead. "I've spent the last four hours contemplating whether or not I should give you a good spanking."

Bad choice of words, he decided as a rash of heated images assaulted his brain. Resigned, he spread his arms. "Go 'head."

"Huh?" she asked, blinking.

"You wanna paddle me?" he asked, the rest of him heating. "Go ahead! You'll get it out of your system. We can move on. Maybe you'll forgive me."

She only narrowed her eyes and measured him close enough to estimate his wingspan. He jerked a thumb over his shoulder, impatient. "What, want me to turn around? Come on! You've been thinking about it all night. *Just do it.*"

Her lips parted. Her eyes shone at him. She panted in the short space between them. Instead of hauling off with her hand, she brought both up to his collar, gripping and fisting. "You really are an effing prince." Jerking him down to her, she went up on her toes, linked her fingers over the back of his head and took his mouth.

"Nmph!" Caught off guard as he rarely was, his arms came up. The sudden force of her and what she was doing knocked him back, between butterfly bushes, up against the wall of the inn.

Their lips broke. He wasn't breathing anymore. His heart rapped the report of his M-60 against his eardrums as she gazed at him with those bright knowing eyes before she looked at his mouth. When she drew close, chest to chest, and rose back onto the points of her toes, he fumbled. "What…" he asked, feeling her arms tie, warm, around his waist. Inviting him into all her fascinating angles. "What…"

"Sh, sh, sh." The urging was remarkably gentle, given her ferocity. The tender part of her that was a mother, perhaps. It lulled him.

Again, she took his mouth. Softer this time, unhurried. "Mmm." He heard the noise rise up. Her head tilted at the encouragement. The kiss went deeper, and he couldn't stop it, the noise or her. Want and need were there, tangled up under the surface. It didn't help when she tried to draw him into the kiss further, taking turns coaxing each of his lips. Tugging the top. Nipping the bottom.

Unbidden, the noise rose through him again, and his hand came to rest on top of her head. Her hair felt like silk. They sank in as his fingers spread to cradle the supple threads at the top of her French braid.

He was compelled by the softness as well as the punch of power behind her. *Give in, soldier*, she said to him, silent, as she coaxed.

Give in, the gluttonous part of him answered and all the tired parts in between. *Give—if only just a little…*

Dragging air through his nose, he raised his chin, confronting her as she'd confronted him. She drew back, startled. She grabbed on to him for balance. The hitch lasted a second maybe. Eager, she parted her lips and met him.

He realized he couldn't give a little. He realized that quick. He realized too late that what had milled inside him, what had grown there, wasn't in the least bit small. In giving, he'd opened the mouth of a flume. The heady breakwaters behind it charged, free to convey through every channel he'd worked hard to close. He had no recourse now but to stay afloat. Kissing Harmony was everything he should've known it would be. Terrifying. Seductive. Death-defying. Crazy. Everything a long-suffering adrenaline junkie like him could ever want, *or* need.

It was Harmony who made noise this time. Not plaintive, but on the brink of triumphal. The sound of rapture. As if at long last she'd hammered through some insurmountable wall, and the view from the other side was spectacular.

She broke away on a trembling, laughing breath. Those angles vibrated underneath his hands. The lines of her face had eased. Something shone through her. Elation. Ecstasy.

He shook his head when she opened her eyes and found his. They were soft like a caress, and he felt hard as Thunderhead Mountain by comparison. "What are you doing?" he whispered into the garden quiet. "What *the hell* are you doing?"

She tried closing her mouth around the smile. It didn't work. She made a satisfied hum and brought his rigidity to proportions only the Crazy Horse Memorial would understand. "You kissed me back."

The laugh was unsolicited. A whisper against his will. "I'm going to hell."

"Relax. At this rate, you'll have company." Her tongue darted across her lips. Leaning into him, she rose up on her toes again. When he snatched his head back from hers, she smiled a pronounced Cheshire cat grin. "Do it again."

She knew him. She knew his inability to stand back from a challenge. Especially one he really... *really* wanted to meet. "No," he ground out.

"Do it," she said, linking both hands behind his neck once again. More summons. Soft and womanly. A siren's call.

"You want your dad to shoot me?" His pulse was ratcheting up in anticipation. "The Glock he hides behind the kitchen cabinets? I know about it."

"Do I want him to use it?"

"You're handing the detective in him plenty of just cause. Is this your backwards way of getting even?" It'd had better be.

"I've wanted to kiss you since I was ten."

He groaned again. "Harm, no."

"The weight of it crushed me," she went on. "I nearly buckled under it."

"You're killing me."

"It's the only thing in my whole life I've done

quietly," she told him. "And I think that's what hurt the most. More than the unrequited part. More than knowing you'd never look at me and see anything other than the kid you used to read to."

"Stop talking," he said with a shake of his head.

"Because it changes things." One deep-bronze brow arched. "Right? And it's scary. It wasn't until I drove sixteen hundred miles to Arizona that the crazy train even thought about hitting the brakes."

"Benji," he reminded her. "You had Benji."

The longing momentarily died in a clutch of grief. "Yes. And he had me, all of me. For a while, what we had eclipsed all the stupid things I felt for you. That is, until you surprised me at the air show. You were there out of the blue, and there went that crazy train racing down the tracks again. Only this time, I thought I might not be alone."

He seamed his mouth, stoic. Stoic was safer.

She nodded, brusque and certain, even as he remained tight-lipped. "I'm not alone," she asserted. "And any doubt I had about that is up in flames now because, Kyle, *you kissed me back*. You wouldn't… You'd have pushed me away if it were different."

When he opened his mouth, then decisively closed it, she challenged again, "Tell me it's different. Lie to me and tell me I'm wrong. You've had five months of fine practice."

He felt the blister of an angry flurry. His jaw firmed. She was back to rankling him to get a response. "It is different." When irritation flared alongside her urgency, he explained quickly, "What you felt for me back then. Christ, Carrots. You were a kid."

"You fell in love with Laurel when you were— what? Fifteen? A kid."

"It's *different*."

"Things hadn't changed for me by that age," she informed him. "At fifteen, sixteen, seventeen, it was still you. Why was what you felt for her real but not what I felt for you? Because I never expressed it like you did with her?"

He shook his head, truly at a loss.

"What about now?" she asked. "Does this not count either because I'm still your little loud-mouthed Carrots?"

"It's standard," he said finally. She frowned. He went on, determined. "It's typical—for a person to turn to the one that was closest to the one they lost. For comfort. For…familiarity."

She blinked at him. Her mouth scrambled. "You are unbelievable. You're so far in denial that you're blaming what just happened on some clichéd 'grieving widow can't stand to be alone' incentive?"

"Happens all the time," he contended.

She brought a hand to her brow and backed off,

reeling. "You son of a bitch," she cursed under her breath. She left him between the butterfly bushes.

He took a second, steeled himself. If Edith was right and there was a Lord, he could use some strength right about now.

He took several steps after her.

She came at him abruptly out of the dark, brimming with renewed fury and bringing him to a halt. Snatching her shoes from his grasp, she trudged off again without a word.

"Come on, Carrots," he said, weary. She'd effectively turned the tables on him—now he was chasing her. As they came around to the front of the inn, breaking free from the lull of the garden, he raised his voice. "Hey, I'm sorry you're upset. This ain't easy for me either."

She stomped up to the entrance and tossed over her shoulder, "Go around to the kitchen door and knock. I'm sure Mom's got some good Roquefort to serve with that whine." At the bite of his sour laugh, she doubled back at the top of the steps. Towering, rod-backed and righteous, she braced her hands on her hips. "I am a grown-ass woman."

He stopped and regarded her because he was a grown-ass man and damned if he could help it. "Ya' don't say."

"I've carried a child." She flung her arms out. "I've given birth!"

"I was there," he reminded her.

"Bea's conception wasn't immaculate. Your friend Benji and I bumped up against each other enough times to bring sperm and egg together."

He grimaced. "It's lucky I've got you, professor. A meatball like me could never have comprehended that one."

She talked over him, vehement. "Luckily, he wasn't half as emotionally constipated as you."

"Oh, thanks," he muttered.

"Regardless, I've had enough experience with the male sex to know when a man is into me," Harmony kept on, lifting an instructive finger. "Further, I've had a man inside me enough times to know where that attraction *leads* when it's *right*."

"Which this isn't," he retorted. "And, for God's sake, lower your voice. Your baby's upstairs."

"I'm sorry. Are you afraid of my daddy or my daughter?"

Kyle advanced up the steps, took her by the elbow and moved her toward the door. "Right now I'm afraid of waking up everybody under your parents' roof, including their good-paying guests, so why don't we call it a night?"

She planted her feet on the welcome mat when he stopped to turn the knob. "At least admit there's more you're afraid of than sharks."

Kyle swung the door open. "Inside."

"No kiss this time?" she asked, testing.

"That's right." He dipped to her level. He spoke

quietly enough that it didn't carry into the lobby when he said, "You want to know something else I'm afraid of?"

"What've you got, superhero?"

"That whatever's happened between us tonight wiped out everything that came before it. Is that what you want?" he asked, mashing it out through his teeth.

"Are you kidding me?" For the first time, he saw the nerves behind the spine. Her chin quavered with them even as she jabbed him with her finger. "Why do you think I didn't say anything before? You think I *want* to lose my best friend?"

Long-held anguish rang through the inquiry. He fell silent.

She lifted her shoulders in a helpless shrug. "But I guess…at the end of the day…I'm not half so noble as you are."

Gentling his hold, he maneuvered her carefully so that the welcome mat at least was between them. *Shit*, he thought when he let go and saw the white imprint of his fingers on her skin. When she only frowned at him, he reached for the knob again. "Stay put. All right?"

She said nothing. Not even when he added, "Good night, Carrots." Closing the door between them, he eyed her one last time through the Belgian lace pattern of glass, reiterating the message. *Stay*.

Backing away, he made it down the steps before he saw her whirl away with a flick of red
braid and disappear into the safety of her parents' house.

CHAPTER TEN

"WHAT DO YOU mean Seb's not in?"

The second mechanic on staff at B.S. blanked. Harmony, already short on patience, pondered speeding up his memory by giving him a decent rattle. "Do you know where he is?" she asked when he continued to goggle at her.

"Mama?"

Harmony glanced back to the door of the hangar. The heat was enough to suffocate. On the tarmac, it undulated off the flattop. She'd asked Bea to wait behind in her office where there was air-conditioning, but in stubby pigtails, purple Timberlands, yellow shorts and a T-shirt emblazoned with the word SASSY, she'd followed. Brow and lips puckered, she rubbed her hands together in a listless manner.

"Bea," Harmony said with a shake of her head. "It's hot. Go back to the office."

"But, Mama…" Bea bounced at the knees, a sure sign of resistance. Her knuckles scraped against her opposing palm.

"Seb went to a meeting," the mechanic recalled.

"A meeting?" Harmony took off her Aviators.

"Maybe you can explain to me why I don't know anything about this meeting."

"Er…" The mechanic fumbled once more for an explanation.

"Mama."

"Bea, please," Harmony pleaded. "A minute."

"But it itches!"

Now Bea was rubbing her hands against the rhinestones on her belt. Harmony lifted a finger to the mechanic and walked to her daughter. Taking Bea's hands, she lifted them to the light. "Baby." The raised skin was damp and rashy. "Why didn't you tell me?"

"It wasn't bad before," Bea said, still bouncing at the knees. "Mama, *it itches*!"

"All right, all right," Harmony said, adopting a placid tone. There was a meltdown in their future if one of them didn't take control. She scooped Bea up and began walking out of the hangar. "It's probably just eczema again. I think I have some lotion in my purse."

"Wait," the mechanic called. "I remember where he told me he was going."

Harmony stopped. Bea whined and began to wriggle. "Well?" Harmony said to him, annoyed.

"Bracken Mechanics," he revealed.

"Why on Earth would they meet there on B.S. business?" And not tell her.

There had been a lot of things people hadn't been telling her lately. It had taken several days for James to get around to telling her everything that had been going wrong with B.S. The advertising. The contracts. As a result, the books. She hadn't spoken to him much other than the standard day-to-day jargon. Because she still felt all the stinging things she wanted to say to him.

She was tired of the people she trusted going behind her back lying and withholding. And she was downright flattened by the prospect that they were doing so again.

Without waiting for an answer from the mechanic, she quickly walked across the tarmac to the office. She dumped out her purse to locate the medicated ointment the doctor had prescribed for Bea's sensitive skin. It was typical of the rash to occur with the changing of the season. Extremes like hot and cold usually brought it on. "Don't scratch," she told Bea as she carried her out to her Grand Cherokee after applying the lotion.

Bea was antsy in the backseat, so Harmony cranked up the air and played one of her Disney soundtracks while she drove. When the gears behind the console began to grind and the air flow staggered, Harmony gave it a sufficient rap with her fist. It ran smoothly until she pulled up in the parking lot of Bracken Mechanics.

"How're your hands?" she asked, pivoting around to the backseat.

Bea's pout answered for her. Arms crossed over her head, her hands hung loose on either side.

Harmony sighed and rushed around to her door. Tugging her out of the booster seat, she patted her on the back. "It's all right," she said and made a beeline for the building. "I'll call the doctor just as soon as I'm finished here."

"No doctor," Bea insisted.

"If the lotion isn't helping, you need to see the doctor."

"Is Kyle here?"

Harmony didn't want him to be. She did not want him to be in the room with Seb and James when she busted in on them.

There was only so much betrayal she could take before she could never look those responsible in the face again.

Don't be here, she thought as she bypassed the men at work beyond the open doors of the garage. The office door was closed, an oddity. She knew Mavis liked to keep it open when she came in. Better to heckle the menfolk.

Through the glass, she saw James sitting on his desk. And Seb. Hick was in there, too, grinding his Copenhagen. She came to the door and nearly pushed through it before she saw the person standing in the corner beyond James's desk, arms crossed and head lowered as he listened intently to James and Seb's discussion. She saw him tugging at the end of his chin. A thoughtful habit he normally adopted when he was trying to fathom something deeply complex.

Kyle's eyes lifted and found hers. Caught, he straightened against the wall. She spared him a mute stare, then barged in.

James sprang from the desk. Seb said her name. Before anything other than shock had time to settle over those assembled, she slapped the door closed with a pronounced thud and shifted Bea to her hip so she could face off with the lot of them. "What's the occasion?"

"Harmony," James began.

"No, no," she cut in. "Don't tell me this isn't a shindig. It's been a while since you boys got the squad together. So come on, pass the Johnnie Walker. Unless this is a *man* thing. In which case me and Bea will get back to the cooktop and let you go back to your Cubans." She ended by giving James a pointed look.

When he only pressed his lips together, she tilted her head, waiting. Bea's arms were tight around her neck. Despite the air-conditioned ride, the sweat was dampening the back of Harmony's shirt, and her irritation level felt like it was about to climb up on to the ceiling fan.

"I'm sorry," James said at last. He looked her in the eye when he said it.

At least that was something. "For what? Holding secret meetings or smoking on the job?"

"Someone's trying to hurt you, ace," he replied.

She looked to the fan for entreaty. "The naughty-stranger-outside-your-house card has been played out. Blame your son."

Bea's head lifted from Harmony's shoulder. She spotted Kyle, gave a relieved sob and sagged from Harmony's hold.

As Kyle raised her into his arms, Harmony made a point not to watch. What had happened outside her parents' inn the other night was still fresh. And the fact that he was here with all the other Benedict Arnolds…it was the worst pill of all to swallow.

"This isn't about what happened the night of the storm," James claimed. "It's a heck of lot more real this time."

She flung her hands out. "What are you talk-ing about?"

Seb spoke up. "You brought the Piper into the hangar a week ago claiming something was wrong."

"I think I remember," Harmony drawled.

"You were right," Seb explained. "There is something wrong and it ain't small." He picked up a series of photographs off the desk and passed them to James.

As James passed them to her, Harmony hesi-tated before flipping them face-up. It took her a minute of rotating to see what they were con-cerned about. "This is the engine."

"Snaps for Red," Hick gruffed from the corner.

She arched a brow at him before flipping to the

next photo. Same one, zoomed in. She brought it closer. "The oil line." Glancing up at Seb and James, she frowned. "Didn't we just do a replacement on these hoses?"

"Per procedure only," Seb said. "Your Piper's a slick piece of machinery. Any damage to hoses would've been unlikely. Replacing the lines was just precautionary."

"So what's with the tear?" she asked.

"Look closer."

This from Kyle. Harmony eyed him over the edge of the photograph. Then she examined the fissure again.

It wasn't ragged. It looked clean. Like…

Another image posted itself against her temporal lobe. A leveled-off tree stump.

Harmony's hand reached for her temples. *"Holy shit."*

Bea's gasp floated through the room. "Mama said a bad word," she whispered into Kyle's ear.

"Sorry, Bea. Sorry." Harmony's hand shook as she thrust the photo back at James, unable to look at it anymore without her stomach roiling. "It's cut, too." When no one answered, she demanded, "Isn't it? Someone tried to cut the Piper's oil line."

James nodded. "We suspect as much."

Seb flattened the zoomed photo against the surface of the desk. "You'll notice it's not a clean slice all the way through. I'm no detective, but I say whoever did this was in a hurry."

"Seb brought the photos here so we could all weigh in," James continued. "Opinion was unanimous."

Harmony found herself looking to Kyle again. He was rubbing Bea's back in gentle circles and roving slowly in the small space between the chairs and the wall as the girl nestled the side of her face against his unshaven cheek. His eyes were on Harmony, and despite the nurturing posture, she instantly gleaned the fighter in him ready to go to the wall.

If what James and Seb were saying was true, someone had wanted to do more than scare her.

Because she needed it, Harmony laid her hand on the base of Bea's spine. She got close enough to smell the sweet scent of her nighttime bubble bath and the medicated ointment on her hands. For a second, a wisp of memory floated across the field of consciousness, and she could smell the Johnson's baby lotion from the early days when it was just the two of them. The crisp aroma of fresh Huggies. She could feel the weight of a sleeping infant against her shoulder and the ongoing question in her mind as to how something so tiny could hold an entire kingdom's worth of treasure troves and possibilities.

A hand slid over hers, hard and reaffirming. Kyle lifted his chin in a minute nod when Harmony opened her eyes. Fragments of another flashback bled together, filling the pockets of her mind this time with chemical hospital cleaner, the rub of starched sheets. A thin maternity gown hung eschew, hardly noticed, over her shoulders. Pain webbed beneath a mild veil of painkillers. There was a newborn in her arms. They had just met. Harmony tried to take in her Gracie Bea's teensy rose lips, her plump cheeks. The softness and fragility of new life. Sleeping, sleeping, trusting. So trusting it awakened something prickly inside Harmony. Anxiety, the sick kind she'd felt once before, the moment she realized she was pregnant.

In the maternity ward freshly minted as a mama, she cradled Benji's baby and felt as though she would fly apart at the stitches. Yet she was paralyzed, unable to so much as move her white-pressed lips and cry out.

Overcome by the task ahead, she'd sought wildly for answers. Her glassy gaze rose to the tall figure at her bedside. Thick, muscled arms crossed over a gray soft-faded T-shirt, feet braced apart in classic Kyle stance, he watched her and the baby steadily with eyes like crystal under the bill of his ball cap. A silent sentry. She didn't speak a word of her anxiety, but he knew exactly what to say in a flat voice that conveyed nothing less than certitude. *Don't be afraid.* And he raised his chin when he saw her seeking the strength behind the instruction. *You've got this. All right,*

Carrots? Then he smiled, small and true, and her anxieties leaked away in a heady stream.

He didn't smile now, but Harmony beat the fear back by latching on to his fighting spirit. Through it, she was able to grasp her own. Her spine straightened and she nodded. "Okay," she said, pivoting to the others. "Okay, what do we do? I hope I'm included in the proceedings at least."

"Of course, you are," James granted. "The next step was bringing the photos to you."

"At the risk," Kyle muttered quietly, "of you and your fifty thousand volts going off seeking your own vigilante justice."

"Is there another kind?" She raised a finger at him. "And I don't remember asking the peanut gallery."

"Is that what I am, Carrots?" he asked pointedly. "The cheapest seats in vaudeville?"

"Yeah, you and Hick look swell up there," she said.

Mirth didn't break the tension packed close beneath his skin, but a longing light did. It reached for her before he diverted his stare elsewhere, turning so that Bea no longer faced the bright rays gleaming white through the vertical window blinds.

"I put a motion down that we take this evidence straight to the police," James said with a frown that passed from Harmony to Kyle then back. "We place it on Detective Johansson's desk, let him proceed from here."

Detective Johansson was the officer who had interviewed Harmony about the fallen tree. Since B.S. butted up against the Brackens' acreage, she had little doubt the events were related. But why? Why had she been targeted, not once but twice? And would this new evidence help the investigation? God only knew when the oil line had been tampered with. She'd been grounded for over a week before she'd flown the Piper and discovered the malfunction. With Seb's handling of the engine afterward, the likelihood of fingerprints would be slim, right?

Regardless, if there was any chance they could get this guy, James was right; they should turn the photos over to Johansson as well as her airplane.

Her inhale wasn't exactly steady, but she gave James a nod. "All right. Let's see what comes of it." To James, she said, "There can be no balance between us if you keep me in the dark. I'm still your partner, aren't I?"

"Of course you're my partner," James certified. "I was just trying—"

"To protect me," Harmony finished with a weary shake of her head. "I get it. But a partnership can't exist if you see me as the weak link. Don't you trust me?"

"Yes. Yes, of course, I trust you. What can I do to earn yours in return?"

"Stop treating me like the helpless female," she told him plainly. "Damn it, James. You're married to a powerhouse woman. You should know better."

"You're right," he acknowledged.

She sighed. "Men. It's just bred in, isn't it? I'm forever to be seen by your kind as someone's daughter. Or someone's *sister*." She tossed a pointed look Kyle's way. He chose to ignore it.

Hick stopped chewing and pushed off the window ledge. "Looks like we won't have to go to the police."

Harmony glanced around. Through the garage, she saw two uniformed officers advancing on the office. She backed up from the door when they knocked. James edged by her to open it. "Can I help you, gentlemen?" he asked, more than a little baffled.

"You James Bracken?" the first officer asked.

"Yes."

The second officer held up a slip of paper. "We have a warrant to search the premises."

"What?" Kyle barked.

James moved away from the door as both officers entered the already crowded room. "Search for what exactly?" he asked.

One of the officers rolled open the filing cabinet under the desk Mavis normally commandeered. The other opened the cupboard doors lining the room, shining a penlight on the contents. "We have reason to believe you're aiding and abetting the use of hazardous materials in your place of business."

"Hazardous materials," Harmony echoed as she gathered Bea to her. She felt Kyle at her back, coiled like a spring. "That's ridiculous."

"Excuse me, ma'am," the second officer replied, scooting around her. "Sir," he said when he came up against the brunt of Kyle.

It took a moment of joint eyeballing, but Kyle finally moved aside so the policeman could get to the cabinet behind him.

"What's going on?" Bea asked, wide-eyed as she watched the officers toss items on to the floor.

Kyle shook his head. "Nothing to worry about." When a series of heavy engine manuals hit the linoleum with a resounding *crack*, he turned sharply, stare battle-ready.

Harmony didn't think about it. She gathered a section of his shirt near the shoulder. With a tug, she brought his attention to her. "At ease, Chief," she whispered. When a muscle along his jaw ticked in answer, she licked her lips and added, "They're just doing their job."

"They'll be lucky if they keep 'em," he groaned.

The officers turned up nothing in the office. Soon they began to search the garage area. Workers stopped to watch them riffle through rolling toolboxes and workbenches. The first officer began searching the vehicles themselves.

James intervened. "They belong to our customers. They're private property. If you want to tear apart some cars, there's plenty of them registered to me outside."

Behind him, Hick whimpered at the idea of anybody rough-handling the sweet sports cars lining the lot.

"What about this one?" the second officer said, approaching a beat-up Trans Am in the work station farthest from the office. The hinges of the driver's door shrieked. He shone his penlight on to the worn seat, bending to get a good look beneath the steering column.

James hesitated. The first officer caught on to him. "Well, Mr. Bracken? Who does the vehicle belong to?"

James used two fingers to scrape his knuckles against his mouth in a rare habit Harmony had seen Kyle, too, submit to in times of turmoil. "I don't know, exactly."

"Not helping yourself," Kyle muttered, pacing from one wall to the other. Head ducked, he rubbed the base of his neck. The skin there was red as Christmas.

"Are you saying this car is stolen?" the officer asked as he palmed his radio.

"No," James said. His stance, the muscles in his face…everything about him looked rigid.

"It wouldn't be too much of a stretch, would it?" the officer ribbed. "Not with priors like yours, Memphis Raines." He held James's stare as he lifted the radio to his mouth. Static crackled. "This is Officer Holmes requesting a plate." After the go-ahead from the operator, he walked around the back of the car to get a look. "Tag number MERCY. M-E-R-C-Y." He fumbled with the trunk latch. It didn't give. Jerking his head at the lock, he asked James, "You got the keys?"

Stiff-legged, James silently retreated to the office. In his absence, Kyle stopped roving to watch the first officer remove the passenger seat completely, tipping it on to the concrete floor. He advanced. "I think we're well within our rights to know more about this warrant and what kind of information led you here."

"Who're you?" Holmes wanted to know, keeping one eye on James's progress.

Harmony spoke up. "Chief Petty Officer Kyle Bracken."

"Who can answer for himself," Kyle told her from the corner of his mouth.

"He's the son," the first officer shouted from deep in the backseat. "Special ops."

"Ranger?" Holmes asked, sizing Kyle up.

The answer came again from the back seat. "SEAL. Purple Heart. Navy Cross. Boy Scout."

"Now what's a Boy Scout doing in the Navy SEALs?" Holmes questioned. His hand went to his belt. "Bar fights. That's what SEALs are well-known for. I knew a guy, in California. Went out for drinks with some buddies, got busted up by a whole fleet of you frogmen. Broken nose. Fractured collarbone. Torn ACL..."

Kyle's body had tuned like piano wire as soon as Holmes touched his belt near the service weapon on his hip. But his countenance was placid. Harmony tried to breathe easier. If he got into it with Holmes, she would have his back. Bea didn't need to see her mama arrested for mouthing off to a police officer, though.

Kyle spoke, sending her hopes into a death spiral. "Guess he deserved it."

Holmes's neck snapped forward. "You got something against cops, boy?"

Jerking a shoulder, Kyle said in a tone that was deceptively calm, "Only when they've got something against frogmen."

Recognition struck Holmes. "Aren't you the guy who got his 'nads blown off several years back?"

"Hey!" Harmony spoke up.

Without even raising his voice, Kyle interrupted smoothly. "You best get back to the jailhouse, Officer Fife. Won't Otis be there any minute to let himself in?"

Holmes's smile curdled. "You got jokes, navy man?"

"Nothing jokin' about it," Kyle claimed. "Especially if you and Juanita want to meet up later with Thelma Lou. I hear her cashew fudge is the bee's knees."

Oh, hell. I'm going to jail, Harmony thought, closing her eyes briefly. Setting Bea on her feet, she whispered, "Go see Pappy for a second, baby."

"Mama," Bea whined, "I want Kyle."

"You both need to get out of here," Kyle muttered sideways.

"Not until they go," Harmony argued.

"You don't need to be here," he retorted, lake-blue eyes peppered with fire. "*Either* of you."

Harmony fought the urge to swear. "Did I not just go over this? I swear! I am always the best friend's baby sister."

"No. Right now you're the little one's mama, and I'm asking you to get her out of here," Kyle hissed.

The stare-down between Harmony and Kyle didn't cease until James approached with a jangle of keys. "Found them."

Holmes moved away from the trunk, inviting James to do the honors. Frowning at Kyle over his father's shoulder, he waited until the lock turned and the trunk lifted. "Step back, please," he said, taking hold of James's arm. Slowly, he poked his head into the dark compartment. There was a rustle as he lifted what looked to be a folded tarp then stood to his full height. "Wilson, get back here!"

"Got something?" Wilson asked, appearing from the passenger cab of the Trans Am.

Holmes had already drawn his weapon. "Radio in and tell them to bring backup." He pivoted on James. "Hands above your head!"

The color drained rapidly from James's face as he gazed, slack-jawed, at whatever Holmes had uncovered.

"Hands!" Holmes said again, lifting the weapon.

Kyle moved in. Wilson crossed to him. "You best back up, son. I don't want to have to arrest a war hero."

"Search him, too," Holmes suggested as he nudged James forward. "Face the wall. Keep your hands up."

As Wilson made a grab for Kyle's arm, Harmony said, "Stop." Pappy came forward to take Bea. "This isn't right. None of this is…" Her voice dropped as both she and Kyle got a look into the trunk of the Trans Am.

An eight-quart pressure cooker lay amid various other items spread out neatly in rows—ball bearings, nails, wires, a kitchen timer… Most damning of all, perhaps, was the lineup of shiny silver, finger-length, torpedo-shaped tubes.

Propane, Harmony realized with a shake of her head. Even as the puzzle pieces fell together, they didn't make sense…

"Dad." Kyle was no more able to look away from the trunk than Harmony. Wilson nudged him toward the wall. His legs locked.

Harmony's attention swung back to James

who had been searched and was now being handcuffed. She tasted bile at the back of her throat. "You can't arrest him."

"Back up, miss," Wilson told her, again attempting to maneuver Kyle toward the wall so he could search him. He palmed the small of his back and tensed. "You got a permit for this concealed weapon?"

"Of course, he has a permit!" Harmony snapped. "He's an active-duty naval officer."

"Harm." Kyle's wallet was already in hand. He took out his ID and gave it to Wilson.

"Thank you," Wilson said. He took a glance and handed it back. "I'm sorry, but we have to take your father into our custody."

As Holmes steered James toward the exit, Hick came out of the shadows. "You'll be takin' me with him."

"Hick," James said. "This doesn't concern you."

"It does," Hick told them. "You want the person who's worked on the Trans Am most? You're lookin' at him."

"On my orders," James reminded him.

"I've got priors, too, if you want to look 'em up," Hick pointed out, offering his tattooed wrists to Wilson. "Stop gawping, neighbor, and use the cuffs like they taught you."

Wilson looked to Holmes for his take on the situation. Holmes waved a hand for him to proceed before prodding James into motion.

Pappy sighed. Passing Bea off to Kyle, he apologized to both him and Harmony. "Take me, too."

"Jesus Christ," James blurted.

Holmes and Wilson stopped once more. The former was starting to look exasperated.

Pappy shed his driving jacket and raised his arms, lifting his brows at Wilson when the officer hesitated to search him as he had Hick. "Go ahead. I don't have any priors..."

"Speaking of Boy Scouts..." James inserted.

"...but if you check the security tapes, as I'm sure you're apt," Pappy explained, "you'll find that both James and I stayed after hours to work on the Trans Am several nights this week. There were no explosives. I can vouch for that."

"We'll see," Holmes said, skeptical.

"A plant," Kyle whispered to himself.

James shook his head at Pappy. "What's Alva going to say about this?"

"'Bout the same as Adrian, I imagine." Pappy frowned. He let Wilson walk him out with the others.

"Wait," Kyle insisted.

Holmes doubled back with a groan. "We've got no room left in the squad car for more volunteers."

Kyle ignored him, snagging James's eye. "I'll call the lawyer."

James gave him a half smile, reassuring. "Call your mother. And Alva," he said with a nod to Pappy. "We'll worry about the lawyers later." He looked to Harmony and his expression tempered. "It'll all work out."

Harmony nodded, though doubt riddled her. As the three men were marched out into the sunshine, her heart rapped loudly. The IED parts were spread out in her peripheral. Unmistakable. Damning. "What is going on?"

"Hell if I know." Kyle sounded dangerous. Now that Holmes and Wilson were out of sight, he let the outward cool wash away. In profile, he looked lethal, skin drawn against his cheekbones.

"What's going to happen to them?" Bea asked woefully.

"Nothing, baby," Harmony reassured her. Finally, she took the child back into her arms. Over her head, she asked Kyle, "Meet you at the police station?"

"You need to take her home."

"I'm going to the police station," she said firmly. "You can't pretend anymore that this doesn't involve me. Besides, I can call Mom and Dad. James is going to need backup. Dad might have some pull. Mom can come take Bea."

"I want to stay with you," Bea said, clinging to Harmony's neck as if she, too, would be taken away. "And—"

"Kyle." Harmony nodded. "I got that." She shrugged at Kyle. "I think she likes you."

He lowered his cheek to Bea's curls and cupped the nape of her neck where a smudgy pink birthmark was concealed. He eyed the bomb parts Harmony could no longer look at and closed his eyes. For a second, a stitch furrowed between them. He straightened and it was gone. "For the last time, Carrots. Get her out of here."

Harmony nodded agreement. "Somebody wants to hurt us. Me. Your father. This isn't a series of random events. Everything's starting to look more like—"

"Sabotage. Yeah." Kyle scowled. "I need to talk to Johansson."

"*We'll* talk to Johansson," she corrected. "*Don't* leave me out."

He touched her, a light brush just above her hip where her shirt was riding up. He touched skin and it answered. "Take shotgun. I'll drive. You can call Cole. Have him meet us there."

As he ushered her and Bea out of the garage amongst the hushed murmur of employees, the afternoon sun was low. The heat baked the asphalt still. If it were much hotter, they would sink right through it, like industrial quicksand. Harmony strapped Bea into her booster before getting into the passenger seat. Kyle cranked the Cherokee. When the vents made a disagreeing noise, he aimed his scowl at them.

She lifted the heel of her hand and pounded the console. The whining ceased and she settled back, feeling a mite better for the catharsis.

He gave her an arched look. Saying nothing, he put the car in gear and backed out of the parking space. As soon as they were on the road, Harmony dialed her father's number. The conversation was brief but loaded. "He's coming," she informed Kyle after hanging up. Then, because it was near time for the doctor's office to close, she called Bea's pediatrician and scheduled an appointment for early the next morning. If James was still in police custody then, she would have to solo their meetings with Solange at midday. She'd have paperwork. James was a high-profile citizen. There would be phone calls, potential statements... They didn't have a PR rep. How was she going to handle that angle on her own?

Harmony tapped the phone to her lips. "Do you want me to call your mother?"

Kyle kept his hard gaze on the road. "She should hear it from me."

"Mama, it itches," Bea said from the backseat.

Harmony stretched her arm back to reach the toe of Bea's boot. "Almost there. Mammy's meeting us. She's going to take you to the inn for an oatmeal bath."

"Can we spend the night again?"

"Yes," Kyle answered.

Harmony rolled her eyes. "If James spends the night in the slammer, your mother won't go home, will she?"

"Not likely."

"So you're going to sleep at The Farm by yourself?"

He lifted a shoulder in response.

She propped her elbow on the windowsill and laid her chin on her fist.

"It's best, all around," he said, making the turn for the station.

Harmony blinked at that. The farmhouse. Just the two of them and Bea. She'd be a moron if she said the idea wasn't appealing.

Ah, who was she kidding? Her blood did more than stir at the prospect of having that gorgeous country house and Kyle nearly entirely to herself for a night. Her libido went into high-octane action. She choked it back, swallowing the potentials. She might as well have swallowed a mouthful of Pennzoil.

Kyle put the car in park, unbuckled quickly and reached for the door handle. Harmony grabbed him by the arm to stop him. "Wait. Just…wait a second," she said when he pivoted halfway back to her.

He released the door.

"Should we tell Johansson or the others?" she wondered. "About the Piper? Think about it. Holmes and Wilson assume James is capable of homegrown terrorism. If we tell them about the Piper, they might think he's behind everything else, too."

"They'd have trouble substantiating it." In a move identical to James's, he scraped the flats of two knuckles across his mouth. "Where's the goddamn motive? The man's clean. He's a good citizen. Sure, he's got a past, but that was brought to light years ago. He moved mountains to get B.S. off the ground. Why would he set out to make it flop when he's never let anything he's involved in fail before?"

"If they know the problems the business has had," Harmony suggested, "in light of everything, wouldn't they come to the same conclusion we have—that none of it is random? There are plenty of people who don't just abandon ship—they set it on fire to save their own asses."

"Not him!"

"Kyle, they think he's building *bombs*," she said, lowering her voice so that the last wouldn't carry back to Bea over the music. "They don't believe in him like we do. There are people in this town who *still* look at him and see what he was when he left your mom."

Kyle grimaced. It was faint, but she knew the tendencies of his face. She knew its tenor and minutiae as well as every contour. He exhaled slowly and mussed the hair growing over his brow. "It might be too late. Hick and Pappy are probably sitting in interrogation by now. Holmes and Wilson had backup called to the garage. They'll search the place again, conduct interviews among the staff and crew. Even if Seb doesn't say anything, they'll find the photos in the office and likely figure it out for themselves."

Harmony mashed her fingers against her temple.

It was several seconds later, but she felt his hand on the one she had lain on the center console. He gathered the back of it against his palm and squeezed. She wondered if it was to alleviate her pain or his and fought the urge to lean her head into his shoulder. Better yet, she pulled his down to rest on hers. "There's Mom and Dad," she said, spotting her father's truck.

Kyle switched off the ignition and gave her the keys. He got to Bea's door first and unbuckled her from the booster seat. Harmony locked the Cherokee and helped Bea shrug the straps of her *Brave* backpack over her shoulders. She gripped her hand tight to keep her from racing across the trafficked parking lot to her grandparents. Her phone was in her other hand. "Here," she said, slapping it against Kyle's front. "Call your mother. We'll meet you inside."

CHAPTER ELEVEN

"THE CAR'S YOURS," Kyle informed his father over the staid interrogation table in the whited-out room with two-way glass behind him. "They pulled its records based on VIN. It was registered to J. Bracken twenty-eight years ago, and it's been in your name ever since."

"I figured as much," James admitted roughly. He looked as if he hadn't slept in twenty-four hours. Kyle didn't blame him. The Fairhope jail wasn't the worst Baldwin County had to offer, but it wasn't cozy. James's beard looked ragged, and his hair had been finger-combed from his brow, but the flickering florescent fixture underscored the bags under his eyes. James drew his shoulders back, stretching them against the width of the chair. "How's your mother?"

He was changing topic. Bracing his elbows on the table, Kyle leaned over it and clasped his hands. "You already know the answer to that."

"Indulge me," James said with a ghost of a smile.

Kyle saw a snatch of yearning behind it as well as concern and chose to put his father out of his misery. "Let's just say I know who I get my fighting edge from."

The smile grew in James's eyes. "She's been a fighter since the day she was born."

"Yeah, well, we're lucky the sergeant on duty last night was a family friend," Kyle informed him. "Otherwise, she'd be warming the brig, same as you."

The humor vanished in a blink. "She's not sleeping at The Farm, is she?"

"Are you kidding?" Kyle asked. "I caught her sleeping behind the wheel in the parking lot. I had to call Olivia and Briar to haul her off to the inn for the night."

"I bet that went over well."

"She's barely spoken to me all morning. She said something about Judas over breakfast."

"How early was she here?" James asked, frown working at the corners of his mouth now.

"Four. I doubt she really slept."

"And you?"

Kyle had never gone to the inn or The Farm for the night, but James didn't need to know that. "I need to know about Mercy."

"She was a friend."

"Specifics."

James shrugged. "There's not much. Every bit's history."

"Then why the mystery?"

"Because a lot of it's still a mystery to me,"

James told him. "And…partly because Mercy—or, Mercedes Gardet—is buried in Pine Leaf Cemetery in Daytona Beach, Florida."

"How do you know that?" Kyle didn't like the suspicion hulling out a home inside him.

"Her lawyer visited me," James explained, "nearly ten years ago. Multiple sclerosis."

Kyle watched his father closely for context clues. "Hard way to go."

"There's no easy way," James granted. "But MS… Nobody deserves that kind of hell, any more than cancer."

Kyle thought of his paternal grandmother, Dr. Mavis Irvington, who'd lost her life to cancer shortly before his sister, her namesake, was born. "What was she to you?" he wondered out loud and hoped the answer wouldn't be too difficult to hear. "Other than a friend."

James read him thoroughly. "If you're thinking your mother isn't the only person I've loved… Well, then, you're right."

Kyle fought the urge to look away.

"But if you're asking me if Adrian isn't the only woman I've been consumed by," James said slowly, "then you're dead wrong." He gave Kyle something of a smile again. "Like you, there's one woman in this entire world who sets me on fire." Reaching for the Styrofoam cup on the table, James lifted it methodically. "Providentially, she's the only one who's capable of taming it."

James was talking about Laurel. However, words like *set on fire* didn't bring a lush form or fair features to Kyle's mind. All he could see were sharp angles. And legs. Legs that went on for days. Honeycomb eyes that challenged and cleaved, just like her elbows.

Kyle could've chalked it up to Harmony's hair. Its red was every bit the essence of fire. Deep down, he knew better. The rub? Tame was to Harmony as an acid was to a base. She was no more likely to tame the fireballs in him than she was to tame the inferno inside herself. Whatever had flared between the two of them since his return made his relationship with Laurel look peaceful by comparison. Safe. A touch modest.

More than a touch.

Kyle tried to get back to the point. "You met Mercy in Florida," he guessed.

"Yes."

"Was this before or after you got clean?"

"Before," James admitted. "She was a trauma nurse. Whenever I was on a bender, I was a regular in her ER. We became friendly, like I said. She cautioned me about the path I was on and tried to wisen me up as others had. I shrugged it off until my big wake-up call."

Again, a fire, Kyle thought. But not the metaphorical kind this time. He spared a glance for the burn marks on James's tattoo-free arm.

"She helped me get the help I needed," James

explained. "She let me crash on her couch for a time, until I was back on my feet. She took care of me. So when it was time for me to move on, I left her the car."

The chair creaked as Kyle shifted against the backrest. "You say she died ten years ago?"

"Thereabouts."

"Why is the Trans Am just now showing up?" Kyle questioned. "Shouldn't it have been delivered to you sooner?"

"By law, yes." James laced his fingers together on the tabletop, mirroring Kyle's pose. "The lawyer mentioned, however, that the location of the vehicle was unknown at the time. There was a PI on the case and there were leads. I guess nothing ever came of them, until now."

"Pappy and Hick said that the car showed up out of the blue," Kyle remembered. "Overnight."

"Mavis found it," James confirmed.

"Are you sure you didn't?" Kyle asked. "Because the reason they've got you at no-bail is because security cams put you in the parking lot with the Trans Am around three a.m. the night before."

James's brow knotted doubly. "That's not possible. I didn't come to the garage until later that afternoon."

"I've seen the feed." It was hard to say. "The cameras never get a clear view of your face or profile. But it's definitely your hat, your jacket. Your height and build—"

"It's June. Why would I have worn a jacket?"

And gloves. Kyle had thought along the same lines when Cole had helped him wheedle Officer Wilson into letting him see the tapes. "Dad. Did you or did you not push the car into the garage?"

"I did not," James stated clearly.

Kyle nodded. "All right." He tapped his knuckles against the table, then flattened them over the top as he considered their options. "All right, here's the deal. There's no evidence you, Hick or Pappy had knowledge of what was placed inside the trunk while it was in house, but Holmes, and—I'm pretty sure—Wilson, thinks you're guilty as hell. Holmes is holding a pack of ATF agents at bay so he can close the case himself. Not your biggest fan."

"There's a surprise," James drawled.

"The same cameras show that Hick and Pappy were telling the truth. The three of you did come in after-hours to work on the car. There's nothing on the tapes to suggest that anyone else came in or out of the garage once you were gone, and it's highly unlikely anyone was able to stash the items in the car during work hours."

"Agreed."

"Wilson and Holmes want to link their files with Johansson's. If they're successful, by the end of the week, there's a good chance you'll be slapped with attempted murder charges."

Even as clarity struck James, his eyes seemed to shrink into his face. "The Piper," he muttered.

Kyle's stomach clutched at James's disrupted mien. Gone was the infamous Bracken poker face. Taking a deep breath through the nose, Kyle went on. "Things don't look good for you. I'll keep reviewing the tapes. I'll go over them a dozen times if I have to because *this isn't you*. There's something big at work here and it goes beyond us. It goes beyond The Farm and B.S. and Bracken Mechanics."

"It's personal," James concluded.

"It's personal," Kyle echoed. "The police aren't looking for other suspects aside from Hick and Pappy. That leaves me and Cole to do the rest."

"And your mother," James pointed out. "And Mavis. They won't be left out of this. You can't forget about Harmony."

Truer words had never been spoken, Kyle ruminated. "She won't let me forget her."

"She's the fire." James shook his head when it was Kyle's turn to look guilty in his own right. "I thought there was a moment, back at the garage... You—"

"It's nothing."

James released a quiet chuckle. "Ah, Kyle. In a way...it's always been Harmony, hasn't it? It might not always have been romantic. But the connection. It's always been there."

Kyle said nothing.

"This is her fight, too," James noted, "and that's hard to argue, considering what whoever's behind it nearly took from her."

"Nobody's going to take anything else from us," Kyle promised, gripping the table's edge. "The lawyer's name. I can start there."

"I'll get Adrian look it up," James said. "There was some paperwork. She'll know where to find it."

"You can't remember the guy's name?"

"Something Irish?" James shrugged. "Did I mention it's been ten years?"

"Yes, but this is important." Cursing, Kyle let the frown weave across his brow.

"You're sure the guy on the security footage was wearing a jacket?"

"Positive."

James opened his mouth, closed it, then opened it again. "This isn't the first time I've had a crime I didn't commit pinned on me."

When his father hesitated again, Kyle leaned in. "Tell me."

"You remember that nasty scar your grandfather had?" James asked, tapping his brow with his knuckles.

"Yeah," Kyle said. The mark was the main reason Van Carlton had worn a baseball cap whenever he'd ventured out in public. "What about it?"

"The summer I left town," James explained slowly, "the court ordered me to do community service at The Farm so that I could pay my debt to the Carltons and avoid jail. It was while I was doing my community service that your mother and me…"

When James fanned his fingers in indication, Kyle nodded away the rest. "Yeah, let's skip the part where you two… You know."

"Okay," James said quickly. He braced his arms on the table. "I began to respect the Carltons. Particularly Van. Edith had made up her mind about me. But Van… He gave me a seat at the table for dinner. He…put trust in me, and faith. He made me think I was more than what society thought I'd become. He made me believe, that maybe I could still be a man like him."

Kyle missed his grandfather all the more when he saw the genuine perplexity and admiration on James's face. Once, Kyle knew, his father had been a lost boy wrestling with the grief and guilt over his own father's death. Even after seventeen-year-old James had wrecked the offices of Carlton Nurseries, Van Carlton had stepped up in a way Kyle knew James had never forgotten. However, Kyle remembered Van's pronounced scar and prompted, "But…?"

James cleared his throat. "But… I'd made a

few misbegotten friends prior to that year. One of them was Dusty Harbuck."

"I've heard that name before."

"Dusty didn't like the Carltons," James recalled. "In fact, for some reason I still can't understand, he hated them. One night toward the end of my community service, he got drunk, walked on to The Farm. I don't know what his plan was, but Van caught him and Dusty hit him hard enough with a blunt object to knock him clean out 'til the next morning."

"And you were framed?" Kyle asked.

"All Van could recall when he woke up in the hospital is that the guy was tall, broad and had been wearing a letterman jacket from the local high school."

"Let me guess. You had a letterman jacket and no alibi."

"Edith threw my name out there," James recalled. "The police decided, with my access to The Farm and the Carltons, that I was the most likely culprit. I was hauled off of my father's boat and taken into custody."

"Dusty let you take the heat?"

"It was long after you were born that Dusty turned himself in for the assault and only because I threatened to turn him in myself once I found out it was him who did it. The Harbucks are hardly known for their integrity."

"So did you go to jail after all?" Kyle asked.

James licked his lips. "Well, as it turns out, I did have an alibi that night. But I wasn't going to cop to it any more than Dusty was going to ride up and admit his wrongdoing."

"Why not?"

James looked pointedly to Kyle as he lifted his Styrofoam cup. "Count nine months from the beginning of August and you'll have a decent answer."

Kyle's chin lifted slowly in understanding.

James shrugged. "Adrian found out they'd taken me in. She went straight over her mother's head to the lead detective and admitted everything. I was released. I left town before she realized…"

"That she was pregnant." Kyle looked to the floor. It was clean but smudgy, like the cleaning person hadn't cared much for what he was doing. "Why the quick departure?"

"I'd done enough to the Carltons already," James answered. There was a patch in his voice that lent itself to more weariness. "I smashed up their place of business. I was an unwelcome presence for Edith through summer as a result. And I knew once Edith and Van knew that Adrian and I were together—that I snuck into her bedroom in the farmhouse to be with her…lay with her… I not only tore apart Van's trust. I drove a wedge between your mother and Edith that they'd never be able to reach across again. I loved your mother, more than I thought I'd ever be able to love another human being, but I left. I left so the Carltons could get on with their lives. Until I came back to town eight years later, I had no idea that that night we made you."

Kyle swallowed because more had come of his father's tale than he'd expected, and the emotions weren't easy-hitting. "I doubt Harbuck's still doing time for the assault on Van."

"He's been in and out of the system," James admitted, the reminiscent gleam vanishing. "Always paroles."

"Where is he now?"

"Last I heard, he was locked up in Escambia County. But that was eighteen months ago."

"If he's paroled again, he'll be bound to the jurisdiction of Escambia. Does he still have family here?"

"Brothers who own a pretty lucrative trucking business. It's where he'd always go for funds when he was low."

Kyle moved up from the chair decisively. "Somebody like him wouldn't hesitate to cross the state line. Let me make a call. I'll get Cole rolling on it. This is good. This could be exactly what we need—"

"Son."

Kyle stopped just short of rapping his fist on the door so the uniforms could let him out.

James's features grew taut and his mouth wavered over a smile. "Thank you."

"For what, Dad?" Kyle asked.

"For believing," James said. The smile grew.

"I've got you," Kyle assured him. "We're going to get you out of here."

"I know. Tell your mother..."

Kyle waved the rest away. "Yeah, yeah. She's paper. You're glue. You want to rub up against her until you stick. I'll tell her."

The low rumble of his father's laughter followed Kyle out of the interrogation room and went miles toward easing some of the ache around Kyle's heart.

USING THE CHILD safety mirror on the Grand Cherokee's passenger sunshade, Harmony did a visual check on Bea. It had to be her tenth check since they left the doctor's office, but she couldn't help it. Not after what the doctor had told her.

It had been a sleepless night at the inn for both of them. Bea's itching hadn't subsided, and the rash had spread rapidly from her hands to her belly and back. Harmony had thought seriously about putting her in the car and taking her to the emergency room. When Bea had dozed off on top of the covers in Harmony's childhood bed, Harmony had lain awake, counting her breaths. Timing each. The pauses between. Measuring them against one another and ready to spring into action at the first sign of difficulty.

Daylight came. And it was the nurse at the doctor's office who confirmed what Harmony already suspected. That this was more than eczema—the culprit was more likely an irritant or allergen of some kind.

They had combed through the previous day, going over it in detail. Bea had eaten nothing out of the ordinary. She hadn't come into contact with any plants. She wasn't allergic to animals.

It wasn't until the doctor sat her down in his office and gave her a juice box that Bea told the story of the caterpillars.

A frisson of unease skittered down Harmony's spine as she drove back to her parents'—she couldn't get there fast enough. According to Bea, if she went back to the mother-in-law suite and looked under her bed, there would be a mason jar. *It has a rusty lid,* Bea had told the doctor while Harmony listened, *and three caterpillars. I named them GiGi, Fur Baby and Stripes.*

What do these caterpillars look like? the doctor had asked in a conversational manner, encouraging Bea to tell more.

White and fluffy with black dots.

The doctor nodded sagely, then exchanged a telling glance with Harmony. *And where did you get these caterpillars?*

Bea piped up with a sunny smile, feeling relaxed after a topical cortisone treatment. She pumped the straw in and out of the juice box and revealed, *From the Caterpillar Man! He lives in the woods, outside our house on The Farm.* Looking askance to Harmony, she mumbled. *I'm sorry, Mama. He told me not to tell. "It's a secret. Keep our secret. Shh!"* she added, pressing a finger to her lips.

Something blurred Harmony's vision. It was swampy. It stung. She blinked until it cleared. Anger blazed. And fear.

She had no doubt Bea's Caterpillar Man was the same man who had chopped down the tree, cut the Piper's oil line and most likely put James behind bars. Bea had claimed that she'd seen him off and on for two or three weeks before the tropical storm *and* Kyle had blown ashore. Harmony even remembered Bea saying something that first night he'd come for dinner. *The Caterpillar Man said the rain's coming, too,* she'd chirped as she chased a comb through Kyle's thick hair. *He said it would rain and rain and rain. I think he likes the rain. It made him laugh real big.*

Harmony gripped the steering wheel harder after making the turn on to Scenic 98. She ignored the view of the pier and the bay and tried to tamp down on the heavy ram beat of her heart. She'd taught her daughter not to be afraid, hadn't she?

Now she was the one who was afraid. Very, very afraid.

She pulled into the inn parking lot, spitting gravel beneath her tires. Bea was zonked in the booster seat, so she sat, clutching the wheel and breathing carefully to get herself under control.

Goddamn son of a bitch.

Hell. What did she know about control? She got out of the car and went around to Bea's side of the Jeep. The roar of a motorcycle drew her attention to the street before she could open the door.

Kyle's hog steered into the lot. It rolled smoothly over the uneven drive and came to a stop in the spot next to her. He dropped the kickstand with the steel toe of his boot and switched off the ignition, reaching for the strap of his helmet. His thick hair stood up as he removed it. His features were cloaked in perspiration, and he regarded her, trouble brewing. "We need to talk."

She nodded. "Yeah, we do."

He paused in the midst of removing his gloves. Quickly, he stood up and swung a leg off the seat, planting his feet in front of her. "Something wrong?"

Again, she nodded.

He held the gloves on one side, the helmet to the other. His body locked in place, laser focus engaged. "Jesus," he whispered and took her arm. "Come inside."

She motioned to the Grand Cherokee. "Bea. I have to get Bea."

"Okay," he said. He set the helmet down on the seat of the motorcycle as she opened the door. He opened it wider. She unbuckled Bea and boosted her into her arms. When he offered to take her weight, Harmony tensed. "No." She shook her head rapidly.

He backed off, acquiescing.

It was a long trudge up to the family rooms. Harmony's arms and calves were burning. It took everything she had not to stay and watch Bea sleep after pulling the sheet up to her chin and closing the curtains to mask the gold-tinged light of the fast-rising sun. Knowing Kyle waited in the next room, she swallowed the sensation working at her throat, threatening to choke her, and lowered her lips to Bea's cheek. She cupped her face for a few seconds and ran her fingers through her curls before backing away to let her rest.

The rooms where she had been raised were quiet. Her father was still at the police station, and her mother was hard at work downstairs with her staff. Party preparations were underway for the anticipated opening of the new wing. Harmony couldn't think about any of it. She couldn't think about anything but the Caterpillar Man who lived the woods.

The hand that came to rest between her shoulder blades made her twitch. She realized she'd been staring at the closed door to the room where Bea slept. Pivoting toward Kyle, she thought better about letting him look too closely and bypassed him. Because her knees buckled, she lowered to the floral-patterned couch. As Kyle stood close by, she willed herself to speak. "I—I think Olivia was right about that tavern delivery service she suggested." *God* could she use a drink, no matter if it made her soft.

"What's going on?" he asked, unable to wait for her to come around to it.

"When you came over that first night and read Bea to sleep…after *Where the Wild Things Are*, what did she ask you to read next? Do you remember?"

Kyle frowned and thought about it. "Eric Carle," he said finally.

"The Very Hungry Caterpillar?" Harmony offered. When he nodded, she sighed. Sweeping a mote of dust off her mother's pristine coffee table, she couldn't bring herself to look at him. "I wondered… She's not a fan of insects, things that crawl. She pulled it off the shelf one night before you came back. That's when the caterpillar stories started. I thought it was her imagination. The books do that. They fuel it—and more power to 'em. But the story kept evolving. The details… I shouldn't have tuned it out as chatter. I should've realized it was more than one of the tales she likes to tell herself."

"What's this about?" he asked, urgent. The sight of her rambling affected him. No wonder. She was straight to the point, always.

"What's this about?" she echoed, growing in ferocity. Her anger turned inward. "It's about me being a horrible mom! Kyle, she told me. She sat at the dinner table night after night and told me. Told *us*, and I just *ignored it*!"

"Ignored what?"

"The caterpillars," she said, down to a hoarse whisper. "Or, as the doctor told me, the Hickory Tussock Moth Caterpillars. They're poisonous. And they've been living in a jar under Bea's bed for *weeks*."

"How did she get ahold of them?"

"They live in trees," she said absently. "Bushes. But she didn't get them from any of those. No. They were given to her—by a stranger—in the woods."

His gaze cleared, homing in. He took a step toward her.

"The person who's doing all this?" she went on, quickly. "The one who caved in my kitchen… who tried to wreck the Piper…who's probably behind all this with your dad—he's out there. Really out there! And he *touched my baby*!" The last bit welled from the base of her throat, thick. It burned coming out, fighting its way through her teeth. A torrent of high-flaming wrath assaulted her. A sob she'd been holding back like her life depended on it tried to punch its way free. Coming to her feet, she took a step to pace. "I'm going to kill him. I swear to God, I'm going to tear his throat out."

"Whoa." Fists closed around her upper arms, trying to lock her in place.

She wasn't having it. There was more behind the anger. Something panicked, writhing and foreign. When it came to the surface, it was going to be ugly and pathetic, and she wouldn't abide it.

"Harm," he said, giving her a small shake. "You're staying here."

Don't look! Don't look at me like this! "Kyle. Move!"

"Whatever you've got," he said, still holding on, "hit me with it."

The familiar words broke through the blinding haze of desperation.

"Hit me," he said again. His eyes pinged from one of hers to the next and back in quickening assessment. "I can take it."

She began to shake her head, even as he eased her toward him. Again, she shook it but found his chest coming up to meet her, his arms pulling her in. Her eyes closed and her body shook, too. "No," she said, fighting what was trying to jab its way free.

Oh, he knew what he was doing. They'd been down this road before, in the visitation room of the funeral home where she'd seen Benji for the last time. She'd tried to escape. She'd tried not to let Kyle see it bubble to the surface like some abominable black smear unlocked from the deep. He'd deflected a well-aimed fist, roped her in, soothing her into letting him see it, letting himself get oil-slicked in the upsurge.

It had hurt. It hurt now. Breaking did that, she supposed. It just hurt.

It took several minutes but the first hard shudder ran aground, the second close behind it. She gripped Kyle by the shoulders, lowering her brow into his shirt. "Oh," she cried as she gave into the sickly fear, the anger that had built and built until she couldn't handle it anymore. "Oh, God," she said, racked by the emotional torrent.

It went on, as it had before. There were few tears, just endless dry sobs. He didn't waver. Like a rock, he absorbed everything, quiet and motionless as she clutched and pitched. When she did subside, his hold gentled from bracing. One arm lowered, warm, around her waist as she hid her face in the hard curve of his bicep, right up against the visible trident on his skin.

Tired, she closed her eyes. It took her several minutes to realize he was rocking her slightly, silent and soothing. She let him cradle her as he'd cradled Bea, one hand on the back of her head, his palm sliding up and down her French braid. She let herself sink into his arms because her legs were jelly, and it felt good. He felt good and sure.

When her breath stopped hitching in the aftermath, she didn't move. She heard his heart thumping through his shirt. She felt the flood of his natural heat. She kept her eyes shut, holding on. "We're going to find him," she whispered.

"Right? We're going to find him. Make him bleed for this."

"Yes. We." It was a whisper, too. An unflinching one.

She pulled back so she could see the unyielding lines of his face. "Kiss me." When the lines eased and his eyes widened, she went up on her toes to make it easier for him. "You said *we* and I need to kiss you for it."

"Carrots." Again, though, he didn't let go. He didn't back off. And, after a moment's contemplation, his gaze flicked to her upturned mouth.

Harmony grabbed on again as his lips lowered. When they met hers, it was a whisper. She folded her arms around his neck, bringing him closer. The rush of weightlessness punched through the wall of gravity. *Lift.*

His mouth parted and hers responded. They merged and meshed, going no further and yet in sync. She hadn't had to dig her heels in this time. He hadn't balked at the chance. He simply kissed her. Underneath her hands, she felt him give and it was glorious, just like the heady palpitating rush of flight.

She stepped into him, though there was no room, scrubbing her fingers through his hair. She stepped in until her thigh was wedged between his denim-clad legs. Until his solid form absorbed her, the hand on her braid latched, digging in for purchase, and the arm around her waist tightened to keep her there. His fingers veered down over her hip, spread and caressed.

The door to the family rooms opened without announcement. Kyle and Harmony sprang apart so fast that Harmony bumped into the coffee table behind her and nearly upended it. Kyle's quick hand around her wrist saved her. It did not save either of them, however, from the look of utter shock on Mavis's face.

"Ew," the latter said in automatic aversion.

Kyle relinquished his hold. "Mav."

Mavis shook her head and backtracked. "Ew," she said, pointing accusingly at them. She grabbed the door and yanked it open. "Ew, ew, ew." She escaped the scene as quickly as she'd stumbled into it.

Kyle laced his hands over the back of his head. "Ye gods and little fishes." He lowered his chin to his chest, blowing out a breath.

Harmony's knees were still wobbly. The sensation was as curious as it was infrequent. *Gotta love a man who mutters medieval jargon after kissing your face off.*

She pursed her lips. *Just once can't he holler "Hooyah" and get back to it?* "Well. I guess that cat's out of the bag."

Hands still on the back of his head, Kyle pivoted to face her. His chin was nearly to his chest, but his eyes reached for hers.

She nearly smiled. He looked guilty but not all ashamed. "Should we chase it?"

That might've been the light of laughter underneath the ice of Scandinavia. He released his hands finally, letting them hang. "I'll go. I might be able to catch her before she stabs her eyes out with a fork."

Harmony stepped to, on his heels. "Maybe it should be me. I'm her best friend. I should've told her before—that things were happening between us."

Kyle reached the door first. "I'm the big brother who hit on her best friend. I should've... I don't know..."

"Asked permission?" Harmony suggested.

"Maybe." Kyle opened the door and took a half step onto the landing before stopping. He turned to Harmony with a pronounced frown etched across his brow. "I don't know how to explain this. I don't know how to explain it to myself."

Harmony gathered a breath, genuinely perplexed. Rarely did she see him anything but definite. "Tell her the truth. Tell her it was a mistake or tell her it's something you meant and intend to do again. The truth's as good a place to start as any."

Kyle weighed the sense in that. Then he jerked his head in a decisive nod.

"And when you're done..." Harmony said before he could even think about closing the door between them, "you could come back here and tell me what you told her. Because I'd like to know."

He stared. And when he only continued to stare, she stepped across the threshold, kissed his slack mouth and reached around to give him a firm pat on the rear. "Dismissed."

He shook his head at her as she backed away, tracing her without touching. Once again, she was the focal point of his intensity as well as a good bit of his heat, so much she thought he would cross the landing back to her and finish what they'd started. "Lock the door," he said instead before shutting it.

She heard his footsteps on the stairs. She listened until they faded out. Then, because the jelly in her knees hadn't solidified yet, she walked from one side of her parents' living quarters to the other. She circled the walls until her strides were long and sure again and she had evened out.

For years she used to lie awake in these rooms wondering if all the violent emotions she felt for Kyle would ever fade like the sound of his riding boots on the wood planks of the stairs. And for a while there, she'd learned what it was like to breathe around him without her pulse racking against her lungs.

Now her child slept and she paced and the timing sucked and Mavis knew and she realized at last that, no, they wouldn't fade. If anything, they were getting louder. Maybe it was the crazy psycho disrupting their lives, threatening everything they mutually loved.

Or maybe life was funny. Maybe the universe had a sense of humor, and it had yet to decide whether to make her the butt of its joke.

CHAPTER TWELVE

"Ew."

Harmony rolled her eyes and lifted her champagne to her lips. "You can cut that out. He's not even here."

"You're thinking about him," Mavis asserted. "You've got that stupid look."

"What stupid look?" Harmony wanted to know.

"The one you wore way back when Kyle and Laurel were joined at the hip. It's like you want to be ticked off but really you're just sad—and *that* ticks you off."

Harmony frowned. "Okay, Cleo." She felt a splat of rain on her temple and glanced at the moody skies. No thunder groused in the distance, but clouds had been moving off and on throughout the day, threatening to bring an end to the glittering festivities at Hanna's Inn. Most of the gala remained outdoors. A long line of silver dishes on pristine white linen covered the buffet table. It was dusk, so there were lanterns, candles and soft summer flowers towering above it all in heady profusion. A string quartet had set up shop on the lawn. White draping festooned low-hanging trees, adding intimacy, and the doors of both the original structure and the new had been thrown wide to invite the well-appointed guests to wander freely. *Don't rain*, she willed. Nothing was going to ruin this day for her parents.

Truthfully, with everything going on, the last thing Harmony had felt like doing was getting Bea and herself gussied up to attend the very public Open House. Bea's rash had gone and not returned. James had been in police custody for over a week alongside Hick. Pappy had been released.

Because of her double workload at B.S., Harmony had barely seen Kyle beyond their trip to The Farm with Adrian so that she could pack a few things. She had opened up the cottage she and Kyle had lived in when he was a boy close to the downtown area and had been staying there with Mavis. Detective Johansson had taken the opportunity to meet them at the mother-in-law suite to gather evidence on The Caterpillar Man. He and his partner found the mason jar under Bea's bed. Despite the vents in the lid, all three varmints had dried up from neglect. When Johansson showed them to Harmony, she'd wanted nothing more than to smash the jar against the wall. She insisted on going with the team and Kyle to comb the woods for prints or other signs of trespassing.

They'd searched for most of the day, turning over a few beer cans and what could've been an old burn pile not far from the clearing where B.S. had been built. Far enough away, Kyle had noted, for the smoke not to be visible from either the farmhouse or the mother-in-law suite.

A sketch artist had sat with Bea for an afternoon. The composite result had sent shivers down Harmony's spine. Wiry beard standard for most lumberjacks. Big tinted sunglasses that had veiled much of Caterpillar Man's face. Bea had admitted never seeing him without them. He had shallow cheeks, not much hair up top and an old flannel shirt that was tattered at the cuffs. "He smiled like a lion," Bea had said.

"How does a lion smile?" the artist asked her.

"With teeth," Bea answered.

Harmony had expected the sketch to look something like the sphinx—a mythological cross-species only the Egyptians, Romans or a four-year-old could've conjured. The artist had seen something different. The face had turned out to be very real. A man. A human being. Smiling and hungry.

Hungry lions were the most lethal. Harmony hadn't let Bea go to bed alone as a result of the sketch.

Despite the artist's rendering, it seemed every lead had dried up. There was a lawyer, O'Farrell, who Kyle and Adrian had tracked down to the east coast of Florida. Unfortunately, his firm had been

closed for some time, the stench of malpractice
growing musty in the air. Adrian had sworn to
keep looking for him. As soon as she wasn't listening, Kyle had muttered, "Bastard's probably
in the Caribbean by now."

Kyle had told Harmony that he was pursuing
another lead. She knew little about it. It seemed
neither Adrian nor Mavis did either. The atmo-
sphere surrounding the inn, the tavern, Adrian's
shop and Belle Brides had been as moody as tonight's sky with the potential for James and Hick
being transferred to county lockup. Harmony suspected only her father's influence and Adrian's
standing in the community had prevented that
from happening thus far.

The town was buzzing with the news of James's
misfortune. Harmony felt the taint of scandal lurking on the fringes of every conversation. No one
had expected Adrian or Mavis to make an appearance tonight despite Flora being closely linked to
Hanna's. When both of the Bracken women did
show, Harmony had stuck close by her friend just
as she knew Briar, Olivia and Roxie had kept loyal
tabs on Adrian.

"It's just weird," Mavis noted.

"Yeah. I got that." As much as she wanted to
avoid talking about Kyle with Mavis, knowing
how much it made the latter uncomfortable, she
wasn't about to force her to let it go. Especially if
it was distracting Mavis from the tittle-tattle. "Is

it any more weird than your childhood obsession with Jack Skellington?"

"There's nothing past tense about it," Mavis quantified.

"Or," Harmony said, smirking at the sight of the first of Olivia and Gerald's sons on the outskirts of the lawn, "the fling you had with William Leighton?"

Mavis pointed sharply at Harmony. "You *swore* you'd never speak of it."

"I'm just sayin'," Harmony said, raising the flute to her lips again.

"It wasn't a fling," Mavis said testily. "It was momentary madness brought on by underage drinking."

"You had *one* margarita."

"It was the Lewis mix. Leightons don't mess around with their tequila."

"He wasn't that bad-looking," Harmony assessed, sizing William up from across the party. "He still isn't."

"Ew!" Mavis said again. "Isn't he like your third cousin or something?"

"I'm kidding!" Harmony laughed. "I just wanted to see the look on your face."

"Tell that to the smoked oysters I ate earlier." Mavis pressed her hand to her stomach. In her black sheath dress with transparent sleeves, she looked svelte and sophisticated, even with the nose ring and the hint of a tattoo on the cusp of her visible collarbone. "They're about to do a magic trick."

Harmony lowered her voice, glancing around to make sure no one was eavesdropping. "Look. Nothing's happened between Kyle and me since that morning upstairs. And if it makes you this uncomfortable... You and I have been friends longer than I've had a thing for him. We'll drop it before it goes any further."

"You'd do that." Mavis had a habit of posing questions as statements. "What I saw isn't the kind of thing you drop like a hot potato. It's the kind of thing that remains an unanswered question. Am I going to spend the rest of my life watching the two of you be ticked off and moony-eyed around each other? That won't make me any more comfortable than I am now. And I'll tell you the same thing I told him...or yelled at him. While I don't care for feeling uncomfortable, it's better than living with knowing I'm the thing that came between you. And thanks all the same for putting me in the middle."

"I'm sorry. I'm sorry," Harmony insisted. "If it makes you feel any better, you aren't the only one who's going to have serious reservations. If Mom, Dad, Adrian or James ever found out about it..."

"If." Mavis chewed over the word for a minute. "So you don't even know if this is something you want to pursue, much less clue everyone else in about."

Harmony's mouth opened to answer, but she remained at a loss.

Mavis frowned, seeming as unsure as Harmony felt. "Forget I'm his sister," Mavis posed hesitantly. "As your friend, what would you rather me do—talk him up or talk you down?"

Harmony shook her head. "I'm not sure. There's a *lot* to think about…"

"He's going back," Mavis concluded. "It's who he is. He's the good soldier who always goes back to the front."

"I know."

"Do you?" When Harmony nodded, Mavis added, incisive as always, "Then how're you doing this? How are you going to let him go, knowing exactly how it feels when he doesn't come back?"

The question arrowed straight through Harmony.

"What about Bea?" Mavis added, lowering her voice. They both glanced around. Bea was sitting on a garden bench, balancing a plate of fruit on her lap while Cole watched her attentively and a contingent of smiling matrons doted on her in her seersucker dress. "She'll feel it this time. He'll be more than an angel or ghost. He'll be the hole in her life that Benji is in yours."

Hard truths. Mavis dealt well in undeniable truths, and as harsh as they were, she meant well by them. "How do you let him go every time?" Harmony wondered out loud. She hadn't had to say goodbye to Benji nearly as many times as Adrian, James and Mavis had had to part with Kyle. "How do you live, knowing that at any moment he could be gone?"

Mavis looked as if she were sinking fast into the gloom that had ridden all of them for the last week. "We don't have a choice. He's the one who decides, and we live with his decision because he's Kyle. He'll always be Kyle. There's no way around him doing the job he was called to do any more than there's a way for me to stop doing mine or you yours."

Harmony hardly had time to digest Mavis's latest dose of reality when a rush of high-end perfume descended on them, stalked by a trim matriarch in a satin suit. "Harmony, *bébé!*"

"Beelzebub," Harmony heard Mavis mutter as she found herself choked into a surprisingly sturdy embrace. "Ms. Marabella," she returned, giving the woman an awkward pat on the back. She was a small lady, petite with regal lines.

According to Marabella's youngest daughter, Roxie, the woman suffered from extreme melodrama. Most of her theatrics were clearly aimed to keep her well-meaning daughter hopping. The rest stemmed from her shipping magnate husband's death years before. Out of the Honeycutt fortune, Leverett Honeycutt had left his wife a small pension—a pittance to what Marabella had been expecting from her spouse of sixty-nine years. "How good to see you."

"Yes, yes. You, too." Marabella held Harmony at arm's length. She hid most every sign of age behind a thick guise of makeup—so thick it could've been mistaken for Sherwin-Williams paint. She might've looked well for her years had she not gone crazy with the Botox. And one too many nip and tucks around the mouth and temples had given her the look of a Kewpie doll on acid. "I almost didn't recognize you. Your hair. Did you get it cut, at last?"

"No," Harmony replied, fighting the urge to touch the tresses hanging in thick waves down her back. She knew the curls she'd painstakingly arranged with the curling iron were wilting, thanks to the evening's overdose of mugginess. "It's just down."

"It's the dress, I suppose. Although..." If possible, Marabella's eyes widened. "It's a bit short for you, isn't it, dear?"

Harmony ran her tongue over her teeth. "Most dresses are. An unfortunate byproduct of being freakishly tall."

"Two of my daughters are as tall as you are," Marabella said thoughtfully. She tapped her manicured fingers to her round chin. Waving them in an airy motion, she indicated, "I'll ask them about their tailors. Give you some options."

"That's...very generous of you," Harmony began. "But I don't need a—"

"I just don't think a mother, even a young one, should show so much skin," Marabella reasoned. She looked to Mavis for an opinion and switched to a confiding octave. "And whoever put this dress together, I think, had someone a little more lithesome in mind."

"Mmm-hmm," Mavis answered. "Who put you together, Ms. Marabella? I'm asking for a friend," she added when Marabella's smile froze. "She's thinking about getting a little work done."

Marabella's eyes narrowed. "Who're you, *chérie*?"

"Mavis Bracken," Mavis reminded her, more amused than insulted. "We've met."

"Bracken," Marabella said and clasped a hand to her throat as if Mavis was liable to lunge for it. She grabbed on to Harmony. "As in *the* Brackens?"

"That's us," Mavis said with a wolfish grin. "Would you like to see my throwing knife collection? It's shiny, not unlike your forehead."

Marabella leaned farther into Harmony. "Is she being facetious?" Because Harmony was choking on laughter and doing a poor job of containing it, Marabella tsked. "I don't find this at all amusing."

"Well, bust my buttons," Mavis uttered.

"You shouldn't jest about things like that," Marabella informed her in good schoolmarm fashion.

"The knives," Mavis wondered, "or your forehead? I wasn't jesting about either."

"How can you stand there making snide remarks with your family in the tenuous position it's in? Have you no respect for the grave set of circumstances your father is facing? Or what everyone's saying?"

"Oh, do shut up, Ms. Marabella."

Mavis and Harmony revolved as one. Harmony felt a jolt at the familiar blonde pressing in on them with a fluid walk in a strappy silver dress and matching lace-up heels. Linking her arm through Mavis's, Laurel aligned herself with the two younger women. "Anyone who's anybody knows the Brackens are less capable of wrongdoing than the bevy of silly gossip mongers this town has to offer."

"Laurel," Marabella greeted, distant. "Shouldn't you be at home with the children?"

"The children are with their father tonight," Laurel answered with a wink.

"Their father. Yes. And how's your grandfather, *bébé*? I hear prison wasn't good for him."

"It was hardly prison," Laurel replied. "Just a handful of nights in the city jail. There were no rumbles, and they fed him three square meals a day. Now he's got a new story to tell at Thanksgiving."

"Your grandmother, Alva, worried herself sick," Marabella reminded her. "I suppose that's what you get for becoming involved with… well…" With a sideways glance at Mavis, she cupped her hand and mouthed, *"You-know-who!"*

"Tom Riddle's here?" Mavis asked, perking up. "This party just got real."

Laurel cackled. "Mavey, I've missed you." Patting Mavis's shoulder, she offered Marabella a cool smile. "It's best you go someplace else, Ms. Marabella. Not only are you talking to a certified Bracken; Harmony works and practically lives with the clan, and I was engaged to one."

Marabella reassessed Laurel. "That's right. You were engaged—to the son." Sympathy touched her deceptive features. "It's a shame you two didn't work things out. Then again, sterility would be a dooming matter in any good relationship."

Harmony frowned. "What?" She felt Mavis stiffen, a flicker of fight coming into her.

Laurel shook her head. "Just as insipidness and narcissism are fundamentals for any good gasbag."

Marabella gasped. "Your children would be ashamed of you, Laurel Louth. Or is it Frye? I can never keep up with you young people and your marital statuses."

"I guess we can't all have the perfect union," Laurel hypothesized.

"Mother." Roxie appeared. She touched Marabella's sleeve. "What are you doing here?"

"You mentioned there was a party at the inn tonight," Marabella informed her.

"Yes," Roxie granted her. "I also mentioned you weren't on the guest list."

"You said it was an oversight."

"And you made half this conversation up. I'll have Byron take you home."

"I thought you weren't speaking to him."

"We're speaking just fine," Roxie said tightly. She threw an apologetic glance at the trio. "Come. You're tired."

"Poor Roxie," Laurel said when they were gone.

"Poor Byron," Mavis opined.

Harmony lifted her hands. "Kyle's sterile?"

Laurel's lips parted, and Mavis's chin drew tight in reaction.

Taking their silence for confirmation, Harmony wove her arms tight over her chest, chilled in ninety-degree weather. "He never—"

"It's not something he advertises." Mavis's mouth shrank inward. "Other than Mom, Dad, and us two..." She looked to Laurel.

"And that's why you left him?" Harmony asked, incredulous. "Because he couldn't have children?"

Laurel winced. "I'd hoped you thought more of me than that. But then you never did like me much, did you, Carrots?"

"Don't call me Carrots."

"Yeah, we're not allowed to do that," Mavis said, using the olive-laden toothpick she stole off a passing waiter's tray to indicate herself and Laurel.

"Sorry," Laurel said quickly. "Only *he* calls you

that." She sighed. "There were several reasons Kyle and I broke off our engagement. His inability to conceive wasn't leading among them."

"Then why?" Harmony wanted to know.

"He chose duty over her," Mavis said, giving Harmony a pointed look. She bit the olives off the tiny sword. With a nudge for Laurel, she inserted a closemouthed, "Mmh?"

Laurel's throat moved. "I asked him not to go back. After his recovery, I begged him to stay. James would've given him Carlton Nurseries to run. The garage. Kyle could've managed The Farm even. But he insisted on re-upping, even when I tossed ultimatums into the mix. The teams or me. That was when a light went off inside him. He shipped out a week later, and then the same light went out in me."

"Just like that," Harmony considered.

Laurel lifted a shoulder. "I used to wonder how SEAL divorce rates could be so high. I thought if two people had enough faith, they could make it last, no matter the circumstances. Turns out, it's not about the separation or the anxieties. For us, it wasn't about injury or recovery. It came down to choice. In the end, we didn't choose one another." She licked her lips. "If you're going to love a SEAL—if you're going to love any military man—that's the best outlook, I guess."

Harmony contemplated Laurel's words. She couldn't be sunk that far, could she? The possibility made her feel the onset of airsickness. Damn it, hadn't she been determined never to fall in love again—*especially* with a military man? "Who says I love him?"

Mavis eyed Harmony, drolly. "She was speaking hypothetically."

Laurel looked from Harmony to Mavis and back, slowly piecing it together. "Oh, my God! You and Kyle are—"

"Complicated," Mavis finished helpfully.

"Go back to your 'ews,'" Harmony suggested. "They were safer."

"You're the one who opened the can of worms." Giving in, Mavis grabbed the champagne flute from Harmony's fingers. "This conversation is stressing me out. And it's not even about me."

Laurel stared at Harmony as Mavis grimaced through the last sips of lukewarm champagne. "I..." Laurel blew out a stunned breath. "I just never thought you two... I mean, you've always been close. But you were just a baby..."

Mavis gave a sour laugh. "Who never liked being put in her corner."

"I was young," Harmony admitted. "But not too young for an indecent amount of jealousy."

Laurel's mouth rounded into an O of understanding.

The next few minutes were marked by stilted silence. Mavis cleared her throat, crossed her ankles and swung the empty flute upside down between two fingers. "This isn't awkward." A waiter passed with another tray. He caught Mavis's eye, no doubt, because of his long hair and the pronounced black plug in each of his earlobes. "Oh, look. Oysters," she said and began to follow.

"Can you check Bea for me, please?" Harmony called after her.

"And bring more booze?" Laurel requested. "A tray, if possible."

"On it," Mavis tossed back before fading into the crowd.

Things felt much more awkward to Harmony *sans* bestie. She felt Laurel's measuring stare and tried not to think about the wet bar or the wine cabinet in the inn dining room. Her mother kept the key in the false bottom of the mantel clock. One benefit of Harmony's freakish stature was that she could now reach it easily.

When neither Mavis nor a tray arrived, she turned to face Laurel fully. "I wasn't jealous because I hated you. I liked you, just like everybody else. Sometimes it was irritating—how likeable you were."

"Oh, good," Laurel said with a dim smile. "Honesty."

"What did you expect?" Harmony gestured to Laurel's impeccable form. "Head cheerleader. City councilman's daughter. The love of Kyle Bracken's life. You were perfect, and I was woefully far from the mark. Age was the least of my problems."

Laurel's smile upended into a quick frown. "What are you talking about? You might've been young, but I always knew there was a part of him that would always be yours. It was intimidating."

"*I* was intimidating?"

"Yes! Factor in the eye-shade you gave me on a regular basis, and I was terrified one day you would tell Kyle you didn't like me."

"He wouldn't have cared what I thought. He was so in love with you, if you'd asked for the moon, he'd've gone all Jimmy Stewart and lassoed it for you."

"Maybe. But you meant so much to him, if you *had* told him you didn't want him to see me anymore, he would've broken things off a lot sooner. Moon or no moon."

That couldn't be true. Harmony dismissed it entirely. "Things have changed."

"They have," Laurel acknowledged fairly. "We're all adults now. We've all led the lives we chose." She paused, hesitant. Then she tilted, considering. "Maybe I'm not all that surprised it's brought the two of you together in the long run."

"No?"

Laurel's eyes took on a reflective glimmer. "Did you know the day you went into labor he was supposed to meet me?"

Harmony shook her head.

"We were going to have a much-needed conversation about our relationship," Laurel revealed. "Since his injury, we'd been stalled. We needed to figure out if we were still on the same page, and I *desperately* needed to hear him say that he was still all-in."

"And instead..." Harmony continued, "you got a call from the hospital saying he was staying there for the night."

"Choice," Laurel said again. "Sometimes, it's a bitch."

Harmony's brows came together. "He was just being a friend."

"I knew that," Laurel admitted. "And I was, of course, willing to forgive him. But then Mavis told me how the nurses tried to stop him from being admitted with you into the delivery room, but he refused to let that stop him. He told them he was the father."

Harmony felt the muscles around her mouth slacken. This part of the story she hadn't known. "He did?"

Laurel nodded. "It bothered me for some reason, no matter how much I tried to chalk it up to Kyle being Kyle and to you needing him more in that moment than I did. I guess you could say I felt a little jealousy of my own—and it never made a tad bit of sense until now." Her gaze passed over Harmony's face. "You've always been bold.

Fiercely bold. It's strange I'm just now realizing how brave you truly are."

"Why would you say that?" Harmony asked. The peep-toe booties she never wore were starting to chafe against her toes and she couldn't wait to kick them off. The uncomfortable conversation with Kyle's ex-girlfriend was making her more and more aware of the fact.

"Because of Benji," Laurel explained. "You've been through this. I know; it must be hard enough the first go-round. Only someone like you would be brave enough to try again."

Brave—or foolish? Harmony caught sight of Bea. Her daughter pirouetted, showing those who'd gravitated to her how her dress billowed in an enchanting circle when she danced. She circled and circled until she swayed and tipped. She tumbled, giggling, on to the grass, cheeks flushed, curls wild and askew. Harmony choked back emotions when Bea clambered up immediately to try it again.

"It runs in the family," Laurel said quietly. She, too, watched Bea, wistful. "Fearlessness."

"I should hope so," Harmony replied. "Excuse me."

As she set out across the grass to pick her daughter up after spilling again, she thought she heard Laurel whisper, "Good luck."

CHAPTER THIRTEEN

THE DISTINCT CLATTER of footsteps above deck brought Kyle to attention in the *Hellraiser*'s cabin. The book open at his waist closed as he rolled toward the shelves above his mattress. On top of a row of abused paperbacks and faded hardcovers, he palmed the butt of his trusty Colt.

The footsteps stopped. The lock on the hatch snicked. Kyle tilted on to his back, flattening the barrel of the Colt against his belly, angled up slightly.

The first leg on the ladder was led by a green bootie and a shapely calf, followed by a second. They navigated the rungs carefully, descending, legs unfurling in all their toasted-almond-coloured goodness. "Knock knock," called a vivid voice.

He let the air in his lungs go, put the safety on and placed the gun quickly back on the shelf. He sat up to greet her, then stopped as she came to stand at the bottom of the ladder.

She stopped, too, when she saw him staring. Her face fell. "What? Did I miss the do-not-disturb sign?"

His hands gripped the edge of the mattress.

"Uh, no." Without explaining further, he lowered his gaze over her.

Devil take him, she looked like sin. As if he hadn't been having enough trouble forgetting she was a woman. With her hair hanging loose around her face, the cat-eye makeup technique making her look more sly, and more than just her stems on display, all the road signs he'd been struggling to read correctly were flashing the same unequivocal message: *Buckle Up.*

As he stared, she pressed her lips together and looked beyond him. Spreading her hands, she said, "Talk, please."

"I did," he responded.

She narrowed her eyes. "No."

"Exactly." He nodded. "I said no.'"

"I meant something more than 'no.'"

He caught his knee bouncing and closed his fist over it. When she crossed her arms and leaned back with one foot in front of the other, he made the mistake of scanning her again—head to toe. Keeping his hand tight on the restless leg, with the other he scrubbed his knuckles across his mouth. "Jesus, Carrots," he said finally. "I've got nothin'." She smelled like the sultry summer night he knew it was. The kind that called for events like stargazing. Better yet, skinny-dipping.

In a gesture that showed how restless she was, too, she dropped her hands to the hem of her dress.

"Nothing's more encouraging than the opines of Marabella Honeycutt."

"Who?"

"Roxie's mother," she reminded him. "She thinks I look like a billboard for promiscuity."

Kyle opened his mouth, closed it. He settled for a mild, "Aha." He wanted to ask what she was doing here, with him, in her green dress. "Where's Bea?"

Harmony's smile returned. "At the inn. I told her she could stay up as late as she wanted. She made it to eleven before conking on Dad's shoulder. I got to watch him tuck her in. He goes through the same bedtime motions with her that he used to with me."

Talk of Bea and her gun-toting grandfather should've straightened Kyle out. But Harmony's face had gone warm, her smile sweet. By turn, her eyes looked deep and lush.

"The party made for some interesting conversation," she said, moving toward him.

"Did it?" He fought the urge to move back. She dipped one knee into the bed, lowering herself to the mattress.

"Yes. With your girlfriend, no less." Gathering the discarded book in both hands, she read the title and author.

Kyle frowned. His girlfriend? She arched a brow, lifting her gaze from the book to him, and it came to him. "Laurel."

"How soon a sailor forgets."

"She's not my girlfriend," he said.

Harmony lifted a noncommittal shoulder, placing the book carefully on the shelf with the others. Tugging the hem of the dress again, she shifted over her knees, making the mattress dip. "She made me realize something I should've maybe considered a long time ago."

"What's that?"

"The grenade. It took more from you than skin, nerves and several pints of blood."

It didn't take him long this time to realize what she was talking about. "Huh."

She gave a small sigh. "You're verbose tonight, K.Z.B."

"What do you want me to say? That I'm thrilled you and my ex were chatting all night about the half of my manhood I had to say buh-bye to?"

"No," she said. "I don't even blame you for not telling me. I just…never knew."

"It makes a difference?"

Her fist balled, and he took the firm blow in the meaty part of his arm. "Seriously? I'm that kind of girl?"

She wasn't a girl any more than she was the superficial kind of woman.

"Do you think, as a man, it makes you less?" she asked.

He paused. "I might've. For a little while, at least."

"When Laurel left."

"It was before. I tried pushing her away." He paused again, spreading his hands and studying the callouses on each. "I tried to take the high road. So she could get what she wanted out of life."

"She stayed. And in the end, you were the one who moved on."

He tried to gauge her chameleon face. In turn, her gaze roved him, discerning. "All this time," she added, "I thought she was the one who got away."

"You thought I was pining?"

"She asked you to quit." Harmony shook her head. "She knew what service meant to you. She knew how hard it would be to deny the call to your brothers if you were able-bodied to do so, and she asked you to choose. After everything, she didn't know you at all. Did she?"

He looked around, saw the wall close enough to lean on and relaxed against it. "I thought it was telling that all I really felt in that moment wasn't so much hurt as disappointment." He gestured to her. "You wanted me to stay, too."

"Of course." Shifting from her knees to her hip, she scooted to the wall behind her, straightening her legs toward him on the mattress. "She thought loving you meant making you stay. But loving you really meant letting you go where you needed to go."

"Like how your family knows loving you

doesn't mean keeping you earthbound. It means letting you fly, however much what you do up there terrifies the rest of us."

A slight smile caught her lips. "She said something else. Laurel."

As much as his thing for Laurel might've been over, the thought of her and Harmony discussing him over champagne and canapés was still discomfiting. "Yeah?"

"She said that if I'd given you the word back when you two were dating, you would've broken up with her."

He watched the conflicting lights of hope and curiosity spiral over her. They were no less subtle than the LED lights on a police car. "It's not much of a question. The real question is whether you would've followed through on your end."

She let out a laugh. "Preteen Harmony was just as selfish, petty and insecure as the rest. I would've loved seeing you send Laurel packing." She sobered when he only smiled at her. "You would've hated me."

"No," he argued. "Resented you plenty. But when it comes to you, hate's not in my vocabulary."

"You would've been miserable." She licked her lips when he didn't deny it. Lifting a finger, she said, "The first time I saw you unhappy, I would've dragged her by the hair and marched her back to you."

He laughed again, a deep resonating rumble straight from the bones. "That I can see." He seamed his lips over a grin as one of her feet touched his. It faded quickly when he saw her hands weave together, when he saw the chewed nails on each, and the frayed edges of her mouth. She struck him as pale and remote. "Carrots." He tilted his head when she met his stare. "What's wrong?"

"Should I be here?" she whispered. A clutch of vulnerability eclipsed her confidence. "Are we *completely* stupid? I've been trying to figure out why I haven't been able to sleep since things started happening. It's because of what might happen. What Dad would say. What James might say. How Adrian would look at me if she knew what I've wanted to do with you since I was old enough to understand." She cursed and swiped a hand underneath her nose. Again not looking at him. "Then I think…what if we ignored all of it and moved forward? What would happen down the road if you…"

The silence gave way to understanding. Kyle, however, felt something thick building at the back of his throat and couldn't find reassurance beyond it. Not when he'd been thinking along the same lines.

"I can't think about losing you," she said, down to a murmur.

He took a breath in. He was what he was. There

was no getting around it. But what it did to his family…to Harmony… None of it was easy to dwell on. Bracing himself, he said with difficulty, "I'll back away."

She frowned at him. "What?"

"Isn't that what you're saying one of us should do?" he asked. "I'll take the lead and bow out for both of us."

"Kyle—"

"I can't put you through what you went through before."

"You *want* to break it off?" she asked.

"No, goddamn it!" Passing his palm over his face, he pinched the sleeve of his shoulder. His hands were sweating. Swallowing, he tried again. "You're the one who said that this whole thing isn't rational."

"No, it isn't," she admitted. "But Laurel told me something else."

"Hell," he muttered, unable to help it when he was this raw.

"It's about the night Bea was born. She said you two had an important date but you canceled to be with me. And when the nurses stopped you from entering Maternity, you said you were the father."

He didn't blink. "Yes, I did," he said. He noted the unabashed gleam, the softness and intensity threading together and the flame building behind the combustive blend.

"Who does that?" she whispered, breathless.

"When it's you in there alone…" He crossed his arms. "Me. I do that."

A steady sigh slowly wound its way out of her. Uncharacteristically motionless, she bathed him in that hard-soft light that was all hers. She took a moment, scanning the spines of the books on the shelf, the boxes of ammo doubling as bookends. "You remember that quote from *Gatsby*—about Daisy Buchanan?"

"It's been a while. Remind me."

"I only read it once," she told him, "in high school. But it's stuck with me. 'He looked at her the way all women want to be looked at.'"

There was no bitterness of unrequited love. Her bitterness had been vanquished by the turn of revelations the night had taken. Still, he saw the ache. And knowing how little she dwelled on aching memories, he ached, too. *Ah, Carrots.* He jerked his chin. "Come 'ere."

There was no further hesitation. She crossed the bed to settle into the crook of his arm. She took off one bootie, then the other, chucking them across the cabin with telling dismissal. Then she pressed her cheek to his shoulder. He tugged her into him as their legs overlapped. He held her, his unshaven chin against her hair, her arm looped over his lap where the book had been. His eyes closed, and he lowered his nose until it was lost in the fragrant reams of Zippo-red that had grown unruly outside.

They stayed that way long enough to hear the lap against the boat's hull joined by the hiss of a rain shower. It was as alleviating to him as the unspoken ease of being with her. The anger that had been fermenting throughout the week…every unsuccessful turn he'd met punching through walls to prove his father's innocence—not to mention the agitation and fear over Harmony and Bea and the very real threats that had come close to extinguishing the fire in both of them… It had nearly been too much. If he hadn't been so busy chasing leads and making sure his mother, sister, Harmony and Bea were well taken care of, he would've hit the gym. Pumping weights was the best way to stave off aggression.

For the first time in days, the fight inside him dimmed. His head grew quiet, and the irritating drum that had been tapping against his temples ceased. He rubbed his lips against the surface of her hair, grazing his thumb over the dip of her spine, down and back up. Then down and up again because it wasn't enough anymore to measure the angles visually. He wanted to explore her by touch.

For a few minutes, he didn't want to think about how futile he'd been in finding a solution to his family's problems. He cut the line to his imagination that had been on a ceaseless loop over what might've happened to Harmony if the real perpetrator had known more about cutting wires.

He just wanted to smell Harmony's hair. Lie with Harmony. Be with Harmony.

There was no going back, he realized. He was supposed to be tough. She had broken him down, bit by bit. And in Harmony's way, she didn't make him feel parceled for it. He felt as shiny as the fallen pennies that never failed to remind him of her.

"Hmm," she murmured, startling him out of the reverie. She made a protesting sound. "Stop jumping like the damned."

"I thought you were asleep," he hissed.

"Not so much." She tipped her face up. There was a thoughtful frown on her.

"Uh-oh," he said. The more time left alone for Harmony with her thoughts was just more opportunity for her to talk herself into whatever it was she wanted.

"Why did you throw me in the mud?" she asked.

"When?"

"I was eighteen," she explained. "You brought Benji and a few other navy buds over when you had a break from training. Mavis and I were swimming in the pond at The Farm when we heard y'all carrying on in the woods."

"You were seventeen," he said at the emergent memory. "And you were parading in front of the guys in the smallest string bikini I've seen apart from the beaches of California."

"I was three days passed my eighteenth birthday," she informed him shrewdly. "The bikini was a gift I bought myself."

"Huh."

"So, why did you?"

"Did we not already establish the bikini's role in all this," he asked, "and the sweaty contingent of naval guys ogling you in it?"

"That's why you tossed me over your shoulder and plunked me into the nearest mud heap?"

"It was a puddle, three inches, max. And yes. I saw them looking at you, Benji in particular, and thought I had no recourse but to teach you a lesson."

"Did you look, too?"

"I don't understand the question."

She brightened. She was impossibly bright. "You *did*, didn't you?"

He frowned. "I used to think it was Benji you were trying to bait that day. Tell me it was him."

"It could've been," she claimed. "By that point, I *was* practically over you."

He read her like a book. "But you had to have the last word before moving on?"

"You looked," she said, smile broadening.

"I looked," he acknowledged, "and, for a while… I loathed myself for it."

Sliding the length of her body against his, she brought her wide-smiling mouth to his. For leverage, she went up on one elbow and angled down to him, her leg splaying farther over his lap. He grabbed the back of her thigh because he'd been thinking about her legs for too long, and he suspected he was going to need to hold on to something. A smug "mmm" emanated from her throat as his touch spread, firm, from the back of her knee to the high hem of her dress. He cupped her neck, encouraging, as she kissed him thoroughly. Tipping his head, he took what she gave, giving back until his mouth was open against hers and they were both breathing in unsteady bursts, their bodies humming in tune.

He murmured, "I like your hair loose."

It was her turn for monosyllabic answers. She stopped because his fingertips were massaging the back of her scalp. Eyes closed, she dipped her head back into his palm, indulgence scrolled in the intriguing lines of her face.

He spread the caress down the long line of her neck, then her back, an encompassing sweep, one hand passing up, the other down. "I like the shape of you," he added.

"Like a Sunday edition caricature?" she ventured.

"No," he told her. He gripped the nape of her neck and the curve of her hip. "Like a wet dream."

She nipped her lower lip into her mouth as she had the night he'd first felt his regard for her slip into something as illicit as her dress. "That wasn't always the case."

"Mmm. It is now." The urge to imbibe her was

far too strong. He gathered her back to his chest and ramped the heat further with a game of tug-of-war for possession of that lip.

A breathless laugh cascaded out of her. "Point Bracken."

"My first." Because he still hadn't explored all of her, he turned his attention to her throat. Here she smelled like sweet grass in a newly minted spring—fresh, trim, invigorating... "You came here in your green dress knowing."

"I don't understand the question."

"It wasn't a question."

"It wasn't." She was practically glowing with satisfaction. Her arms were underneath his shirt, hands dancing lightly, tacitly over his abdomen and pecs. She swept a thumb across his nipple. It hardened instantly and she beamed. "Yes. After learning everything I did tonight, after these last few weeks of you running around me and Bea, doing your stupid alpha-male dance... I guess I wanted to take care of you, too, for a change."

"How're you certain?" he wondered. "That this is what's right?"

She raised a brow, brushing her thumb across his nipple again and laving the seam between his lips briefly with her tongue. "Feel that?"

"Hmm," he groaned, trying to catch the end of her tongue. She pulled her head back to keep him from latching.

"What could be more certain than that?" She

sobered quickly. So quickly it knocked him off balance. Under his shirt, her touch ranged from his sternum to his ribs, loving. "You're the most certain thing I've ever known."

He saw the snatched longing again, all the years she'd bottled it inside her. He swallowed. Fire was certain, sure. But it was hardly stable and was almost never safe. Diving into it, into her, called to him. She'd culled out a place in him now cheerfully inhabited by a mercury cloud of lust. Everything about her appealed to the risk-taker he'd been since youth.

But the thoughtful side of him, the analytical part that always measured and kept him calibrated and controlled in the heat of battle, didn't know how either of them would get through this without burn marks. Still, when her mouth sought the ridge of his jaw and began to wander, his eyes rolled and he closed them, raising a knee as she kissed him, unreserved, in places that had been taut for too long.

"You know what I want?" she asked him.

"What do you want, Carrots?" If he held her tight enough, could he make the fire more stable? Could they get away without hurting themselves or others?

"I want to see."

He'd felt her touch slip from under his shirt and glide to his hip, over the leg of his shorts, and underneath where she found the first surgical scar. "You sure about that?" he asked.

Harmony didn't shy. She showed him by tracing the scar up, closer to his groin. "On your feet, soldier."

"Ma'am." He waited for her touch to fall away. She flattened against the mattress, letting him plank over her and find the floor on the other side. He rose and stepped to the middle of the small open space of the cabin. He reached back for the neckline of his T-shirt and tugged. "I feel like DJ Snake or Tone-Loc should be playing."

"Another time," she said, muted. She was sitting on the edge of the bed when he pulled the neckline over his head.

Shrugging the shirt from his arms, he let it fall. "Another time, huh?" he asked and gripped the elastic band on the shorts and boxer briefs underneath.

She only raised her brows, waiting with the heels of her feet propped on the box spring. With her toes pointed down, she was the picture of anticipation.

Kyle heard his pulse ratchet up in answer and didn't waste another minute. He pushed the bottoms down quickly. Shaking the shorts off one ankle then the other, he kicked them out of the way and propped his hands on his hips.

Harmony's mouth slackened and air rushed between her lips. She gripped the fitted sheet.

They'd come full circle. Only he was naked and she was still wearing the dress. Shifting to the balls of his feet, then back to his heels, he told himself to relax under her commanding assessment.

It had taken some getting used to—months of getting used to—after the surgery, but no longer did the dead nerves on his inner thighs give him pause. Neither did the tight sensation of sewn skin around them bother him overmuch. Only now did it draw his attention because he was exposed, and aroused.

The arousal had loosened its grip at the idea of her seeing what he'd allowed so few to see. When he'd finally disrobed in front of Laurel after recovery, she'd wept—buckets of tears.

That had been a hard one to forget. So much so that afterward, any cozy time with a female had rarely come with a full disrobing.

He tried to ignore the blood washing against his eardrums in pounding strokes. He ignored the prickled skin at the base of his neck and spine telling him to put his shorts back on, damn it, so Harmony didn't have to see him like this. Not because he was determined to man up and get over it. Because of the way she was looking at him, at all his damage. Because though he saw her throat move on a swallow and he knew her perusal hadn't yet gone beyond the scars and the element missing from his undercarriage, she wasn't

tearing up. True to form, she held to him fast, unblinking. More, she seemed to see him in a meri-
torious light. It took him a moment to understand
that the expression growing over her was one of
approval.

When her eyes roved from his junk to his abs
and farther up his torso, the prickles at the base
of his neck trickled to the base of his spine, where
they gathered in ranks. She licked her lips, and he
thought he might lose his mind.

She gained her feet, and he planted his to the
floor. Closing the gap, she traced the line of his
shoulders with her gaze before lifting her eyes
to his face. She lingered on his mouth. Then her
stare fused to his. There was admiration in numbers, and he took it, growing taut in places, thick
in others. His heart was about to bang through
the wall of his chest and cling to her like static.

Slowly, her hands lifted. His entire body went
still. "I want to touch you. Can I?"

Was that a question? Kyle jerked a nod. It was
going to take a nutcracker to pry his jaw open.
He was locked down, his grip on his hips hard
enough to keep from reaching for her first. His
breath did not come steadily anymore.

She placed her hand flat beneath the wall of
his heart. Slightly damp, it didn't quaver. It was
hot and sure. She left it there for several seconds
before her fingertips trickled their way down the
center line of his abs. The dark hair that grew

thick below his navel was practically standing to attention when she reached it, every short strand tingling on end. He firmed his lips as she ventured lower. He watched her. Her hair had fallen halfway across her face, but he could see that her bottom lip was between her teeth again.

He didn't open his mouth, but he let out an involuntary noise when her perusal reached the base of his erection. It was swollen. Veins pushed toward her, blue and singing. *Stop. Don't stop.* Both entreaties swam through him, and he nearly closed his eyes. He watched her lip instead as she suckled on it. He saw the points of her teeth digging in, and his arousal heightened.

She flattened her palm against the length of his rod. A smile pulled at the corner of her mouth when she wrapped her thumb around to the tip and gave it a quick strum. The base sound in his throat was a groan and gulp all in one.

"You're lookin' pretty spry for all your damage, K.Z.B.," she murmured to him.

"Harm…" He was holding himself together by skin alone. The muscles in his temples flexed as those around his jaw packed against the bone.

"Just a little more," she whispered.

He locked his mouth up tight because she ventured lower where the damage had been done. Now he closed his eyes. She cupped her palm around the empty space where scar tissue lived.

Her lips came to rest against his breastbone. She began to massage.

He made another sound. This one was softer. Longer. Her ministrations tugged it from him. "Shh," she entreated, using her other hand to massage the loner free of scarring. Then, with her brow resting against his chest, she traced the web of scars down both thighs.

An epiphany sprang from the depths of his mind. *Kintsugi*, a philosophical nugget he'd learned from his travels. Instead of throwing out broken pottery or ceramics, the Japanese considered damage part of an object's history. Not only was lacquer used to fill the cracks or joints. It was mixed with gold, silver or platinum to create something of value. A plate or dish could not only be useful again, but the breakage became art.

Kyle felt golden in the cracks of his skin, in his damaged tissue and surgical lines. She made him feel golden and rejuvenated. Everything that was resilient and finite.

"Take off your dress," he said, rough.

Her chin touched his chest as her eyes lifted. There was wonder in her. Light, wonder and hunger. She scarcely nodded, smile blooming. It was saucy and wide. "Aye, aye."

CHAPTER FOURTEEN

HARMONY MADE A few unladylike noises peeling the dress from her hips. Why did these things never work in a hurry? She heard Kyle's chuckle. Blinded by lace, she wiggled to bring the dress all the way up. His arms wound around her, and he joined the yanking.

She felt the dress give. Happy to be shot of it, she flung it to the floor. Flushed, flustered and unbalanced, she moved her feet around to confront him. Before she could blow the hair out of her eyes, he was there, swiping it away with tender palms.

Touch had a memory, just like taste and smell. Someone could blindfold her, force her to take half a dozen turns on The Zipper carnival ride, and she'd *still* know it was Kyle's fingertips grazing her skin. He'd brushed hair from her face a thousand times. A thousand nothings. Here, in the place where he came for reprieve, the gesture felt deeply intimate. It dug deep inside her. There was no pain. Just the sweet ache of knowing, the impact reverberating through every inch of her.

His head bowed, hands cupping her shoulders.

She felt his breath on her skin and it brought a fine coat of gooseflesh to the surface. He gently blew each strand of hair from the line of her shoulders. He traced her then, from bicep to neck, a barely-there tease, and tipped her mouth to his. She let him lead because up to this point, he'd been uncertain.

She wanted him certain. He'd given in to her wishes, letting her see and touch the pieces of him that were no longer whole. Not many women had come this far with him, she sensed. *Let it be me*, she wished. Crazy psycho lunatics aside, her cup was pretty full these days. She didn't have to wish for much other than her child and family's safety and the success of the business she reveled in being part of.

She wished now with a vigor she realized she'd stopped wishing with because wishes had a tendency to be stripped once granted. Hence, Benji's death. James's downfall. B.S.'s misfortunes. Her own near brush with death. Wishing was excruciating.

Maybe she couldn't handle Kyle certain. The ache took on diamond strength and bent her to its potency. *Dear God*.

She'd promised herself. No falling. That part of her soul was supposed to stay with Benji. Only Benji…

Panting, Harmony closed her hand around

Kyle's wrist as the hives of fear droned loud in her ears.

"Harm." The tip of his thumb circled the point of her chin. "Something's wrong."

He said it like he was armed with his 60, and her fear was a live thing leering in the corner. All she had to do was point and he'd render it obsolete. The image brought laughter to her throat. It never made it out. Her mouth was too full, too empty, too dry.

"Are you nervous?"

Ha. Nervous of being with him? Nervous of being naked with him? "No," she answered.

"What is it?"

She sighed because he framed her jaw, and his thumbs passed over her cheeks in a soothing caress. "Nothing. I'm just..."

"Scared?"

She winced. *Scared.* It might've been an ordinary sentiment for others. To her, it seemed paltry. Pointless. It was most definitely in the way of her getting everything she'd ever wanted...

Everything she'd ever wanted...

"Oh," she said out loud. Yes, she had promised not to fall for anyone else...because aside from Benjamin Zaccoe, there had only been one person for her, hadn't there? And up until recently, she'd been sure she could never have him.

That man was standing with her, skin to skin. Heart to heart.

Trust. The far-off voice struck her off guard.

Trust Kyle? Trust fate? The first was easy. The second, not so much…

Trust in this man and everything that's led you here together.

She put her hands on him. *Can I really have you?* she wondered. *Really?*

"It's not nothing," he confirmed. "What's going on?"

She shook her head. "This matters."

"No shit." He nearly laughed under the weight of unspoken things. "Why do you think it's taken me so long to come around to it? I've walked into firefights with less deliberation."

"What changed your mind?" She wanted to know, gathering every detail of his face.

"I love you."

She might've made a noise. After long, stunned silence, she uttered, "Oh, God."

"And I know," he went on, the muscles tight around his neck and jaw, "I know you love me."

Well, she couldn't deny that, could she?

"Whatever happens…" he continued, careful. "Whatever comes of this… I guess it's knowing I'll take care of you."

She nodded and concluded, "And I'll take care of you."

Emotions sprang to him, more than she normally saw him give. "That's a promise."

"I don't need promises," she said. "I *know*. We're a team."

He nodded solemnly. "Exactly." He touched his brow to hers. "Better?"

"Yeah. My knees are like jelly, though. So unless you want the possibility of a large woman-shaped hole in your cabin floor, I wouldn't go throwing words like 'I love you' around like cannelloni."

"Here." His arms wrapped around her waist, and without so much as a grunt, he lifted her off the floor. As she flattened against his torso, he arched a brow. "How's this?"

Her feet dangled and her heart knocked. "Taller. How the hell do you breathe up here?"

"Lately, around you?" he asked. "Not at all." And he kissed her again, hard and hot enough to ensure neither of them would be breathing for the next good while—and that was okay.

It wasn't until the elevation changed that she realized he'd carried her to the bed. His hand closed over the back of her neck and her tongue tangled against his. Neither of them broke away as he helped her arrange herself, straddled, over his lap. Arousal consumed her as her core came up against the brunt of his erection. She felt the bite of heat inside her thighs. When he brought her center against his, the heat seared, rising to the surface of her cheeks. He was hard and she was wet. Now, that was promising.

She planted her hands on his shoulders and lifted, ready for eclipse.

"Nuh-uh." A quick overturn and he had her across the bed beneath him. He ranged himself over her on hands and knees like a predator on the brink of ending a hunger cycle. "My bed." The words came rough again as he bared his teeth in a grin. "You don't get to lead in *my* bed."

She grinned, too, and stirred. Knowing his composure, seeing the warrior come alive with the door closed and the sheets down was thrilling as hell. She stretched her arms over her head, submissive, and parted her legs. He nodded at the move. She tipped her head back, inviting him to the weak spots. His fingers twined with hers, flattening them against the mattress.

Can I really have this? she wondered. Her mind was floating, up and away.

The wandering rush of his touch was deliberate and encompassing. Her body rose in a wave beneath the possessive sweep of hard hands, from her breasts to her thighs and back up. Her leg circled his hip, calf leveling across the small of his back. He tried to hold her arms back, but she wasn't done touching him for the night.

"This is new," she murmured, finding the indented ring on the back of his shoulder.

"Hmm," he answered. His brow rested between her breasts, and his hands were beneath her hips, kneading.

She blew a sigh through her nose when he pressed his mouth to her stomach and said nothing more. Only one kind of weapon left a telling indention like this one. She reared up as much as she could without making him give up any of his seductive progress below. Tossing her loose hair out of the way again, she lowered a kiss to the bullet wound that had healed but was fresh enough for color. She doubted he'd shown it to his family. She was the first. The hot extraction he'd described came rushing back in stark detail. Had he gotten this trying to bring her brother back to her alive?

Just a little lower, she mused, and he might've taken the shot between the lungs. She pressed her hand against his left shoulder blade, her cheek to the top of his head, cradling it and turning her head away.

Here we go, she thought. *Damn it.*

She'd done this before, hadn't she? She'd learned quickly she couldn't torture herself through the roller coaster of what-ifs and what-might-bes.

She was too lost now. His hands were everywhere. His essence was paddling through her blood. His grip slid to the inside of her knee, bracing it outward. She couldn't stop. *Too deep in him now.*

She let him press her leg to the top sheet. Lowering back to his sheets again, her hips rose as his stubble rasped against the sensitive skin beneath her navel. A noise ground against his throat.

His breath blew hot against her flesh. He breathed a light kiss across her center. Arms rising from the bed in humming rapture, Harmony placed them above her head. *Surrender*. This is what absolute surrender felt like. It turned her into a bubble—furnace-forged and molten. Searing, translucent. Easily shattered.

He groaned again, lifting his head to shake it. "I love that you make noises like that."

"Like I'm coming apart at the seams?" she said. She shivered because there was dew on her skin and more gooseflesh beneath it.

"Like a feline locked inside a dairy wagon." He rose to her for a mouth-to-mouth revival.

She raked her fingers through his hair and brought him down again for more kisses. More, she wanted. More of his breath, his taste. Just more.

His knees dropped from the bed to the floor, and he hooked her beneath the legs, pulling her to the lip of the mattress. His grip ventured up the back of one thigh and cupped her bottom, lifting a fraction, just enough.

Harmony licked her lips. Again, he was in charge. With anyone else, she would've chafed at the submissive stance. But this was Kyle. Naked, aroused, concrete shoulders rising above rebar chest and eyes flickering with need and promises and a touch of something else—something naughty that made the parts of her that had long trembled for him crow loudly in answer and her tongue press against the roof of her mouth.

Angling her hips up to his, he filled her, quickly. Harmony caught herself making the sound he loved. He used the hand on her bottom, the other beneath her knee to slide out, in. His nostrils flared, and a muscle moved on the ridge of his cheek. "You don't always need wings to fly."

She gasped, flexing around him. He quickened the pace and she cried out. It felt good, so good that a fork of pained longing jetted through her. He bent over her, hardening. She absorbed him. That vital glass ball inside her was about to splinter into a million tiny fragments. She doubted there'd be any refitting. She continued on anyway. Climbing alongside him, ladder rung by ladder rung.

His body tightened, and he arched his back, closing his eyes as he lifted his face to the ceiling. Rapture rode him, like Helios in his sun chariot.

Beautiful. Everything about the man was so beautiful, it nearly broke her.

Then it did break her. She hissed as the waves of pleasure took on an electrical pulse, surging from her curled-up toes, lighting up every nerve in her body in a pyrotechnical ode to the Technological Age. She broke for him, the terra cotta particles of her falling apart around her like fragile Technicolor rain.

Only this time breaking didn't hurt. It was affirming. She didn't mind so much that she'd likely never glue all of those pieces back together again—not when she watched him break, too. A man not used to breaking. She linked both legs around his waist, folded him into her, inviting him to lie down beside her in the wake of loving havoc and wait for recovery.

KYLE STOOD ON the deck of the *Hellraiser*. The rain had moved gentle swells to shore. The vessels bobbed lazily around him. The air was cool and breathable, odd even for three o'clock in the morning. Mist hung around him like suspended precipitation, dampening the skin of his torso as he leaned on the starboard rail.

The gentle pitching of the boat had woken him. Harmony was still passed out on his bunk. He liked her there, he'd thought as the low light of the cabin had feathered across her features, the sheet tucked around her middle, her bare legs visible.

He'd wanted to stay. He wanted to climb back below, take up his place beside her and disappear once again into the safe ebb of tranquility.

Safe? Since when was any of this safe? What had happened in his bunk tonight was a lot of things, but safe? No.

Still, he'd woken to a face-full of silken red hair.

He'd lain stationary, weighing whether he should slide back into sleep or slide his hands over her until she stirred for the next round.

The face of the clock had brought him up short. It was mere hours to daybreak. She'd have to go back to the inn early enough perhaps to sneak by Briar and Cole in the dress she and Kyle had both left a little worse for wear.

He'd wake her and take her back to Hanna's. But first, he needed a minute.

The phone was in his hand. Turning on the screen, he got beyond his pass code and into his text messages.

Pettelier. The former teammate had been the key Kyle had needed to unlock the whereabouts of one missing frogman. Kyle eyed the jumble of numbers Big Pete had last sent to him. He tapped it and selected the Call option before he could talk himself out of it. He heard the echo of the first ring, then put the phone to his ear.

The connection wasn't great, but the call went through. It rang enough times on the other end for Kyle to anticipate voice mail.

The line clicked. "Who the hell's this?" a hard sleep-muffled voice answered.

Kyle gave it a second. Two. Then he replied. "Bad time, boo?"

A wave caressed the underside of the boat once and again before a whispered curse blew through the speaker, and Gavin answered. "Kyle."

It wasn't a question. Kyle waited for more.

"Maybe you could tell me why you're callin' me at four a.m."

"'Cause I knew you'd bitch about it and give away your location," Kyle noted. "Good to know you're still somewhere along the Eastern Seaboard. Let's talk about the weather."

"What do you want?"

The gruff mumble brought a rush of blood to Kyle's face. His knuckles whitened over the rail. *What do I want?* Kyle took a moment to cool before he replied, "You're not back, and I'm havin' to answer for it. So it'd be super-duper if you'd pack your little bags and put in an appearance on the home front."

"You're back."

"Yep." Kyle nodded. "You starting to see the picture?"

"They know." Gavin scoffed. "What'd you hold out for, a day?"

"No. I just got tired of doing your dirty work."

"It was Harmony. She got to you."

"No, the point is—"

"You *looked* at her and caved, didn't you? Some brother in arms you are."

"You're raking *me* over the coals?" Kyle asked, incredulous. "When was the last time you talked to her or your dad and told the truth? How long were you going to wait before telling them you're no longer in service, that you've been home for six months, or that you need help crossing the goddamn street?"

"Screw you, Bracken."

"Before you hang up," Kyle said in warning, "there's one thing you gotta know."

"What?"

"Your family loves you." Kyle let it sink in before he went on. "I had to look your father, Briar and Harmony in the eye and tell them what's really been going on. All they've wanted since is to get their hands on you. Not to ring your big stupid neck like you deserve. They want to see you for themselves. They want to know that you're okay. Harmony—I had to see her crying. *Crying.*"

"Shit." Gavin sank once more into weighted silence.

"Come home," Kyle said. "If you don't, they'll find you. They'll forgive you. They've already forgiven you. They just want to take care of you. Give them what they want, Savitt. Or so help me God, I'm going to hunt your ass down and kick it all the way back to the Hindu Kush."

"Affirmative."

Kyle narrowed his eyes. "Say again."

"I said affirmative, dickhead. Just hold off telling them. I don't want them—"

"—to be disappointed when you don't show?" Kyle nudged. "No, I wouldn't dream of setting them up like that. Just let me know if you need transport."

"No thanks."

"Call Mitchum at Little Creek. He can fly you. If you need a driver—"

"I've got it. Anything else?"

Kyle went over what he'd thought he would have to say. If the harsh dose of reality didn't bring Gavin home, Kyle had been prepared to play his ace.

If Gavin found out what Kyle and Harmony had been up to lately, he'd come home, all right— faster than he could say "k-bar" or "haversack." From there, it'd be Kyle's ass buried in Alabama clay. Not that there'd be anything to find once Gavin was finished with him. The man might be legally blind, but he still had hands, he still had training, and Harmony was still his baby sister. It was discomfiting, knowing Kyle was taking a leaf from Gavin's book and lying by omission.

Letting the confession fall away and setting the guilt aside, he decided to hold on to that ace until he was sure Gavin *would* return.

By then, maybe Kyle would have a better grasp of what was happening between him and Harmony. Gavin would at least want to know his intentions. Before he killed him.

Kyle cleared his throat. "We'll talk when you get back."

"She deserves better," Gavin said suddenly.

Kyle's stomach took a steep dive. "What?"

"Harmony. She deserves better than this."

Kyle shook his head. "I don't—"

"I know what she's been through, and I still let her find out the wrong way about my eyes. She cried? Really?"

Kyle fought the urge to release a tumultuous breath. "Yeah." He knew her eyes. He'd known they were wet that night on the bay. She'd looked the same after crumbling on his shoulder the day the Caterpillar Man's story came to light. "She does deserve better."

"I hurt her, and she deserves a life without pain."

"You're right."

"Tell her I can do better. Tell her she won't have to go through this again and that I'm sorry."

Kyle nodded slowly. "I'll do it."

"I owe you—for taking care of her."

"I wouldn't—"

"Shut up. I'm grateful. I'm only going to say it once."

Kyle scraped his knuckles across his closed mouth. "You're welcome."

"If it were the other way around...you know I'd do the same for you. Right?"

He fought a wince. "I wouldn't go that far."

"YOU'RE QUIET."

"Nope." Kyle drank his beer and kept to himself, training his peripheral eye on the corner of the room where a clutch of men huddled. It was several days after his phone call with Gavin. After his night with Harmony.

He'd made another call before waking her and driving her back to the inn to beat the sunrise. Like Cole, he had a few contacts. Through the years on the teams, he'd rubbed shoulders with government officials. After a high-profile mission in the Persian Gulf, one had offered to be of service to Kyle should he ever need a favor. Kyle had cashed in that offer, seeking information on the whereabouts of a parolee from Escambia County Prison.

Olivia Leighton plunked another draft on the bar in front of him. "You've been nursing that one since you got here." She took the first glass glazed with the tavern logo from him and set it aside. Then she leaned on the bar, planting her chin on her hand. "You know who they are?"

"Who?" he asked, vague. He took a sip of the house ale.

"The people you've been spying on since you got here."

"I don't like the word *spy*." He kept his voice muted under the crush of rock 'n' roll.

"My spouse, the living thesaurus, headed home an hour ago," she informed him. "Spying's as good a word as any."

"I'm gathering intel."

She grinned. "And I'm butting in." She reached over the bar to comb the hair over his brow with her crimson nails in maternal fashion. "You never come here solo. You always meet someone. Or bring someone."

"Hmm."

"Like Harmony."

The name nabbed his attention. The muscles around his navel clutched. Heat built behind them. He did his best to look unaffected at least. "Huh."

Olivia was as incisive as his mother. Also, she'd known him his whole life. He closed down the line of thought on Harmony and tried to tune out the low hum of lust he'd been harboring since she left his vessel. Going back to his subtle review of the corner table, he returned with, "Do *you* know who they are?"

"The one who's built like a forklift is your dad's old pal, Dusty Harbuck," Olivia confirmed. "I hear he's on parole again. Your father did time at the end of high school, as I recall, 'cause Dusty let him take the fall for something he didn't do."

The details were identical to those his father had given him. "The one to his right—which of his brothers is that?" Kyle wondered.

"Clint, the womanizer," Olivia said. "He took a shine to Briar. She steered clear, and wisely. Not the type you want to bring home. Cole taught him a lesson, too, and Clint's hardly looked at her since."

"What's his rap sheet look like?"

"Did a nickel," Olivia revealed. "Can't remember what for. This was fifteen years back. Something to do with the Kennards."

The Kennards. Kyle drank his beer, slowly. He ran his tongue over his teeth as he lowered the pint back to the bar. "And the last guy?"

Olivia met Kyle's stare with the grim conviction that, he was sure, mirrored his. "Can we leave him at bad news?"

He waited, unblinking, as he took another glug from the pint.

Olivia sighed. "You believe in step-uncles?"

"Depends," Kyle answered. He tipped the pint toward her by the handle. "I believe you're as good an aunt as any. If not by blood, then kismet."

A smile touched Olivia's mouth. Affection shone from her as she touched her hand to his wrist.

"But if that man there's Radley Kennard's brother," Kyle considered, "then he's no uncle of mine, or ever was."

"True that." Olivia turned her head to William who edged by her to fetch more customers on the other end of the bar. "Shooks, bring your mama a whiskey."

"Comin' up," William acknowledged. With a nod to Kyle, he went back to work, choosing not to eavesdrop.

Kyle tipped his chin to the man, then focused again on the operation at hand. "Which brother is he?" Kyle asked. "Radley had several."

Olivia nodded. Radley, Adrian's first husband, had been part of an unrefined tribe of lowlifes. "Cecil, the youngest. That's all that's left of the brothers Kennard now—Cecil and Liddell. Emmis is dead. Shooting accident. Dorsie went to county for murder one. Tarvis up and disappeared sometime within the last decade, but rumor is he's dead, too, and it was the family that did it. And we all know what happened to your stepdad."

Kyle remembered well the night Radley Kennard had met an ugly demise. He remembered the yelling and pounding at the cottage door. He remembered the glazed fear in his mother's eyes even as she made him run to his room, lock the door and call for help. When Kyle heard the kitchen window shatter, he'd gone out the bedroom window and run to James's house. Later, he learned that Radley hadn't just broken in. He'd entered with a buck knife and intent to kill.

Adrian had held him off as long as she could, giving him the fight Kyle wished he could have given him for her. James had arrived in time to finish it. Radley was sent away, first to a hospital with fairly serious injuries, then prison.

Olivia spoke up again, quietly. "I'm sure you know the rest of the story, too—how he paroled out at some point?"

"Yeah." James had kept track of him, even if Adrian had moved on. Kyle had done his own tracing, too, using some of the same official channels to supplement his father's old underworld connections. "Something about 'good behavior.'"

"There's little justice in the world," Olivia noted. She took a topped-off jigger from her son and raised it to him before tapping it to the lip of Kyle's pint. "And won't be, unless lawmakers figure out that wife-beaters and sex offenders are too softly penalized."

Kyle felt a strike of emotion as Olivia threw the whiskey back and set the jigger on the bar, unflinching. Radley's break-ins had been regular events from the time Adrian had left the marriage and bought the cottage near the bay. Olivia had been there, loaded with her granddaddy's double-barrel shotgun and no qualms about shooting the worm bastard. She'd been there to calm Adrian and reassure the small boy who'd felt helpless to protect her against the Marvel-worthy villain screaming on the other side of the door. Kyle turned his hand into hers and held it firmly. "They say he's dead, too."

Again, Olivia nodded. "Heart disease or some such thing?" She clicked her tongue when he acknowledged it. "Too easy."

Indeed. Something far more painful and imaginative would've been more apropos to Kyle's mind. He spun the pint glass on the bar. "Here's a question for you."

"Hit me, baby."

"You believe it's as small a world as they say?"

Olivia offered Kyle a teeth-baring grin. "Honey, I've been around far more years than I care to admit."

"You're the best-lookin' thirty-five-year-old I know," he said and grinned back, wide.

She laughed her big booming laugh and chucked him beneath the chin. "I ever tell you you're like my own son?"

"Hey now," William said as he prepared a margarita close by.

"No favorites," Olivia claimed, holding up her hands. "To answer your question, yes. As little wooden Dutch children have been known to say, 'It's a small world.'"

"Hey. Big guy."

Olivia straightened as Kyle turned his head slowly to the whip-thin gentleman behind him. Kyle had seen him move away from the corner, flanked by his burly Harbuck counterparts. "Talking to me?" he replied.

"You're damn right I'm talkin' to you," Cecil said. Up close, Kyle saw he looked as mean as he was rumored to be. He had a prominent eyetooth and hard, industrial gray peepers. "You're the son of that Carlton she-bitch, ain't ya?"

Kyle spared a glance for the hand Cecil pressed into the top of his shoulder. "That's me, I guess," he mused as he blindly chose a toothpick from a small crystal bowl on the bar. He lifted it, tested one of the pointy ends. "The son of a bitch."

Cecil guffawed. It was seven-thirty and the man already smelled like the inside of a distillery. "Everybody says you're that POS James Bracken's boy. But we know the truth."

"Oh yeah?" Kyle asked, feigning interest.

"You're my big brother, Radley's kid," Cecil informed him. The hand hardened on Kyle as he looked to Clint and Dusty Harbuck for agreement. "Look at him. He's the spittin' image of Rad."

Clint didn't seem to care one way or the other as he shrugged and took a slow pull from his longneck. Dusty studied Kyle with grim curiosity.

Kyle pursed his lips. "Huh. Well, sure, if you mean big, dense and liable to scare ticks off a dog."

Cecil stopped smiling abruptly. His brow furrowed. "What'd you say, boy?"

Clint spoke up. "He's callin' your brother ugly, dumbass."

"Not ugly exactly," Kyle amended. "Every one of you Kennards are bound to look similar." He spread his fingers in front of Cecil's head and rotated his palm in circles. "And I think I speak for everyone when I say we've seen prettier on Rocky Balboa after he got the shit kicked out of him by Apollo Creed."

"Heh," Dusty cracked. "He's got a mouth on him like Adrian."

Kyle ignored him and offered Cecil a come-hither motion. "Come on. Once. Let's hear you say it."

"Say what?" Cecil asked, brow wrinkling further.

"*Adriiiiaaaaan!*'" Kyle prompted. Behind him, Olivia laughed. William began crooning the *Rocky* training medley.

Cecil's facial muscles twitched. He leaned down to Kyle's seated level and lowered his voice. "I know you don't want to take this outside."

"Now who would want a thing like that?" It was *exactly* what he wanted, but he trusted Cecil and his Harbuck tagalongs to stay upriver on that point.

Cecil sniffed and ran a finger under his nose, propping one foot on the bottom rung of Kyle's stool. "You'll show some respect and apologize."

Kyle looked around in consideration. The jukebox was still crashing loud into the night, but the verbal skirmish had drawn the attention of most of Olivia and William's patrons anyway. "I'm sorry, man." He clapped his hand over the one Cecil still had locked on his shoulder. "I had no idea you were so sensitive."

Cecil snatched his grip out from under Kyle's. Kyle took a hurried sip from his pint as a cacophony of laughter spread around the tavern. Then Cecil raised his voice over the crowd and music and said, "It's a shame your mama's such a whore she don't know which of your daddies is the real one."

Then the music did stop. The amusement dried up. People came to a standstill. Kyle spared a glance for Olivia who looked as tightly wound as the bullies at his back. Any minute she'd hunt up that old shotty. He set down the pint and pushed up from the stool, bringing himself to his full height. Shoulders back, he pivoted to Cecil, levity diminished. "Now it's you who needs to apologize."

"Why?" Cecil asked. "Your feelin's hurt?"

"No," Kyle told him. "I know who my father is, and he isn't a scumbag like you or any of the rest of your ill-bred kin. But if you're going to insult my mother, you'll do so facing her so she can speak for herself."

Cecil shook his head and bared his teeth. "If Radley'd raised you like he shoulda, you'd know a man's best served when his woman ain't speakin' at all." He looked to Olivia who glared back. "That's what's wrong with this world, you ask me."

Olivia gave a sour laugh. "Oh, Cecil. Nobody ever asks you anything."

"Shut your pie hole," Cecil clipped, pointing at her. "You think I don't know who keeps this bar goin'? Everybody's thinkin' it; I'll just say it. You honey-trapped that writer so you could steal his millions. Ain't nobody in this town doesn't think you're a stone-cold, gold-diggin' floozy."

Kyle's fist closed over Cecil's forearm, hard enough to restrict the blood flow. "I'm starting to think outdoors is the best place for nut jobs like you."

Cecil raised his brows. "You're not gonna be a pussy and bring any of your woman friends, are ya'?"

"Let's go," Kyle said and nothing more. He released Cecil, so he could file out silently with Clint and Dusty at his back. Pulling his wallet from the back pocket of his jeans, Kyle peeled out a crisp twenty-dollar bill and set it on the bar. He took off his hat, his favorite, and set it next to the money.

"Kyle."

He lifted his eyes to Olivia. When she said nothing more, just looked at him in warning, he winked at her simply and clamped the toothpick in the corner of his mouth. Then he moved through the crowd the other boys had parted for him and followed them out into the torrid night.

CHAPTER FIFTEEN

THE COTTAGE ON the bay was well-kept. The mail-box was still painted red with the name CARL-TON artfully scrolled on it in his mother's schoolgirl cursive. The grass and small garden beds in the postage-stamp-size yard were kept up religiously. It was his father, Kyle knew, who'd made sure of it through the years after reselling the house he'd lived in next door. He'd redone the cottage's front porch one weekend while Adrian was away, building a covered deck from the front door to the end of the house and replanting all her bushes and buds around it. Kyle remembered how, before they moved to The Farm, the couple used to swing there on warm lazy evenings like this.

The swing was empty. He could hear voices within. The door was locked. He used his key, the one he hadn't given up. He wasn't sure he ever could. Then he pushed through it into the place that had been the primary home of his childhood.

The voices were high and happy. His mother and Mavis sat on the sofa. They were both smiling. Miracles, he mused. He got a jolt when he realized that the center of their attention belonged to the laughing girl sprawled on the living room rug with Harmony, fiery untamed hair loose again, and in matching pajamas. She tickled Bea mercilessly.

Kyle watched for a moment from the shadows. Bea's rolling, high-pitched giggles and Harmony's singsong voice as she counted Bea's ribs one by one in a familiar ditty. One of the straps of Harmony's pajama top had slipped down an almond-hued shoulder. He could see the path of freckles trailing down her arm, the bare curve of her throat.

There was too much tangled up inside him already. And the thoughts for Harmony he'd tried to harpoon earlier, the feelings and the slippery knot of need, rolled together, nearly choking him.

They had hardly been together, much less *together* together, since their night on the *Hellraiser*. From that point, she'd spent her time between her daughter and the airfield, while Kyle split his between the family businesses, helping Adrian and Mavis keep them in shape. He'd never noticed how big of a balancing act it was until his business-minded father wasn't there to juggle with them. Any spare time had been spent at the city jail between visits with James, investigators and lawyers, dodging the local press or digging up past wrongs.

He wanted her. Again. And again, at that. For now, he looked and needed and wished that circumstances were normal. That they could've found more time for unguarded moments. For touching. Just her hand. He wanted to hold her hand like normal people did walking down the street. He wanted his fists all up in that tumble-down hair. He wanted to lose himself in her. It had felt *so good* to lose himself in her, however short a while he'd spent there.

Not tonight, he reminded himself, finally catching Adrian's eyes. She jerked hard when she saw his figure lingering near the door. Recognition struck and she closed her eyes briefly. She gave him a tight smile.

Before she could speak and alert the others to his presence, he nodded to the door in invitation. She got up quietly and began to walk to him.

He opened the door, glad his father kept it WD-40'ed, and held it so she could pass in front of him. Glancing back, he caught Mavis's eyes. He touched a finger to his mouth. She rolled her eyes and went back to watching the game. It was Bea's turn to tickle Harmony.

Harmony's brassy, wild laugh floated to him even as he crossed the porch to where Adrian stood close to the swing. She tilted her head. "You're bleeding."

He lifted his fingers to his face, pulled them away from his cheek. Damn it, he *was* bleeding. He cursed and muttered, "Damn Harbuck's a slippery mother—"

"Harbuck?" Adrian repeated, struck by the name. "*Dusty* Harbuck?"

"Well, it wasn't Clint," Kyle said, dabbing at the cut. "He's slower than Dutch Gold syrup in January."

Adrian's eyes flared. "Why exactly were you fighting Clint and Dusty Harbuck?" She wrinkled her nose. "And why do you smell like the underside of a bridge?"

"It rubbed off of the other guy," he explained, offhand.

She goggled at him. "There were three? And the Harbucks! Are you *kidding* me, Kyle?"

He placed a hand on her arm. "Mom. You need to sit down."

When he gestured to the swing, Adrian frowned and lowered to it. It wasn't so much an acquiescence. Not with her spine like a dowel and her mouth a thin line.

Kyle let out a breath. Then he lowered to the seat next to her. Neither of them rolled their feet to send the swing into motion. They sat with the established cozy neighborhood nestled around them. The air was thick enough to spoon to their mouths. It would taste like bay water and seep lukewarm into their bellies like fish stock sprinkled with topsoil, loaded with sea salt and a pinch of ozone. They could still hear the shrieking giggles and the singsong voices from inside the house. He was touched—that Harmony had thought to bring Bea to the cottage in an effort to take his mother's mind off everything.

He didn't know how to deliver this. So he just put it out there, as gingerly as he could. "Dad's set to be transferred to county in five days."

Adrian said nothing, arms locked over her chest.

He couldn't watch her fortify herself. There was more, and he wasn't sure she'd be able to bear it. She was strong. Rock solid. But he'd seen her broken. It was what he feared most—seeing her break again. Kyle scraped his knuckles over his mouth. "My CO called this morning. I'm back in training the Monday after next."

"So we're running out of time," Adrian concluded. She licked her lips.

"It's more than that," he said delicately. "Mom… we've turned over every stone. Johansson's tried. It's not going his way, despite the departmental resources. Cole can't unlock any more networks than he has already. Holmes and Wilson have attempted to trace the explosives. They tried to trace the car. They've done fingerprints. Interviews. Door to door's. They've combed the woods again. Harmony's even turned over the Piper."

"Are you trying to tell me that it's time to throw in the towel?" she asked, quietly. "I won't be done until your father's free. I don't care where they take him. I don't care for how long. I won't stop until he is home."

Kyle caught his knee bouncing. "I've been following a lead. A small one."

"And why don't I know about it?" Adrian wondered out loud. The bite under the words was clear.

"Bear with me. When I told Dad someone had likely disguised himself as him to place the Trans Am at the garage, something popped. A memory."

It took a moment. Then she said, scarcely breathing, "Dusty."

"The guy just paroled, and he's bound to the jurisdiction of Florida. I got a call, though, earlier tonight. He was spotted at Tavern of the Graces. By the time I got there he was meeting Clint." It was here Kyle hesitated once more. "And Cecil Kennard."

Adrian's lips parted.

Kyle looked away. The skin across his knuckles was cracked. He turned them out of the light so she wouldn't see. "They recognized me. Tried to bring your name into it. We decided to finish it outside."

She said nothing, although he could practically hear the gears shifting again. She was a staunch military parent, but she hated the idea of fighting. Likely because she'd been on the wrong end of it.

"If it makes you feel any better," he said experimentally, "I dropped them off at the hospital, after."

She shook her head at him. "And what if they

press charges? I assume there were witnesses. Do you think I can afford to have you thrown in jail, too, Kyle Zachariah?"

"Give me some credit. There were witnesses to the jawing that led up to it, but I didn't want Olivia or William to follow. And as good a backup as I'm sure he is, I wasn't keen on bringing Cole into it either."

"What exactly was the point in fighting them?"

"They weren't likely to give up the information I wanted with sweet talk," he indicated.

"This isn't about vengeance, is it?" she pressed. "The years we spent under the Kennard yoke? Or Dusty's betrayal? Have I taught you nothing about life? You might not forget. Sometimes you can't forgive. But you *have* to move on or you won't survive."

"Tonight I was more concerned with the present," he said tightly. "Though if I made Dusty Harbuck squeal, don't think it didn't give me a snatched bit of pleasure."

She sat, mouth folded in disapproval. "They could still press charges. You dropped them off. They'll have your marks on them."

"Who says I left any?" When she only sighed, he went on. "I wanted Dusty's confession. But after I saw he was meeting a Kennard, it was Cecil who made me most curious. It didn't take much to get him to tell me he and his family know about Dad's transfer. And when he gets to county…"

Kyle sucked in another breath because the blood was swimming back, fast, into his ears. Releasing it, he said, "When he's moved into general population, someone will be waiting. Someone who's got no bones whatsoever about finishing the job."

"Job," Adrian echoed. She pressed her fingertips into his shirtsleeve. "You don't mean..." A ragged shudder took her by surprise. "James. Oh, God, James." She stood quickly. "Detective Johansson. We need to call him."

"I've already gone down that road," he said, watching her pace. "There's not much he can do, or anyone else in the department, for that matter." Before she could argue, he cut in. "Mom. A forced confession wasn't going to get us anywhere with the police."

"Then *why* did you do it?" she argued, anger white-hot in contrast to her depthless gaze. "You could've taken your suspicions to Johansson first. You could've used legitimate channels. Now your father's going to prison, his *life* is at stake, we're out of time and your actions have painted us into a corner!"

"We're not completely out of time," he said, level and cool under her censure. "Nor are we completely out of options." He spread his hands. "Remember to be open-minded." When she only narrowed her eyes, he revealed, "We finish this ourselves. Here and now."

"Kyle. No."

"You *want* Dad to get shanked by Radley's brother in the prison yard?"

"No!" she said again, firm. "We can warn him. But I'll follow whatever means I have to in order to save you from confronting Papa Smurf. Do you know how many people have walked into Osias Kennard's swamp and disappeared? Even if you don't wind up as some kind snack for his gators, he'll have you hauled off for trespassing. Can you trust yourself to keep a cool head in the face of the man who molded the one that tore our lives apart?"

"I'm going in without arms," he admitted. "I've spoken to Cole. He'll be there, too. Tomorrow morning. He'll utilize some of his old diplomacy tactics. I'll…utilize restraint."

"Bullies see neither diplomacy nor reason," she said.

"I'm doing this for you," Kyle told her, standing, "as much as I'm doing it for Dad. Let me finish it, or at least try."

Adrian pressed her fingers between her eyes. Her head lowered, and he watched her chest lift and settle on an unsteady breath. "I'm going with you."

The statement sank like a ship to the deepest realm of him where only blind sea cucumbers and other wrecks lived. It carried tsunami-size ripples everywhere else. *Well, shit.* "Sure?"

She was pale and clear-eyed. They could hear

the laughter inside the house dying and the soothing sound of Mavis's subdued tones as she read from *The Gruffalo's Child*. Bea responded in titters to Harmony's sound effects.

It nearly hurt to listen because he knew now whose hand had brushed up against Bea's as she was given her caterpillars. He knew who'd set out to destroy the Piper and Harmony. It had taken a *great deal* of restraint not to lay into Cecil Kennard more than necessary. "There's one other thing," he told her. "There's a reason why they chose now as opposed to all the time they've had before."

Adrian embraced herself wholly, and Kyle wished he wasn't the one to have to tell her how close to home it really hit. "The Farm has expanded under you and Dad's ownership. It's tripled in size and value since Granddaddy's passing. When you add B.S., it's an impressive chunk of real estate. It borders on another wooded enclave. I've heard Dad talk about bidding on it, but it wasn't until I spoke with Byron Strong a few days ago that I realized who he'd have to bid against."

"Let me guess," Adrian said dismally.

"It's why he hesitated," Kyle expounded. "There's only a few acres of pine between B.S.'s airfield and Osias Kennard's swamp. I didn't think it was enough motive at first. Not for everything we know that the Kennards have done up to this point. But then I think how far Radley took things years ago, despite the divorce or the restraining order. It turned him into something animal."

Adrian swallowed. The top button of her blouse had been left undone. She gathered the lapels of the crisp linen together at the base of her throat. "He was animal. Bred by one, too. Only Osias could incite such viciousness over a simple land dispute."

"We're doing stovetop popcorn if anyone's interested."

Kyle's body tuned itself to Harmony as she ventured out onto the porch. Cautiously, he turned his eyes to her. He couldn't handle her in the pajama plaid any more than he could handle her in her godforsaken green dress. She seemed to sense the enormity between him and Adrian. Her smile was muted. "Neither of us can seem to get the little fire-breather to wind down for the night."

Adrian moved herself to smile back. "Popcorn sounds fine."

"Great." Harmony looked to Kyle for a second motion.

He was already moving. In light of everything, he couldn't stop himself from going to her. He tossed an "excuse me" to Adrian before taking Harmony's face in his hands. His mouth clashed against hers in a hot, longing surge.

Something caught in her throat, breathy. Her legs locked, but she didn't buckle or bow. Chin lifting, she offered her lips to him, parting them and letting him take a long, strong draught.

When he broke away, he wasn't any more steady. Damn it. He was never steady around her. "I missed you," he whispered. "Sorry." Gentling his hold, he skimmed his palms from her cheeks to the line of her throat. He lowered a simple kiss to the plane of her shoulder next to the renegade strap already slipping toward the slope of her arm again.

"I missed you, too." Harmony's reply was ragged. Her eyes closed, and her arms tightened around him as a high-wattage grin broke out on her face.

"Well."

Harmony jerked at the sound of his mother's voice. Kyle lifted his head and turned it slowly to Adrian.

She licked her lips. "How long has this been going on?"

"Um." Harmony pushed the hair back from her cheek in an uncharacteristic nervous gesture that was ridiculously cute. "A week or two, I guess."

"Longer," Kyle admitted. "For me."

Harmony's gaze warmed to his. She rubbed her lips together, trying to contain the grin. "Me, too," she murmured. She rose to her toes and kissed him as he'd kissed her, clearly not finding Adrian's presence all that awkward after all.

"Mama?"

AMBER LEIGH WILLIAMS   313

This time it was Kyle who snatched away. He set Harmony back a step to put a safe distance between them, but by the look of Bea's face, it was too late.

"WHY DO YOU kiss him like that?"

Mavis came through the door, assessed the situation and made a grab for Bea. "It's time to butter those kernels, kiddo."

"Why?" Bea demanded. Her eyes seared into Harmony, the flush of laughter dying on her cheeks.

Harmony glanced at Kyle, blank. When he appeared to be just as lost as she felt, Harmony cleared her throat. Bea waited for an explanation and it was Harmony's job to give her one. "Um. Bea…" Feeling like she needed to be eye to eye with her, Harmony went to her knees. "Kyle and I… We just…" She searched and searched for the right justification.

Bea's bottom lip began to quiver. "*You don't* kiss him like that!"

"Bea," Mavis said.

Bea's lips pursed. Harmony had never seen her eyes burn so bright with indignation. "Say you won't kiss him, never. Say it."

Harmony spread her hands. "I'm sorry. I had no idea it would upset you like this."

"I'm not *upset*," Bea said. The quaver was in

her chin and she was beginning to tear up. "I'm mad. I'm mad at you, Mama!"

"Okay," Harmony said, nodding. "Okay. You can be mad."

"No," Kyle said quickly.

Harmony felt him beside her. He bent at the waist to snag Bea's attention. "Don't be mad at your mother. Be mad at me. I...kissed her first."

"No," Bea said with a shake of her head. She stamped her foot. "No. Don't do that. I don't want you to do that."

Harmony closed her mouth carefully. She had *not* seen this coming. There had always been a serious attachment between Bea and Kyle. Harmony hadn't thought that seeing her and Kyle canoodling would offend Bea so. Everyone could feel the tantrum brewing. With anger and crocodile tears building on the rim of her sweet, round cheeks, it was bound to be the epic, devastating kind.

Harmony reached out to her, wanting to console her. Hoping it would be enough.

Kyle spoke instead, bringing the devastation. "All right. I won't do it again."

Harmony looked up at him. "What?" she nearly blurted. Thankfully, Bea jumped ahead. "Promise?" she asked. "Promise you won't ever again?"

Kyle met Harmony's stare. She glimpsed regret and apology and blinked rapidly in succession.

"Yes," he agreed. "I promise."

"Good." Still, Bea's bottom lip protruded. She sniffled, rubbing the stuffed unicorn in her arms under her nose. Eyes squeezed shut, they remained so for several seconds after she lowered the soft-haired toy. Yes, it was bedtime.

Harmony touched her cautiously on the wrists. "Why don't you go get ready for bed?"

Bea's eyes opened. They were tired and red. Her nose had started to run at the onset of emotions. "No. Popcorn. You said I could have popcorn. I want popcorn, Mama. Now."

"Easy," Adrian said, stepping into the fray. She offered Bea her hand. "Come with me. I'll get you the popcorn. Then we can brush our teeth and make a big pallet on the living room floor."

A smile quavered on the edges of Bea's mouth. "Okay." She folded her hand into Adrian's and turned quiet and slump-shouldered for the door.

When it slowly shut behind them, Harmony didn't move. It took her several seconds to realize neither Kyle nor Mavis had either. *What just happened here?*

Mavis cleared her throat. "That went…swell."

Harmony couldn't be out here. Not with her stomach churning and something happening in her chest. Something heavy. She knew grief could strike quick as a viper.

She stood, finally. Arms hanging heavy at her sides, perplexity webbed through her. She sidestepped Kyle, aiming for the door. "I should go in and help."

He started to stop her. He began to touch her. He didn't. "Wait. I need to be up-front about something."

I can't. Mavis always said Harmony reverted to pissed-off mode when she felt moony. She was right, Harmony realized. Like Bea, she felt a bad moon rising and wished Kyle would let her go before she turned it on him.

Mavis asked, "Are you going to tell us how your face got messed up?"

Harmony focused on him. Sure enough, there were marks on his features, some blood along the wide point of his cheekbone. When the urge to touch rocked her up to her toes, she planted her feet back to the porch boards and chastised herself.

"Mom's decided that tomorrow morning she'll be traveling with me and Cole to Kennard territory," Kyle admitted.

"Kennard?" Mavis struggled for what to say.

Harmony helped her out by inquiring for both of them, "Why?"

Kyle gathered himself. In a flash, he'd disappeared behind the hard bulwark that made him look both battle-tested and battle ready. "We're confident they—or some of them—are involved in this."

They stared. Beyond the knee-jerk horror and

incredulity, Harmony recovered the impulse to speak. "They'll kill you. They'll take one look at you and Adrian, shoot and kill you, even if you shoot first. An eye for an eye. So what's the point?"

"Yes," Mavis reiterated. "What's your point?"

"They're going to crush Dad," Kyle said carefully. "That was the master plan. Beyond making B.S. fail or putting The Farm to auction, they knew if they did things right, he would wind up going to county where he'd be rubbing elbows with hard killers like Dorsie Kennard."

Mavis made a noise in her throat. Automatically, Harmony put an arm over her friend's shoulders. She offered silent commiseration when she felt Mavis shudder. Mavis never shuddered. Not unless she was on the brink of a seizure, Harmony knew as much as any other member of the family.

Kyle scanned Mavis's complexion. Underneath the dark freckles, she was a shade beyond porcelain. Kyle cursed and tugged her to him. He wound an arm around her waist and hugged her against his side. "Steady, baby girl." He hugged her tighter. "Steady."

Mavis jerked a nod, breathing carefully. When Harmony made a move for the door to retrieve Adrian, Mavis snapped, "No." She shook her head when Harmony looked back. "No," she said, more gently. "I'm fine." It took her several minutes, though, to gather herself. "When are they moving Dad?" she asked him.

Kyle didn't let go of her. "We have some time," he said. He'd dropped the battle veneer. Right now, he was nothing more than a big brother doing what he could to protect his baby sister. Trying uselessly to defend her from the illness that lay within her and the never-ending slew of Bracken woes. "A few days."

"What about the detective?" Harmony asked quietly. "Johansson. Have you told him any of this?"

"I've got nothing solid to substantiate it. Just word of mouth. Coerced."

"I want to go with you," Harmony informed him, taking a step toward him. "You'll let me come with you." When he said nothing, she said, "We're a team. We stand together. We fight together. No matter what. *Right?*"

"You can't, Harm." She gaped at him, and he hurried on to explain, "You're capable. I've got no doubts on that score. I know this is your fight, too, and that it's personal…"

The scowl wore in. She felt dead inside. "Then what's the problem?"

"They need you," he returned. "I need you with Mavis. Preferably at the inn. And Bea. Carrots, you cannot… *We* cannot leave Bea in a position with the only parent she's got left walking into a situation you might not walk out of."

She searched him, darting back and forth across his set features. "This is crazy," she breathed. She said it again, louder, the words piercing, fractured and thick.

"I don't know any other way," he admitted. "I've tried thinking my way around it. The only real course we've got is going in there without arms and showing our cards. Maybe some bluffing…"

"I don't like it," she said.

"I never said I liked it," he returned. "Knowing what we know of Osias and the rest of them, it'll likely be a shot in the dark. But it's the only chance we've got. That is, without breaking into city lockup and breaking Dad out ourselves."

Mavis spoke. "I like that plan. I'll drive the getaway car. I pick the Shelby."

"Sure," Kyle weighed, thinking it over. "It's rare, conspicuous. Perfect for our flashy *Back to the Future* escape plan. You're short and scrappy. You can be Marty McFly."

"Yeah, but where are we going to get the plutonium?" she asked. "Without the plutonium, we could never achieve the 1.21 gigawatts necessary…"

"…to make time travel possible." He nodded defeat. Closing his eyes briefly, he circled his thumb over a small space of her sleeve. "This is heavy."

"This sucks," Mavis amended, and the sentiment was heartfelt.

Kyle sought Harmony over Mavis's head as he lowered his chin to her hair. *It sucks. In so many ways*, he said without words.

She made herself look away. She made herself keep the anger from slipping.

Because to be without anger, to confront either the dismal pangs of loss or the mounting anxieties over what could happen to him tomorrow... she'd never make it through the night with heart and mind intact.

BEA FOUGHT SLEEP. She fought it like a person drowning. Her anger toward Harmony lasted through their bedtime routine. She turned away from the storybook Harmony tried to read. She stayed facing the wall while Harmony silently switched off the light, leaving the glow of the night-light. It had been Kyle's at some point, but neither of them needed to think about Kyle...

Bea remained tense when Harmony cuddled her. When Bea didn't relax, Harmony rubbed circles over her back. She sang softly, wishing she knew how to sound on key at least. Still, her daughter didn't sleep or speak.

Almost against her will, Bea eventually sank into dreamland. When Harmony heard her inhales elongate and her small body ease, she swallowed hard against the knot in her throat. "I'm sorry," she mouthed. She kissed Bea's curls, wishing she could assure her child that things would be better tomorrow.

She wanted to forget that things wouldn't be. She wanted not to think. Sleep, she thought. It would bring her one step closer to the next day, but it was the easiest route of escape. She felt weary enough for it, the weight in her chest dragging her from the small corner bedroom.

A shadow formed in front of her as she opened the door. She jumped, then settled when she recognized the beard and mass of torso.

"Sorry," he said simply.

"You're still here," she murmured, closing the door quietly at her back. She couldn't see his eyes in the dark. "Have you been waiting?"

She saw him nod. When he didn't breach the silence, she leaned against the door. Their situation was knotted between them, but neither of them could untangle it. How could they after everything?

"That day at the airfield," he began, "when we saw each other again, you asked me what I was afraid of."

Harmony nodded.

He hesitated. "There is something."

"Tell me," she insisted.

"Mom thinks I'm afraid of change, but there's something bigger." He reached back for his neck and scrubbed. "I'm not afraid of death. I'm prepared to die in service to my country. But the thing that's kept me up nights is wondering what it would do to Mom. What if it pushed Dad back into the bottle? Mavis. Her health. And there's you. Even if we hadn't crossed the line, it would hurt you. When I saw the look on Bea's face, I remembered. I've put you right back where you were five years ago."

He grew restless in the short hall between bedrooms, pacing. "If we took this where I think it could go, I'd be setting you up for what happened to you before. Only there'd be no one to stand beside you when I'm gone. As much as I like to think Gavin would step in, his behavior has left me skeptical."

She closed her eyes. Slowly shaking her head, she lowered her face into her palm.

"I can't leave you alone," he went on. His hands were in his pockets, his posture caving. "I can't leave you to go through what you went through with Benji. It kills me just to…just to think about it, Harm. I should have been a man and let you go after our talk on the *Hellraiser*."

"Yeah," she uttered, dismal. "It's a pity you're not a prince."

He stopped pacing. She knew it was foolish, like not letting go of him when she realized she was falling, but she touched him. The flat of her hand skimmed from his shoulder to his elbow. She closed the distance, answering the call to rub her lips against the trident beneath his sleeve. "Kyle."

"Carrots." His fingers sifted through the reams of her hair to embrace the back of her scalp.

She turned her cheek to his skin when his thumb found a place behind her ear to caress. They leaned. Rescuing a ragged exhale, she tortured the both of them further by asking, "Say the extraneous details didn't exist. Say your father wasn't in danger and the Kennards weren't in the picture. Say it was just Kyle and Harmony, and Bea was all for it. Do you think this could've had the legs? Do you think you and I could've gone places?"

"Great big places," he acknowledged sadly. "All the places I never thought I'd see again." He ducked his head against hers, tilting his face away so as not to tempt himself. She held on, nestling when he didn't extract himself from her. "You're not saying all this now because of where you're headed tomorrow," she hoped aloud.

He backed away, edging along the wall toward the dim light from the living room. "Look after Bea and Mavis tomorrow. I need you here, Harm. I need you." He seemed to want to say more but moved on instead.

She trailed behind as he beelined for the door. Mavis and Adrian had gone to bed. She followed him on to the porch.

Don't let him go, you idiot! the voice inside her screamed when he went quickly down the steps. "Wait," she demanded.

He stopped. "I need to hash things out with your father. We're going to need some strategy…"

She feared for him. She feared the possibilities. All that fear and anxiety she'd felt in the wake of Benji's death and the face of impending motherhood rained all over her. It was torrential. She lunged. From the steps, her face was level with his. She confronted him as she had in the inn garden, only this time there was an ardency behind the kiss that made her gasp. His lips parted. She'd caught him off guard again, and she didn't mind taking advantage, deepening the kiss until she was sure she got her point across. She wanted to kiss him until she got her fill, but then they'd still be here when Bea woke up and her father drove in to pick him up for their ill-fated jaunt to Kennard lands.

He grabbed her by the arms and latched. Panting between them, he seemed to brace himself from her. Buoy and buffer, he held her up when she felt like sinking.

"Sorry," she said. Then, "Screw it. I'm not sorry. I love you. I love you, Chief Petty Officer Bracken."

A furrow appeared between his brows despite the flicker of hard need that turned lakes into oceans. They swept over her and she found a thread of courage, enough to smile. "Don't worry, K.Z.B. You can still keep your promise to Bea. After all, *I* kissed *you*." Grabbing his face, she kissed him again one hard final time before backing blindly up the steps and telling herself *enough*.

Inside, she locked the door and looked out through the window to watch the darkness swallow him whole as he disappeared down the road.

Darkness took hold of her, too. The hell she'd thought she'd learned not to toe pulled her in. And once more she was back to contemplating a life without the person her spirit had chosen.

CHAPTER SIXTEEN

KYLE PEERED THROUGH the windshield of Cole's pickup at the rutted dirt road leading up to the Kennard house. On either side, a marshy wood had grown thorny and uninviting. The road was straight-up Alabama clay. Standing rainwater inside the ruts had been stained the glaring red-orange that was a regular menace to anyone used to cleaning the underside of vehicles. If he rolled down the window, he was sure he'd be able to hear the drone of mosquitos.

The farther the truck bumped along the back-country lane, the farther any of them felt from the pleasant streets of downtown. Kyle checked the GPS as Cole slowly navigated the truck around a particularly pitted section. "Two hundred yards and closing," he announced.

"Remember," Cole said, "as we discussed, do not engage."

"Yep. And don't walk like a cop." When Cole only frowned, Kyle nodded at him. "You know what I'm talking about."

"It's been thirty-two years since I quit the force…"

"And you still walk like a cop," Kyle informed him.

"All right," was Cole's measured response. "I'll trust you not to walk like a commando on a take-down mission."

Kyle fought the compulsion to check his weapon. True, he was carrying—he always did. But he planned to keep his sidearm at the small of his back. Even with its comfortable weight there, he felt as if he were going in naked.

This is crazy.

Harmony's words kept floating back to him. His Spidey sense was listlessly plucking the strings of his nervous system. And Mom was sitting in the backseat, unarmed, unspeaking and generally out of place.

He hadn't argued her decision to come. Nor had he tried talking her out of it. He'd wound up stuck in the boggy middle between sons sho knew better and SEALs who operate better without attachments. For years, he hadn't been a part of ops involving Gavin or Benji. Now his mother was doing a ride-along to the homegrown equivalent of Kashmir.

Damn right, this was crazy. He chanced a look at her. Dark sunglasses in place, she struck him as small in her commonplace choice of jeans and a button-up. If not for the fact that she was wor-

rying her lower lip, she would've looked unflap-
pable. "Mom," he said, drawing her gaze from the
side window. "Holding up back there?"

"I'm fine. Cole's right. Don't engage them. No
matter what... Please don't give them a reason to
draw on you."

"Scout's honor," he responded, lifting two fingers. She'd be standing beside him the whole time,
he assured himself.

The brakes squeaked slightly. "We're here,"
Cole said.

Kyle took a look around. The drive was packed
but unpaved. A handful of vehicles had gathered.
Two of them were out of commission. The first
was jacked up on cinder blocks with its tires missing. The other was older, rusted and missing its
right quarter panel.

The rough-hewn house looked old yet unfin-
ished. The porch was a step up from the ground
and uncovered. It sagged in the center. A half-
assed, single gable drooped over the point of entry.
The whole place looked to have been added on to,
likely as Osias's household expanded. Rooms had
been tacked on to either side. The farthest rooms
to both left and right had never been walled off
by plywood, leaving the sheathing exposed.

Kyle noted the sound of mean barking. There
were two muscly canines confined to the circum-
ference of a gnarled tree. Chains kept them at
bay. There was a heap of broken and discarded

furniture. A couch showing its innards. A retro white, orange and green patio chair, a busted rocking chair that looked as good as kindling. Kyle thought he saw a paint-chipped crib and turned his attention elsewhere.

The front door was open. As Cole put the truck in Park near the mouth of the dirt lane, the spindly screen door opened, and a young man stepped out, shouting brusquely to the dogs. Neither Cole nor Kyle moved as they watched the boy of about sixteen realize that he had company.

When he ducked back inside, Cole asked, "Ready?" Kyle waited for Adrian's go-ahead. It took her a second. The sound of the latch on her door answered for her. Kyle got out. The air was like soup, and the breeze carried the swampy odor of sweet sewage. Kyle sniffed and circled the truck to meet Adrian, placing her between himself and Cole as a line of males ranging from mid-teens to mid-fifties filed onto the porch.

Cecil himself stepped off the porch to meet them. There was no evidence on his face of his skirmish with Kyle, but he looked a shade gray. He spat on the ground in front of the trio, shining with malice. "I hear you ain't got but one ball, boy," he said to Kyle. "You'd have to have both made of cast iron to come here."

"We just want to talk," Adrian explained in a voice that was neither shaky nor cool. Almost normal. "Can't we do that, Cecil—talk things out like rational human beings?"

Cecil took another step, all but leering at her. Kyle felt the hairs on his neck rise when he saw the assessment linger in all the wrong places. "Adrian Kennard."

"Bracken," she corrected, firm and placid. "My name is Bracken."

Cecil's mouth twisted. "You expect us to talk rational after the crap you pulled on my brother? Drove a knife through his back is what you did. He was never the same after you. Just a broken pile of bones."

"Is Osias home?" Adrian asked. "We'd like a word."

"That's about all she'll get," said someone behind Cecil, similarly tall, on the lean side and around the early- to mid-fifties. Cecil was mostly talk. This one had more of an edge to go with his drawl. The men that flanked him sniggered.

"Liddell," Adrian greeted.

The man used his middle finger by way of salute. His gaze toyed with her. Like a cat batting a mouse between its paws.

Kyle shifted slightly forward and to the right, placing himself in front of Adrian. He had no doubt that every man on site was armed and every member of the Kennard faction was eyeing her like the prized buck they wanted mounted on their wall. "Look, we didn't come here for trouble. All we want is to talk to the old man."

"Who's askin'?"

The men crowding the porch parted, giving way to a stocky, bowlegged gentleman. His beard was full and raggedy, gunmetal gray. He wore snakeskin boots that thunked and twanked across the distressed porch boards. It took Kyle a split second to realize that the twanking was made by shiny spurs on the back of each. Actual spurs. His thin, buttoned shirt was tucked into faded jeans and a bit baggy around him, though he was somewhat fleshy around the middle. The jeans were held up by a wide suede belt with a gleaming buckle. It looked like a prize from the rodeo.

Where's your ten-gallon hat, Marion? Kyle nearly said out loud. One of the few things that stopped him was the Peacemaker hanging from the gunslinger holster on the belt. An antique that had no business slumming it on Osias Kennard's hip.

Was this Bea's Caterpillar Man? Kyle's Spidey sense reached fever pitch. He felt the tension in Adrian double.

Osias's advance halted at the porch edge. Cecil fell back to give him precedence. Osias crossed his arms. His voice didn't rise above a scruffy tenor. It didn't have to. Kyle watched every single one of the rough-ridin' Kennard males tune their frequencies to catch what he had to say.

"You never did have any smarts, child. It's a shame you didn't ever grow enough to know comin' back here was as good as suicide."

"Hey," Cole said, stepping forward just as Kyle had. Palm down, he stuck a hand out low and shifted one foot forward in classic, peacekeeping motion. *So much for not acting like a cop.* "Let's not take shots here. We just want to lay some things on the table, then leave you to your own."

"In other words, this is a negotiation," Kyle struck out. "Not an ambush."

Osias eyed him, amused. "Not the way I see it." He lifted a finger and pointed. "How's your daddy doin', sonny?" There was a chorus of titters behind him.

"That's what we've come to discuss," Cole said as he propped his hands on his hips. "We have information from one of your own regarding James and the events that led to his arrest."

"A shame, that one," Osias mused. "A pillar of the community falling so far from grace." He sniffed and squinted at the sky visible through the open oval of thick trees. "Far and fast enough to break the sound barrier, wouldn't you say?"

Kyle's heart rate pumped up by a serious fraction. Who could miss the allusion to B.S. and Harmony's close call? Retorts burned on the back of his tongue. He went so far as to open his mouth but felt contact. Neither he nor Adrian turned to one another, but he could understand what she was saying by passing a hand over his spine.

Do not engage them.

Then again, he didn't need a weapon to achieve that. Kyle shifted his feet apart and matched Osias by crossing his arms over his chest. "How long have you been planning? Since my father bought up acreage for his new application business? Or since the day he put Radley in a prison hospital?"

Though the amused smile remained, a glint appeared in Osias's flinty gray eyes. Again, he spoke low and slow. "You gonna walk up on my property and talk about my son like that? What the hell d'ya think gives you the right?"

"He did," Kyle answered. "Every time he snorted cocaine at the kitchen table and knew I was watching. Any time he backhanded my mother in front of me. Each and every time he blocked the door to my room from the outside so that I couldn't get to her when I heard her scream at night. We lived in that trailer with him for three years, and I don't need a hand to count the number of times he met my eye. Because I knew what he was, and he knew it, too. Even if you didn't."

"And what was that?" Osias asked as everyone else on the scene seemed to hold a collective breath.

Adrian's hand was now balled in the back of Kyle's shirt. Kyle ignored it. "Your son was a verified monster. Not the storybook kind, either. He was the sort they send me overseas to put down. What do you say, sir? Do you think it's wrong of me to see his face every time I pull the trigger?"

"Kyle," Adrian said, nearly inaudible.

A knife could've cut the strain. Everyone assembled stayed very, very still as Osias weighed and measured, the Peacemaker likely growing heavier on his hip. Kyle saw the *tic-tic-tic* of a nerve in the space beneath his left eye. Then Osias barked a laugh. It cracked through the quiet like a whip. Adrian flinched. Osias laughed mirthlessly until his brethren joined in, the dogs started baying and howling in response, and he himself began to double over and wheeze.

When the laughter wound down, Osias reached up to his reddened face and rubbed an imaginary tear from the underside of his eye. "Ooo wee! You're about as stupid as your mama, soldier boy." Then the Peacemaker was in his hand. He didn't raise it. He simply held it, admiring its simple lines. "You're outnumbered. Outgunned. They train you to be this stupid in the military?"

Kyle chose not to answer, watching Osias's trigger finger. Was he a quick draw? He handled the gun well. Their luck, all the Kennards were trigger happy. Kyle shifted another inch in front of Adrian.

She placed a hand on his arm now. "Osias. Put the gun away. This has gone far enough."

"My land, my rules," Osias noted. "Matter of

fact, I think it's time my boys here showed y'all the family arsenal. How 'bout it, Cecil? This one's a pretty piece. Smith & Wesson. Circa 1930s. My grand-mammy wanted to sell it for pennies during the Depression when ain't anything was worth much. My grand-pappy was smart and buried it 'round back yonder. Hold it up, son. Let 'em see it in the light."

They went through one by one, taking out their weapons. Pistols, handguns, a few engraved hunting knives passed down through swarthy generations of Kennards. One guy went inside the house and emerged with a Revolutionary War musket. "Still works," Osias boasted. "Though Waymon doesn't get much use out of it. Accuracy's off. I'd let him demonstrate, but one of ya's bound to wind up with a ball of lead. By accident, of course. Heh!"

"What do you want?" Adrian shook her head in a way that signaled defeat. "You want B.S. to relocate? You want the deed to the land between it and your property? What's it going to take for you and Dorsie to spare James and the rest of us?"

Osias handed the musket back to the teen, Waymon. "Is this you hagglin'?"

Adrian pressed her lips together. "My family's well-being is far more important than any bitterness or feud. So, yes, I'll deal. This is some dispute over territory so let's redraw the lines, not blow it out of proportion by staking a man's life."

Not the plan. So not the plan. Before the self-satisfied smirk painted across Osias's face, Kyle knew that dealing with the devil rarely changed anything for the better. The devil always took his. Cole dipped his head to hers and whispered, "Adrian. This is not what we discussed."

"I don't care," she said. "I told you reasoning wouldn't make a difference. He wants something. It's always something."

"Blood," Kyle muttered. He'd seen Osias's type overseas. Militant leaders. Warlords. The architects, instigators, and rabble-rousers that preferred to stand over the chessboard, not on it. "He wants blood, and not the metaphorical type." *Which he'll get, one way or the other.*

Unless I stop him.

A splashing noise over the din of silence accompanied the growl of a deep-throated motor. Kyle pivoted sideways, keeping Osias and the Kennards in his line of sight as he watched an orange, '80s-model truck park next to Cole's. He glimpsed the blonde in the driver's seat and cursed. The brutal admission died, however, when he saw that she was accompanied by someone with flame-red hair. His mouth ran dry.

"No," Cole breathed.

Harmony stepped down from the truck cab, her thick-soled duck boots confronting the mud-slicked drive. Olivia at her side, she stalked forward, fearless and fixed, shoulders back and eyes firing.

Osias barked another laugh. "Behold! The cavalry!" He slapped his knee and guffawed as the others joined. A catcall went up from their ranks. Harmony didn't slow. She slipped from Cole's grasp and spun out of Kyle's, moving into the marked space between both parties. She didn't stop until she'd reached the porch.

When Osias stepped down in anticipation, Kyle dove for her. He pulled her back, an arm wrapped across her front. But her feet dug in, finding purchase in the grass-riddled clay. "You Osias? Never mind. I could spot the belt buckle and machismo from over there. I wanna know how you sleep at night, creep."

"Harm." Cole's fingers closed tight around her left upper arm and tugged. "Stand down."

"No, no," she said, trying to shrug both him and Kyle off. "He's going to explain himself to me."

"Who's the tiger girl?" Osias wanted to know. The Colt was still in his grip. It rested against his thigh.

"My name is Harmony Savitt. I'm one of the founding members of Bracken-Savitt Aerial Application & Training. I fly a red Piper Pawnee Brave 300 bearing the symbol of a water bearer. But you already know that. Just as you know I'm the person who lives in the little white house in the woods with a four-year-old girl. You've been there. You or one of your two-legged dogs walked into a B.S. hangar and tampered with my plane, just as you've been lurking around my home for the last two months watching me and my daughter and threatening my life and hers. You want to know who I am, old man? Good. I'll tell you. I'm the woman whose face you're going to see every night you sit rotting in a jail cell because it'll be because of what you did to me and my daughter and the family you see standing behind me that put you there."

"Strong words," Osias considered after a stretch. "Righteous and hot." The corner of his mouth moved. He reached out, fanning his fingers out to touch her.

Kyle hissed and drew her back against his chest.

Osias missed the mark, letting the fingers fall away. "You know how you fight heat, child?" He tucked his chin into his chest in an admonishing manner. "You snuff it, just like that. Before it gets wild. Fire's best left contained. Just like a woman."

"We get it," she claimed. "You're a coward and a bigot."

"Coward." Osias turned cold. "You wanna elaborate on that?"

"Well, sure," Harmony said, relaxing enough to loosen Cole and Kyle's hold. "First, you've got a Napoleonic complex as wide as Elba. I mean, come on. I've seen tiny men with egos, but yours is like Waterloo and Russia combined. Second, when you use subterfuge as a warhead and a string of unctuous minions to carry it out, you think it's ass-smart, but all the rest of us see you hiding behind their stupidity. And last, but not least, any man who says women are best left closemouthed and limited, only do so because they're Stage Five, shit-your-pants scared of them. And that, sir, is the definition of cowardice."

When Osias and the others only glared and gawped at her, she mirrored him by tucking her chin to her chest. The fact that she was taller than him hit the censorious nature of the gesture home. "Did you understand the first time, or do we need to review?"

The muscle below Osias's left eye twitched in rapid-fire succession. "Soldier boy," he said. "You wanna see a round go into tiger girl's forehead? Tell her to open her trap again."

Harmony opened her mouth, and Kyle used his hold under her arm to jerk her around to him. When her gaze fell on him, round and blistering, he whispered, *"Carrots!" For Christ's sake!*

She frowned at him deeply, but her mouth closed. She was close enough to feel his heart tapping a breakneck march on his sternum. Out of view, her palm skimmed his navel, a bare brush above his sensitive belt line. The gesture was small, but he recognized it for what it was. Assurance. She assured herself—that he was alive and standing and the situation hadn't yet come to a deadly junction.

Kyle realized what had led her here with Olivia, the same Stage Five fear she'd spoken of. The same fear he was trying to contain with both her and Adrian close enough for grips.

Team. Stand together. Fight together. His hand found hers, again out of sight. He kept the link hidden between them as they confronted the assemblage of thugs and the mixed munitions among them.

"Go home," Osias said to Adrian. "Go back to your farm while you still have it. My boys are a hair jumpy. A sudden move by any one of y'all and they're bound to drop ya. All of ya."

"The time for making threats is over," Adrian insisted. "We know what you've done. These things have a way of coming out, however well you think you've prepared."

"You're the trespassers," he told her. "The only people who've done wrong here is the five of you. I'm well within my rights in defense of my home."

"I'm defending mine, too," she argued.

"What do you know of home?" His voice climbed to a shout as he lost his tightly wound poise. "My son put aside everything to give you his name. I told him, 'Rad, don't you marry that whore or you'll spend the rest of your life raisin' another man's son.' He wanted you, bad enough to defy me. And he paid. You had a home, and you as good as burnt it to the ground. The one you got now, the life you think you built on it with that no-account Bracken and your bastard kids will go up in smoke. I'll be smilin' when it does. What goes around comes around, bitch, so take Soldier Boy, Fire Crotch, Sheriff and the gold-miner and *get off my land*!"

THE DRIVE AWAY from the Kennard house was silent. Cole drove two miles up the highway, turned the truck on to another unpaved lane and waited for Olivia to pull in behind him. "Oh, boy," Olivia said when Kyle jumped from Cole's truck first, slammed the door and took determined strides toward her.

Harmony had known this was coming. She threw her shoulder into the passenger door as she unlatched it. Her feet came to rest on the ground in time to meet him. "I know you're ticked off, but—hey!"

Kyle grabbed her by the elbow and tugged her around the bed of Olivia's truck. There was a thick patch of honeysuckle hanging over the shoulder. He moved her into the shade, conveniently out of sight of other members of their party. "Careful," she said. "Your alpha male's showing."

"What the hell?" he said. "What the actual hell, Harmony?"

"Don't you think we should regroup with the others before we do this?" she asked.

"They can wait. *I told you* to stay with Mavis and Bea. How do you expect me to *think straight* if you put yourself in the line of fire? He was going to shoot you!"

"He didn't," Harmony reminded him. "Now, while we're on the same page, I'll ask how you expect *me* to sit on my hands waiting for a call from the city morgue."

"We had *everything* under control. You just had to have a piece of him."

"Yes, I wanted a piece!" She flung her arms out. "I did it for me! I did it for Bea! I did it for your family and everything they've given me! I needed to be there when we tied him to this because, if everything goes right, he *will* sit in jail for most of what remains of his life, and I wanted him to know me. It's women he's put down all his life, and he'll know it's women that helped put him down."

"It was reckless," he certified.

"I don't expect Mr. Navy SEAL to understand anything about recklessness, do I?" she countered, shouting.

"Jesus, Kyle, it was brilliant." Olivia strolled into the fray. "Admit it."

When Kyle pivoted on his heel and scowled at her, Olivia lifted her hands. "Just thought you might need a ref. Your parents can hear everything, by the way."

"Oh, that's great," Kyle muttered. "That's just great."

"You said we were a team," Harmony reminded

him, unhindered by the interruption. "I tried to stay behind, but I couldn't. For twenty-nine years you've had my back, Kyle. Don't lambaste me for returning the favor." She didn't care who heard. She needed to yell at him. Maybe the force of shouting at him would singe the last dregs of fear she'd felt driving to the swamp, not knowing if he would be alive or dead when she got there. "It's all your fault, anyway! Last night, with your damn hero goodbye speech. Was I supposed to say, 'Okay, pumpkin,' and wave you off?"

He moved into her space, closing off the gap. *"You were supposed to stay safe!"*

She watched a cannonade of breaths roll through him like thunder. Defeat claimed him, and he lowered his head. Harmony saw the vein pulsing blue against his temple and the pallor underneath his sun-bronzed skin. While the last of her anxiety drained, he was still getting sucker-punched by his, she realized.

When he crouched underneath the honeysuckle canopy and laced his hands over the back of his neck, she didn't hesitate to drop to the grass beside him. She listened to his careful inhales. She listened to the silent storms in his head. Like Gavin, there had always been storms in Kyle. His skill at containing them was unmatched. She saw his effort not to give in costing him now and placed her hand on his knee. "I let you go last night because I was scared of going through everything I did

before, like you said. The danger's been too real.
It was real today. And all the possibilities will be
there tomorrow and especially the day you report
back to Little Creek. My whole adult life has been
a tangle of tribulations. Days like these make it
easy to believe the universe is against you and the
hardest lesson's coming around." She shrugged.
"But I can't live like that, and neither can you."

His grip eased from his neck. His chin lifted
by a fraction.

She placed both hands on his knee, insistent.
"From the moment I flew for the first time in your
father's Cessna, I stopped being controlled by fear.
It's why I love flying. The world falls away and
I'm in control. No fear. Just flight and freedom.
I'm raising my daughter to never let fear stand
in front of her. It took five games of Go Fish this
morning at the inn waiting for you to call to realize I couldn't let you go without giving myself
to you completely. I've lost many things, but I
don't have much regret. If something happens to
you…if I let you walk away again, regret's never
going to leave me alone. I don't have to be in control anymore. It's not like I ever have been with
you, anyway. This is me. I'm in, and it's up to you
whether you want to call shotgun."

The air didn't move. The sun had reached its
pinnacle, and the heat had tripled. Bees hovered,
drunk off honeysuckle. The scent of it infused the
hellish clime with something pleasant. The sun

fought through coverage to dapple him, and the lost freckles on his nose and cheekbones raised themselves to the light. If not for the beard, he could've been the Kyle who'd read to her and played with her. "I swear sometimes *you're* the soldier," he said softly. He took her hand and bent to kiss the back of her wrist. She teased the hair on the back of his head in answer, until he raised it, eyes hooded. "Bea. I promised her."

"You did. Prince." With a sigh, she added, "Our prince."

He shook his head.

"Who knows?" Harmony said. "She could still come around. Once, last year, she asked me if you and I were ever going to get married."

Kyle's brow hitched as the word *married* dropped between them. "What'd you tell her?"

"After I peeled myself off the tarmac," Harmony recalled, "I asked her why she was asking. She said that if I married you, you might not leave anymore."

Pain worked across Kyle's features.

"I told her it's your job," Harmony continued. "You sacrifice the time you have with us to defend the place we call home. To her, that meant The Farm."

A ghost of a smile flickered in his eyes. "It's The Farm for me, too," he revealed.

"She thinks you're out there fighting in her name and defending the homestead like some noble fairy-tale knight." When the smile grabbed his mouth at the corners, Harmony added, "I don't blame her. It's how I see you, too. Without the sword, of course."

"I'd have done well with a sword today."

"Me, too." She wanted more but settled for gliding her hand along his jean-clad thigh. It came to rest on the outer seam. He felt warm underneath and she yearned. "She loves you—like she loves sunny days, storybooks and Disney show tunes. And it makes me love you more."

"You're making this harder."

"There's more. Watching you defend your mother against Osias makes me love you, too. And, because I'm twisted and backwards and a glutton for punishment, knowing what you promised Bea ramps it up further. You've kind of ruined us." She swallowed because the next wasn't an easy admission. "This is it, for me. Neither she nor I have much patience to wait for you to deliberate over whether you're going to keep bowing out like a good prince or grant all our dreams and make us threefold."

"I'd like that," he revealed. "I want every piece of that."

Harmony closed her eyes. A tremor went through her. "Give me a second."

"Was that the right answer?" he asked with a smile in his voice.

"Yes," she breathed. Her heart was no longer heavy. Her spirit no longer afraid. "Oh, yes."

"I want to go places with you," he acknowledged. "I want to chart a course and fly there. You can be in control. I'm that crazy."

She laughed. In a loving motion, her hand roved up his hip and didn't rest until she'd pressed it to the center of his chest.

"You really think that's what Bea wants, too?" he wondered.

"I do." Harmony nodded. "I think we just went about it the wrong way."

He nodded. Feather-like, he traced the curve of the outer shell of her ear with his thumb. "You told me you'd never love anyone but him," he mused quietly.

Benji. They couldn't leave out Benji. "Yes."

"What changed?"

"Nothing," she explained. "I never wanted to love another military man again…unless it was the one I loved before. Turns out, I don't stop loving, no matter how many goodbyes we have to say."

"Ah, Carrots," he said, nudging the tip of her nose with his, "it's really hard not to break my word and kiss you. Right now."

She linked her arms around his neck and shifted her knees forward, between his. "Let me."

Before she could lift herself to him, a shadow

fell. "Don't you think it'd be wiser to ask my permission first?"

Harmony groaned. When Kyle tensed, she pulled him closer. *Not yet.* "Not a good time, Daddy."

"Fine timing from where I'm at," Cole observed. His arms were crossed. His feet were spread. A perplexed frown rode his serious jaw. He pointed from Kyle to Harmony and back. "How?" he asked. The question was loaded.

Kyle stood, helping Harmony to her feet with her hand tight in his. "Sir. I take full responsibility—"

"Oh, quit," Harmony interrupted. "I jumped *you.*"

The muscles in Cole's face slackened. Kyle pressed his lips together and winced. Adrian moved in. "Cole," she said, placing an equanimous hand to his shoulder. "Don't ask questions you may not want answers to."

"How long have *you* known?" he asked her. "Didn't you think me and Briar should know our daughter and your son have been…frisking each other?"

Harmony snorted. When Cole aimed a glare at her, she covered her mouth with her hand and let her shoulders shake silently with repressed laughter.

"They told me last night," Adrian said. "In their own way. I shouldn't have thought it was smart to tell you before this morning's excursion. The ride over was hardly the time for you to give Kyle the third degree."

Cole eyed Kyle. "Can't say the same for now."

"Game on," hazarded Harmony.

"I'm not sure how a certain young lady feels about the arrangement, in any case," Adrian pointed out.

"So Bea knows?" Cole assumed.

The humor fell away quickly. "Yes," Harmony answered. Her hand lowered from her mouth to her throat.

"Good." Still, Cole cursed.

Olivia raised a brow at him. "You realize this was inevitable?"

"No." Cole jerked his chin at Kyle. "What's with you Bracken boys falling for all the tenacious redheads, anyway?"

"Um," Kyle said by way of response. He glanced over his mother's natural red crop, then Harmony's braid and settled for, "Hmm."

"Is this too weird for you, Daddy?" Harmony asked.

"It'll linger," Cole considered. He fought a grimace. "You're adults. Reasonable enough to make up your own minds. Usually."

Harmony narrowed her eyes on him. "If that's the case, we don't need your permission."

"Uh, at this point, I might," Kyle stated.

Cole continued to measure him, then Harmony

by turn. Finally, he conceded with, "As long as it's all right with Bea, I don't see any reason to stand in the way."

Kyle nudged her. "Thank you, sir. Bea is, of course, our top priority. I'd actually like to be the one to speak to her."

"You would?" Harmony asked, stunned.

"I think I know why she's unhappy," Kyle said. "It would help if we waited until she's clear to go back to The Farm." He took her hand in a loose hold. "Would that be all right with you?"

"I trust you," she told him. "First, we need to cut the noose from your father's neck and use it to tie up Osias."

"Hallelujah," said Kyle.

"We'll go back to the inn and regroup," Cole decided. "I'll call your mother and let her know we're bringing good news."

"EVEN THOUGH THE confrontation with Osias was fruitless, there's evidence to consider," Adrian announced when they had all returned to Hanna's to gather with Briar and Mavis around the kitchen table. She looked to Cole to continue.

"We didn't get an admittance of wrongdoing," he explained. "Just threats he'll likely slip by a jury thanks to us trespassing. However, the still you mentioned, Adrian, was visible from the front of the house. It's been lost, somewhat, to weeds, but it looked to be in working condition. I'd say Osias remains a bootlegger."

"Is it enough?" Mavis wondered.

"Is anything enough?" Harmony asked.

"Domestic production of moonshine will get a lengthy sentence," Cole calculated, "but making meth out of house and home will extend that considerably."

"What?" Adrian said, surprised. "Where did you find meth?"

"I didn't," Cole said. "I came up on enough labs in my Narcotics days. You never forget the smell. The kitchen window was open. And the roof over it looked to have had some recent burn damage. We'll have to act fast. If Osias is as smart as he thinks he is, he might order the others to ditch the evidence in the event of a raid."

"Do you know anybody in Narcotics at the Fairhope PD?" Kyle asked.

"Detective Bedding," Cole replied. He pulled out his phone. "Hang tight. I'll give him a buzz."

Adrian licked her lips as Cole left the room. "What if the raid doesn't come through? What if it does but it's already too late?"

This was the civilian world, Kyle knew. It had to be enough. Else, he was going to have to call in a few favors from buddies in his unit and flush every Kennard out of the swamp by force. "Dad's coming home," he assured her. "You might want to call Roxie and figure out how to bring him back in style."

"Oh, Kyle." The tension finally washed away. Adrian's face cleared. "You were right. I thought it was pure recklessness, but if all works out, you've just given your father the justice he deserves."

"What you did today was about the bravest thing I've seen anybody do," he told her. "You didn't have to face them again, but you did. You're amazing, Mom."

Adrian swiped the wet from the undersides of her eyes. "Men. I'll never survive them."

"Oh, yes, you will," Olivia opined. "In another life, you were one of those giant cockroaches that never die."

Adrian emitted a strangled laugh, pressing the handkerchief Briar passed across the table under her nose.

Cole came back, his walk clipped like his voice. "Bedding's taking it to his superior. He wants me to come in and put everything on paper to make it official. They'll need a warrant. That could take a few days."

Mavis swore. Cole held up a hand. "They'll get it. There's not an officer who's been around within the last fifty years who hasn't had a run-in with the Kennards. The entire department will push it through."

"Hopefully not after James's transfer," Adrian muttered. "Our timetable's shrinking."

"What about everything else?" Harmony asked.
"So they'll go down as drug dealers. That won't
clear James."

"Osias may choose not to brag about his under-
handed achievements," Cole said. "But the same
can't be said for the rest of his kin. With the right
amount of pressure, one of them is bound to cop to
recent wrongdoings, especially if they have something to gain from it."

"They sell out Osias, they get less jail time,"
Kyle detailed when his mother and Mavis only
frowned. "They follow him like puppies, but I'm
pretty sure Cecil at least will be willing to trade
Papa Smurf to save himself some hard time."

"It's a good plan," Harmony said.

"All that's left is to wait," Kyle concluded.

"Great," Mavis said with a roll of her eyes.

Kyle looped a supportive arm around her shoulders. He tightened it when she didn't pull back
immediately.

"Just think," Harmony said. "This'll all be over
soon. And we can all go home."

"Home," Adrian murmured, hopeful.

Mavis relaxed enough to lean against Kyle. His
gaze lifted to Harmony's across the table. He was
impressed with her. When was he ever *not* impressed with her? Her spiel against Osias had been
everything he knew her to be—crazy, inspired,
remarkable, fierce. He'd wanted to kiss her even

as he'd wanted to haul her over his shoulder and rescue her.

I love you, Carrots. He couldn't stop thinking it. Her eyes were hot. When she was righteous, she was luminous—as luminous as she had been in his bed.

The woman drove him so crazy he was breathless with it. All he wanted was to leap into her fire—the fire Osias had wanted to snuff. He wished he could live there, breathe her fire and not have to worry about all the things that made better sense in this world.

If they went home… *When* they went home, he wanted to go with her. When he reported for duty, she was what he wanted to come home to. More than The Farm, he wanted to come home to his two tiger girls in the woods.

The future hinged on Bea. Precious Bea. Kyle had more promises to make and keep.

Briar refilled each of their tea glasses. When she had finished, she set the pitcher down and folded her hands in her lap. "If you don't mind, I'd like to share a bit of news. It's good news," she added.

"We could all do with some good news," Olivia piped up.

"Yes, please," Adrian agreed. "Go ahead, Briar."

"I had a call while everyone was away." Looking to Cole, Briar exclaimed, "From *Gavin*."

"Gavin!" he said.

"Gavin?" Harmony repeated.

"Yes." Briar nodded vigorously.

"Did he say where he was?" Harmony wanted to know. She was practically across the table, gripping the edge.

"More than that," Briar expounded. "He says he'll be here within a few short weeks." She beamed at her husband.

Surprise melded into his stolid features as Briar patted his cheek. "How did he sound to you?" Cole asked.

"Yeah, is he okay?" Harmony asked.

"I think so." Briar's grin extended to Adrian. "Can you imagine James and Gavin coming home at the same time and everything back as it should be at last?"

As the others offered their enthusiasm, Harmony's attention shifted to Kyle. White midday light spread wide in the window behind her. "Did you do this?" she mouthed.

Kyle lifted a shoulder. He'd made a phone call. But Gavin had made his move all on his own. Kyle felt nearly as surprised as Harmony that he was following through, finally, on his word. And he was relieved. Home was where Gavin should be, much like The Farm was the medicine the Brackens, Harmony and Bea needed.

The same relief shone from Harmony. As he watched, her irises darkened, the lashes wet. Finally, her lips moved. "Thank you."

Finding her foot under the table, he planted the sole of his boot next to hers. *Anything*, he conveyed to her on a silent plane he knew she'd understand.

CHAPTER SEVENTEEN

THE RED BRAVE was flat-hatting.

As Kyle spectated, shading a hand over his eyes to block the afternoon glare, he watched the plane climb and dive, climb and dive. As it leveled out and chased its shadow over the runway at B.S., he glimpsed the water-bearer mark on its cockpit door.

Harmony was showing off.

Although he hadn't seen her outside the dinner table with his family and Bea, he had heard plenty of her. The hum of the Piper was audible from the farmhouse, especially in the tranquility of the early morning. It roused him from bed, smiling before he cracked his lids. Every time, he'd gone straight to the window to see the red flash of the Piper scale above the treetops.

The playfulness of the Piper's flight brought to mind a playful Harmony, shouting and sprinting to keep up with Kyle and Gavin as kids. It made him grin even as his stomach clutched, and he swore profusely on her next dive.

He heard singing and looked around for his pint-size companion.

Adrian had spread seedlings for wildflowers in the short field between the border of The Farm and B.S. when James had bought the parcel for its use. Both she and Bea were gathering ripened blooms into the flat basket tucked against her side.

Now that everyone was under the right roof, Adrian was in serious nesting mode. No one intended to call her out on it either. In fact, it did Kyle good to see his mother back in her element. Relaxed and happy among her flowers.

The warrant had come through, and the resulting raid on the Kennard stronghold had confirmed Cole's suspicions. The moonshine still and meth lab had led to the arrests of every adult residing in Osias's den. Liddell had rolled over on his father first in exchange for parole, further explaining the timing behind the threats and charade. Apparently, the old man had felt his illegal enterprises threatened by the activity of James's new high-profile business. It hadn't helped when James began making noise about buying the acreage that remained between B.S. and Osias's swamp.

Dusty and Clint Harbuck were arrested, too. Liddell identified Dusty as the culprit who disguised himself as James, planted the Trans Am at Bracken Mechanics and returned to the scene, shortly before Holmes and Wilson were tipped off, to load it with IED materials. James was exonerated and released before authorities could pro-

ceed with his transfer to the county house. He'd
returned to The Farm to extended fanfare.

Kyle missed most of the festivities due to scheduled training. By the time he returned, his father
had caught up on some much-needed rest—and
shaving—and was eager to get back to work. He
and Harmony had had to hit the ground running
at B.S., particularly once she received the Piper
back from Evidence. Several farmers had had a
change of heart about not doing business with
Bracken-Savitt after news hit that Osias and his
crew had intentionally sullied negotiations.

Timing was everything. Kyle had let Harmony
and Bea move back into the mother-in-law suite.
He'd kept his distance. He'd kept his promises to
both Cole and Bea. He'd hardly touched Harmony,
though he'd wanted to.

He neglected to count the times he'd caught
himself placing his hand on the small of her
back. Or the time they washed dishes together
and a plate slipped between his handling and hers.
They'd both caught it before it hit the floor, his
arms underneath it and hers wrapped around his
as a barrier.

With the rest of the family in the living room
tuning up instruments for their Saturday night
musical round, they'd hovered, the plate pretense
as they kneeled together, knees bumping, thighs
brushing. "That was lucky," she'd said, grinning

widely and managing to sneak a brief, stolen kiss before leaving him reeling on the floor.

He hadn't touched her intentionally in over a week and still her vibrancy captivated his soul. He'd thought she could bring only wildfire into his life, but the last few weeks had been hell, and still she'd smiled through it. She'd brought the smile out in him when he'd needed it. She made him laugh. At times, she made him forget.

She was fire, true. But she was also calm. She was strength. She was cease-fire.

She brought harmony to a life that, despite his best efforts, had always been rocky. That was the way it was, he'd learned. Life was chaos and evolution. He'd just needed balance. Her spontaneity to spice up the unchanged portions of his home life. Her passion for everything to make him forget things that, for a soldier, were often far too real to forget.

Her dogged faith in times of uncertainty. However much she complained about her thighs or elbows, to him she was perfection.

How could something so fast and frenzied feel so good? How could he be looking at this person he'd known for twenty-nine years and be contemplating a life with her? A full one. How could he want it so badly he could taste it like honeysuckle?

He smiled again and lifted his hand at the Piper as it soared overhead. There she was, the woman who'd take him—all he was, all he wasn't—and proudly build her life around him.

Training his attention to the ground, he kicked at the old burn pile. He toed aside ash that had grown as damp and heavy as the wood's leafy carpet. Osias had never admitted to being the lumberjack in the woods. Neither had any of the other Kennards. Kyle couldn't dwell on how the Caterpillar Man had come close to truly destroying them all.

"If you stand there long enough, you might drive yourself crazy," Adrian cautioned.

He considered. "Define crazy."

The Piper peeled overhead, and Adrian lifted her face to watch the flyover with him. When the noise of the plane faded, she said, "She doesn't make it easy for you not to."

"Nope," Kyle said with a laugh.

"It's the same with him," Adrian complained. "Your father." The complaint was tempered by a soft warm smile. "He can hardly keep his feet on the ground for a single moment."

"When you're with him, are yours ever really planted?" Kyle wondered out loud.

Adrian beamed. "No. Not really."

"Huh." He scanned her. "You look nice today, Mom. You look happy."

"I am happy," she said truthfully. She focused on him again. Shaking her head, she observed, "You look a-bothered."

Bea danced in the field, her knees marching high over the heads of wildflowers. She was singing about "peace like a river." It charmed Kyle to his toes.

Adrian patted his arm. "You've got patience enough for a saint, Kyle Zachariah."

"I'm just waiting," he shrugged. "There's a time and a place."

Adrian flicked her gaze up to the scattered clouds. "Today's a good day as any."

"Maybe," he said after a beat.

Adrian hitched the basket. "I want to ride these back to the farmhouse before your father brings himself home. We're doing dinner again tonight, all of us. I need to redo the centerpiece for the dining room."

"Do you need us to come with you?" he asked as she gathered the reins of the horse she'd rode from the barn.

"I know the way." Touching one of the flower blossoms to her nose, she raised her brows at him before clambering up on her big Tennessee Walker. Positioning the basket carefully across her lap, she contemplated out loud, "You should take her to the mound. The one where you, Gavin and Harmony used to play as kids. She'd love that."

Kyle thought about it. "You might be right."

"Of course I am." Grinning, she nudged the horse into a walk and trotted into the woods in the saddle.

KYLE HAD WANTED to bring Bea back to their woods. Both he and Harmony had discussed letting her reacquaint herself with the safety of the pines, the importance of not holding her back. The woods had been their place, years ago. Now it was all Bea's.

"Why did you name Fury, Fury?" Bea queried as they picked their way through the forest on the back of Kyle's stallion.

"For Colonel Nicholas J. Fury. Director of S.H.I.E.L.D."

"The one with the pirate patch?"

"That's the one." He gave her hands clasped over the saddle horn a pat. Harmony didn't know it yet, but to distract Bea from all that had been going on throughout the summer, he'd been telling her stories of superheroes and supervillains; good guys versus bad guys. He'd also begun to contemplate how young was too young when it came to kids handling comic books.

They'd helped him chase bad dreams as a kid. It was only natural to pass on the escape.

"Why does he have a pirate patch? He's not a pirate."

"No, he's not." There was a hanging branch over the path ahead. "Watch your face, sweetheart," he muttered, leaning around Bea to bend it out of the way. "He was in a war."

"Like you?"

"His war was bigger. He was hurt, by a grenade."

"What's that?"

Kyle picked through his explanation carefully. How much did she really need to know in order to retain that perfect halo of innocence? "A little ball about as big as your fist. It packs an explosion."

"Oh. Is that how you got hurt?"

"Yep. But a different kind got me."

"There're more?" she asked, and he heard the unease.

"We have special tech specially trained to find them."

"*Before* they get you?"

"Before they get us," he answered. Seeing a break in the path, he tugged on the reins. "Whoa, Fury. You see that little hill with the flowers on it, Bea? This is the special place Uncle Gavin, your mama and me came to when we were kids."

"It's *preeddy*," she breathed.

"Wanna get down and explore?" he asked. At her nod, he shifted, flicking the reins over Fury's head. "Let's go."

He let her trudge around freely, knowing she needed to feel as much as before that it was all her own.

"I LIKE IT HERE," Bea announced cheerfully after her fourth high-stepping trek through a dandelion patch. "It's like *The Gruffalo*. You know? Where the mouse walks in the woods? I like that story."

Kyle grinned. She'd brought the book to the

farmhouse a handful of times over the last week to have Mavis read it for her.

Bea sat down in what was left of the dandelions. She watched tufty motes lift on the balmy breeze. When he knelt beside her, she handed him a white seed head on a stem. "Make a wish," she told him before picking one for herself. When he only looked at her, she ordered, "Close your eyes!"

"All right. Say please."

"Please," she said and batted her eyes.

Talk about *ruined*. He closed his eyes and did as he was told.

"Now take a deep breath," she instructed. "And *blow*!" She cackled when he gave a great huff, clearing the seed head completely. The motes wafted, then scattered, parachuting across the glade. And so their *preeddy* piece of the world grew.

Clapping for him, Bea asked, "What did you wish for?"

He looked at her, resisting the urge to chuck her small round chin. He noticed she tried to suppress the mischievous gleam, the same he'd glimpsed often in eyes shaped just the same as hers. "Wouldn't you like to know?"

"Tell me!"

He leaned down to her, dropping his arms on to his knees and said, "No." Then he kissed the tip of her nose and drew back.

"I know already," she bragged.

"Oh, yeah, Goldilocks?"

"It's about Mama." The mischief orbited into something more knowing...and only slightly admonishing.

Kyle treaded carefully again. He planted his knees in dandelions, then shifted them out from under him. He sat beside her, cross-legged just as she was, and plucked a lone yellow jonquil. Handing her the flower, he watched her bring it to her nose for a cursory sniff and skimmed a hand over her hair. "Would you mind me talking to you about your mama?"

Bea pursed her lips. Her shoulders lowered as she experimentally skimmed her flattened palm across the fleecy seed heads. "This tickles," she said and did it again.

Kyle waited a beat, then joined her, touching the dandelions. "They change eventually," he said quietly.

"Into what?" she asked.

"Flowers. Yellow ones. Over there," he pointed out, "In the sun."

"Why do they do that?" she asked. "I like them soft, like this."

"It's just nature."

"Hmm." Bea picked another dandelion and shook it. "They're still preeddy."

Kyle opened his mouth, closed it. He considered his options. *Don't push.* "You know who else loves dandelions?"

"Mama. But not as much as honeystickle."

"Honeysuckle." He smiled when it occurred to him that *honeystickle* sounded much better.

"She says the bees like it best. You like them, too."

His combat flashbacks had grown less frequent. Another benefit of Osias's arrest and James's homecoming. So this time around, most of his nights at The Farm had been lost to honeysuckle dreams. He'd found Harmony there, every time, and—without striking a match—they'd burnt it down together.

A slight pout came to Bea's mouth. "Do you like kissing her much?"

"Yes, I do." When she only frowned, he shifted on the forest floor. This time, he picked a blade of grass, tore it in half, folded it, tore it again. "I don't expect you to understand... Not yet, anyway."

She shrugged. "Isn't that what grown-ups do?"

"Ah..."

"Talbot tried to kiss me."

Who the hell is Talbot? "Who's Talbot?"

"A boy. He goes to my day school."

"A boy." Kyle lobbed the word like a grenade.

"I told him no."

"Good."

"I felt bad. He cried."

"He's fine." Kyle dismissed Talbot with a brusque shrug. "You've got your whole life ahead of you. You and Talbot can save the kissing for later. *Way later.*"

"Is that why you kiss Mama—because you're old?"

"I'm not that old." Amusement crept along the seam of his mouth. "Am I?"

Bea beamed. "You're old in a good way."

"Thanks." The conversation had gone off the beaten track. But then, what had he expected with an astute four-year-old? "I, uh, I think I know why you didn't like seeing your mom and me kissing."

Bea's frown returned.

Kyle swallowed. "We've been good buddies, all of us, for as long as you've known."

"I've never seen you kiss," she mumbled.

"The kissing's new." She was quiet again so he went on. "Are you afraid that it might change things?"

Bea's shoulders lifted. She batted a fruit fly away.

"I was afraid at first, too," Kyle admitted. "I still am, in some ways."

"You get afraid?" she asked.

"Oh, big tough guys like me are the biggest 'fraidy cats," he admitted. "But that's our secret."

She grinned but still didn't lift her eyes. The grin melted away by gradual degrees, and she sighed. "You have to go away again."

"Not right now," he assured her. "At some point…"

She nodded understanding. "I don't want you to stay away."

"Why do you think I'd stay away?" he asked, brow furrowed.

"My daddy stayed away. Mama said she loved him too much, and he stayed away from us."

Oh. Comprehension struck Kyle like an armored truck. *Damn.* "Bea." He lowered his head. "You listen to me. Your daddy would be sitting right where I am if he could. He wouldn't have walked away from your mother, and he especially wouldn't have walked away from you. He doesn't stay away because your mama loved him too much. He stays away because he doesn't have a choice."

"Because he's dead," Bea said, finite.

Ah, it hurt. It hurt left, right and center. "Yeah." The monosyllable was riddled and grated. It hurt, too.

"Are you going to die?"

Kyle blinked again. Then again, quickly. "Not if I can help it."

"You're going to come back?" she asked hopefully.

"Let 'em try and stop me." He soothed the small line of her back. "So long as I'm able, I promise I'll always come back for you and your mother."

Finally, she looked at him again. There was a thoughtful glimmer in her eyes. "You want to kiss Mama again. Don't you?"

He let out a laugh. "I've been thinking about it."

"Are you going to marry her?"

Quick. To the point. Just like Harmony. It was his job to keep up. After a pause, Kyle asked, "How would you feel about that? Mad at us again?"

Bea glanced up at the stir of pine needles, the song of the forest. "No. Not mad."

"A little happy, maybe?"

"You'll live with us? In our house in the woods?"

"If we're married, yes."

"You'll keep reading me stories—like *The Gruffalo*?"

"As many as you need."

She smiled again at last. "You'll make Mama laugh, not yell?"

"There'll likely be both." He told the truth, knowing Harmony and their passionate natures combined. "We'll try and keep the shouting to a minimum. Can I tell you something else?" He pointed at her, then himself. "You and me? We'll always be buddies. That's one thing I can tell you *won't* change, ever."

Slumped, curious, she propped her elbows on her knee and cupped her chin in her hands. She scanned his face, smiling some more. "You're preeddy, too. The hair on your cheeks gets real soft, but I like it best when I can see them."

He'd remember to shave. "Do you feel like asking me anything?"

Bea shook her head, making the curls around her head, springy with heat, bounce. A butterfly flitted between them. Her eyes widened, and she gasped in delight when it landed on the back of his hand. It opened its pale yellow wings once, twice, before crawling to the knuckle of his middle finger and lifting off.

"That was awesome!" she hissed.

"Yeah, it was," he said, watching the butterfly frolic from one flower to the next, flirting with their open faces before veering to the next. Carefree playing, just as he'd seen Bea engage in.

"Caterpillars change into butterflies."

He frowned, then scrubbed the portents from his mind. "They do."

"And white dandelions change into yellow dandelions…" she riddled slowly. "What will *I* change into?"

"Whatever you want," he told her. "You can be Wonder Woman, Supergirl, Buffy, Ms. Marvel… just so long as you promise your buddy Kyle one thing."

"Okay," she anticipated.

He narrowed his eyes. "You keep telling those boys not to kiss you. They're bad news."

Bea cackled, falling back to the grass. "You're silly!"

"Wait a minute, Gracie Bea," he cautioned, only half kidding, "you didn't promise…"

THERE WAS A phone jammed between Harmony's ear and shoulder. She juggled the mail in one hand while balancing a casserole dish her mother had dropped off at the farmhouse in the other, all the while trying to slip her keys into her bag so she didn't lose them again... Her father and Kyle had both been adamant about her locking her front door at night. She'd blown them off because A) they were both still planted in alpha male mode, and it was annoying, and B) she'd caught Kyle sleeping on her front porch twice since her and Bea's return anyway. He was practically her own live-in sheepdog.

She wished he were live-in. Oh, God, how she wished. The first night she found him, they'd had a very near miss with the stun gun she kept strapped to her ankle in her sleep—because *reasons*—and the commotion had startled Lucy, Bea's bobcat mix, who'd clawed her way up his T-shirt and nipped him in the ear.

After administering first aid, Harmony had invited him into the house. More specifically, into her bed. He'd looked at her for a long time, wanting, considering. Without a word, he stretched out on the wicker lounger that was a foot too short for him, lowered the bill of his ball cap over his eyes, crossed his arms and said, "Good night, Carrots."

Frickin' prince, she'd thought as she threw her arms up and stalked back to bed.

"We're fine, Dad," she said into the phone. She

groaned when Cole kept jabbering off in alpha-male speak. "No, I didn't read the brochure. I have a life. And I told you, I don't need a security system." She cursed when she tripped over the metal, airplane-shaped wind-spinner leading to the front door. "Ow," she gasped. *That'll bruise.*

Meanwhile, her father kept talking. "It's not a question of money," she responded, stomping up the steps to the porch. "I just don't want one." She stepped over Bea's scooter and the edge of the lounger. She bobbled the casserole because she'd forgotten she needed the keys to unlock the door they insisted she lock. "Look, if it makes you feel better, I'll get a dog." She dropped the bag, dropped the mail, and thought about tossing everything except the foil-covered baking dish in the garbage. Screw the bills. She'd just sit on her porch in the thick of late afternoon and gorge herself on casserole. She was famished from extending flying time through lunch.

The forks were inside, however. She went back to rooting through the bag. "Shit! *Where are they?* No. Ignore me, Dad. It's nothing. I just can't get through the damn door." When Cole started harping on about the present-day marvels of home security systems and smartphones, she found herself groaning again. "I'll get a wolf. A mean one. We'll call him Cujo and teach him to pick locks with his fangs. Aha!" she said as she felt the jangle of her key chain and yanked it out. She stood, unlocked the door, swung it open and spun back around to scoop up the discarded items…

She stopped. A big, brown stallion was walking up the lane to the house. Bea bounced on Fury's saddle while Kyle led them both by the reins. He pointed. Bea waved and called out.

Harmony lifted her hand numbly in return. "Uh, Dad? I'll call you back. Bea's home. And Kyle." At Cole's next inquiry, she grinned wide. "No. I definitely don't plan on behaving myself. Nope. Love you, too. Bye."

By the time Kyle had guided Fury to the small garden gate, Harmony had tossed the mail, bag and keys inside. She watched Kyle swing Bea off the horse and into the air before letting her go.

"I'm telling, I'm telling!" Bea streaked up the steps of the porch into Harmony's arms. "Guess what, Mama! I rode Fury. We went to the woods. These are for you." She passed a clutch of dandelions to Harmony and swiped curls from her cheek. "Guess what else! Kyle says I can be a superhero. We saw butterflies. He's going to read *The Gruffalo*, and he's going to marry us."

"Marry…" Harmony faltered. Looking askance over Bea's shoulder, she watched Kyle lead Fury to the steps before letting go of the reins so the horse could roam the inside of the neglected garden.

"Don't eat the airplane, old boy," Kyle advised

with a pat. "She'll skin us alive." He stayed at the bottom of the steps, looking up at them. His gaze collided with Harmony's and stayed. "Hi."

"Hi," she returned.

Bea wrapped herself close against Harmony and turned her lips into her mother's ear to whisper, "He's going to kiss you and read me a book. He's coming back after he goes away, and he says he'll live in our house with us. Mama, *he's going to live in our house*!"

"I…heard." Harmony swallowed when Kyle only continued to gaze at her.

"I have to peepee!" Bea cried and abruptly leaped out of Harmony's embrace.

"Need help?" Harmony called after her.

"Nope!" Bea replied, racing through the house.

His boots thunked up the steps. Harmony stood quickly in response and stepped back so he could enter the porch. She felt the lounger close behind her and made a mental note not to spill over it, even as his towering frame shrank the porch down to scale-model size. "Busy day," she assumed. Somewhere in the house Bea was singing—loud, off-key and very merrily.

"Nah." He slid his hands into his pockets. "Just productive."

His intensity struck her. Pulse washing, she felt her blood hum at the promises his Scandinavian blues held. "So the talk went well."

"The talk went very well," he said with a nod.

"What changed her mind?"

"She was worried I might stay away if you loved me like you loved Benji. I assured her that wasn't the case."

"That I don't love you like him...or that you aren't going to stay away?"

"I'm not staying away," he told her, and his intensity softened until he was looking at her tenderly. Quickly, she realized she couldn't handle that any more than his magnetic concentration. "God help the person who tries to make me."

"I like that." She realized she was whispering. Then she gave herself a mental shake. "Just to clarify, the kissing ban has been lifted?"

"I'm told kissing is acceptable."

"Thank Jesus," she expelled. His laughter swept over her, into her. She edged closer, every part of her aware that it was no longer forbidden by the resident sass-meister. "How about...touching? Is it all right if I touch you?"

Her hand closed around his wrist. He let her tug him closer. He dipped his head toward hers, and he placed his hands on her hips. "I speak for myself when I say, yes, woman, you better touch me."

"What about this?" She slipped both palms beneath the hem of his shirt. The hard abs on the other side greeted her warmly. Rolling her palms into her fists, she felt the soft brush of his chest hair on the back of her hands. "Is this okay?"

"More than." His eyes had closed at the naked caress.

She moved farther into him, pressing her middle against his. It felt *so good* to be close. Going up to her toes, she took him off guard by raking his chin lightly with her teeth. "This?" she asked, gliding her mouth along the rim of his jaw.

"That," he decided, down to a whisper. She nibbled again once she got near his ear, and he tilted his head, laugh ragged. Fingers linking through hers, he lifted them to either side. "Carrots."

She sighed. Opened her eyes. Met his. "Yes?"

"Ask me."

Their feet were moving, circling in some kind of shuffling, absentminded dance. "Ask you what?"

"How I'm certain." He raised their linked hands higher. "How I know this is it."

This is it. Yes, buddy! "Do tell."

"Because you're my best friend," he told her. "Because you drive me crazy. Because you burn me up. Because I can't imagine ever wanting to come back to anyplace but you and Bea. I don't want it to be any other way. I meant what I said on the *Hellraiser*. I'll take care of you, Harm. Both of you. So let me. I need you to let me."

She shook her head. Was this really happening? Hell, yes, it was! She'd waited. Convinced herself to stop waiting.

After all that and everything in between, he was here. They were both here—in the same place—at the right time. "Let me," she said back. "Let me make you crazy." She kissed his nose and pressed her cheek against his. She breathed him in, absorbed the line of him into herself until she felt joined with him in every way that mattered. "Let me keep you wild."

He gave a convincing snarl, and, cackling, she linked her arms tight around his neck. He boosted her up, holding her above the floor so her legs wrapped snug around his waist.

Her brow arched when he still didn't kiss her. "I'm not going to beg."

"No?" He grinned.

"Mama! Where's Miss Poppinbobbles? It's time for tea!"

"Okay," Harmony decided instead. "Kiss me. Quick."

He stopped her just before her mouth swooped down to his. Curving his fingers into the braid at the nape of her neck, an ardent line built between his eyes. He closed them.

She followed suit and felt swept away when his lips brushed across hers once, then again. Her hold tightened. Shuddering, she let him take his time.

Kyle drank from her and savored, deepening

the kiss and tilting his head by gradual degrees until she was flying so high she'd forgotten what gravity was altogether.

A close nicker startled them apart. Harmony gave a breathless laugh when she saw Fury's head poking between the porch rails. He nosed against Kyle's pant leg and nuzzled his way up, looking for sugar cubes.

Bea came out on the porch. "Mama! Miss Poppinbobbles!"

As Harmony laid her head back and sighed, Kyle pressed his face into her throat. Lips grazed her skin, smiling.

"This is the new normal," she revealed. "Are you ready for it?"

"Baby, I'm livin' it." He didn't put her down as he made his way to the door. "Come on, little wing. Let's find that missing uniform. You." He set Harmony down on the kitchen floor, letting his hand span across the back pockets of her jeans. He kissed her again, until his shirt was rolled up in her fists and her foot was off the floor. "Mmm. I'm comin' back."

"Yes," she said.

As he joined hands with Bea and walked farther into the house, he tossed a wink over his shoulder. "What's for dinner, Mama? 'Chitlins and dumplin's'?"

"Mac-and-cheese!" she called after him. When he tossed his head back and guffawed so that the rich sound of his laughter rang through the rooms, Harmony sagged a bit at the knees. She was beaming so broadly, her cheeks hurt.

They'd live, she realized, from one moment to the next until they all converged into one great forever here in their little house in the woods.

* * * * *

Get 2 Free Books,
Plus 2 Free Gifts—
just for trying the Reader Service!

YES! Please send me 2 FREE Harlequin Presents® novels and my 2 FREE gifts (gifts are worth about $10 retail). After receiving them, if I don't wish to receive any more books, I can return the shipping statement marked "cancel." If I don't cancel, I will receive 6 brand-new novels every month and be billed just $4.55 each for the regular-print edition or $5.55 each for the larger-print edition in the U.S., or $5.49 each for the regular-print edition or $5.99 each for the larger-print edition in Canada. That's a saving of at least 11% off the cover price! It's quite a bargain! Shipping and handling is just 50¢ per book in the U.S. and 75¢ per book in Canada.* I understand that accepting the 2 free books and gifts places me under no obligation to buy anything. I can always return a shipment and cancel at any time. The free books and gifts are mine to keep no matter what I decide.

Please check one: ☐ Harlequin Presents® Regular-Print   ☐ Harlequin Presents® Larger-Print
                          (106/306 HDN GLWL)   (176/376 HDN GLWL)

Name _____ (PLEASE PRINT) _____

Address _____ Apt. # _____

City _____ State/Prov. _____ Zip/Postal Code _____

Signature (if under 18, a parent or guardian must sign) _____

Mail to the Reader Service:
IN U.S.A.: P.O. Box 1341, Buffalo, NY 14240-8531
IN CANADA: P.O. Box 603, Fort Erie, Ontario L2A 5X3

Want to try two free books from another series?
Call 1-800-873-8635 or visit www.ReaderService.com.

* Terms and prices subject to change without notice. Prices do not include applicable taxes. Sales tax applicable in N.Y. Canadian residents will be charged applicable taxes. Offer not valid in Quebec. This offer is limited to one order per household. Books received may not be as shown. Not valid for current subscribers to Harlequin Presents books. All orders subject to approval. Credit or debit balances in a customer's account(s) may be offset by any other outstanding balance owed by or to the customer. Please allow 4 to 6 weeks for delivery. Offer available while quantities last.

Your Privacy—The Reader Service is committed to protecting your privacy. Our Privacy Policy is available online at www.ReaderService.com or upon request from the Reader Service.

We make a portion of our mailing list available to reputable third parties that offer products we believe may interest you. If you prefer that we not exchange your name with third parties, or if you wish to clarify or modify your communication preferences, please visit us at www.ReaderService.com/consumerschoice or write to us at Reader Service Preference Service, P.O. Box 9062, Buffalo, NY 14240-9062. Include your complete name and address.

HP17R2

Get 2 Free Books,
Plus 2 Free Gifts—
just for trying the Reader Service!

♦ HARLEQUIN®

HEARTWARMING™

Get 2 Free Books,
Plus 2 Free Gifts—
just for trying the
Reader Service!